AWAKEN

A NOVEL

Awaken

Copyright © 2020 by Tracy Tripp

This book is a work of fiction. The names, characters, places, and incidents are products of the writer's imagination or have been used fictitiously and are not to be construed as real. Any resemblance to persons, living or dead, actual events, locales or organizations is entirely coincidental.

ALL RIGHTS RESERVED. No part of this book may be used or reproduced in any manner whatsoever without written permission from the author.

For information contact Tracy Tripp, tracytripp.com

Formatting by Bella Media Management

AWAKEN

A NOVEL

TRACY TRIPP

"The Clod and the Pebble"
By William Blake

"Love seeketh not itself to please,
Nor for itself hath any care,
But for another gives its ease,
And builds a Heaven in Hell's despair."

So sung a little Clod of Clay
Trodden with the cattle's feet,
But a Pebble of the brook
Warbled out these metres meet:
"Love seeketh only self to please,

To bind another to its delight,
Joys in another's loss of ease,
And builds a Hell in Heaven's despite."

Written by William Blake

PROLOGUE

Brent

FBI Field Office
Jacksonville, Florida
Present Day

SWEAT DRIPPED DOWN the back of my neck and numbness spread through my hands as they gripped into fists. Everything over the past year played through my mind—the case, the feelings, the relationship I'd trusted Skylar and I had formed. I questioned it all, every word, every tilt of her head that had made her look innocent.

I couldn't get out of the briefing room fast enough. All eyes had been on me, watching me squirm in my skin as Ryan, our Senior Supervisory Special Agent or SA, had reviewed the facts. The findings were incriminating; that part was undeniable. But how—how had I missed so many clues?

I shut the door of my office behind me and slid into my chair. From inside my bag, I pulled out the journal Adam, Skylar's fiancé, had slipped me earlier. To give him credit, I'm not sure I'd have done the same, not with our history. He'd made it no secret that he blamed me for her disappearance. I placed my hand on the journal, felt the smooth leather cover, and wondered about the book's contents. No one else needed to know about it. Not yet.

Again, my mind scrambled to find the answers that could erase everything I'd just heard during the briefing. But if Skylar was innocent, if the facts weren't proving her involvement, then where was she? Why had she disappeared without even giving Adam a clue as to where she might be going? Unless, of course, she had. I looked down at the journal in my hands. I had only read the first page, but I already knew the answers would not reveal themselves without a fight.

CHAPTER 1

Skylar

Journal Entry

I'VE NEVER JOURNALED. Personally, I find the idea terrifying, as if my mind will be exposed. I'd officially be giving prying eyes a flashlight to shine on the darkest parts of my mind. I'll say it again; the idea is terrifying. So why would I expose myself? I've realized I don't have a soul in the world to discuss private matters with, which leaves me with empty pages of a journal waiting to catch the secrets the world can never know, or at least, not yet.

Adam, if you ever find this diary, please understand that while I share my life with you, there is still a piece of me that is solely me, and you might not care to know that side of me. I would like you to close the journal now and allow me to have this private conversation with myself, and hopefully, if all goes as it should, I will talk some serious sense into myself, and you will never know any of this conversation took place. If you choose to continue, then I guess we'll deal with the consequences. Here goes…the first dream.

From the back seat of the car, I stared at the man driving. My heart pounded. Who was he? Friend or foe?

Snarling noises came from outside. The zombies were closing in on us. A half-dead man, slamming into the rear door near me, clawed at the car. Sweat dripped down my forehead and the distinct feeling that a premonition was demanding attention closed in on me, much like the creatures running at superhuman speeds outside my window.

Something large landed on the roof of the car and banged and scratched at it like an animal. My heart beat against my ribs until I thought it might bust out of me. And then a decaying hand ripped through the roof. I slid from one side of the car to the other, knowing that no matter what, this creature must not latch on to me with its rotten teeth.

I pressed myself against the door. The zombie's face emerged through the roof. My breath stuck, making it impossible to let out the scream building inside of me, as the creature breathed the smell of death into the air. I squeezed my eyes closed, and the zombie's teeth sank into my shoulder.

Suddenly, I appeared in the guest bathroom of my home, studying myself in the mirror. I slid the shoulder of my shirt to the side and saw only a small trace of the bite mark. Bringing my face closer to the mirror, I searched for changes and found none. However, something about me was different.

In the master bathroom, Adam innocently got ready for bed, not knowing that a new beginning for me was sprouting. A mysterious happening was taking place just a short distance away from him, and the woman he sometimes spoke of marrying would be changed forever.

The bite hadn't turned me into a zombie, but instead, had made me powerful. Confidently, I stared at myself in the mirror as something enormous started banging against the closed cabana bathroom door. I watched my image staring back at me from the framed alternate world. Soon my power would kick in, and I would puff up to my immortal self, allowing me to demolish the being that threatened from the other side of the thin door.

I waited, yet my transformation didn't happen. The banging noise got louder.

My confident, knowing smirk faded, yet I had not completely lost faith.

A clawed hand smashed through the door. I got my first glimpse of an enormous, alien-type being pushing its way into my happy home. Again, in the mirror, I stared at my unchanging appearance. I wasn't big. I wasn't powerful. I wasn't immortal.

I screamed "I'm scared!" But I didn't just yell, "I'm scared." I called out his name, and almost in the same moment I heard his name leave my lips, I jolted awake and realized I was in my bed with Adam beside me.

Why do I care about this dream? I care because I can't forget it. It was vivid, as if I watched a movie, which is not how most of my dreams unveil themselves. It also made me ponder why I would dream about changing into a powerful being. Finally, I questioned the name my sleeping mind called out in the night; my cry woke not only me, but Adam as well.

I'm backtracking and writing some of these dreams from memories because, in the beginning, I thought the vivid imagery was only a one or two-time occurrence. Then I had another vision and another. I hope that by writing them down, I'll make sense of the events triggering them.

I find myself running to Google to understand the meanings better. Why does someone dream about changing into something else? According to my sources, metamorphosis dreams represent that a transformation has already begun. I've thought a great deal about this interpretation and the feelings the visions have stirred up. For the first time in many years, I sense movement in the thick, heavy drape that has darkened my world. A warm breeze has lifted the edges, and I'm suddenly curious about what lies on the other side.

CHAPTER 2

Brent

Jacksonville
Three Months Earlier

I AWOKE TO THE image that still haunts me. Henry's yacht, captained by the unknown person of interest, was slipping away to some far-off country. The strange part was I'd never actually seen the boat during the investigation or the arrest. Henry and the speed boat driver were taken into custody, but the yacht waiting for the two of them to return, was never found. Voice analysis proved the man arrested with Henry at the drug bust was not the same man in the recorded conversation involving Adam's kidnapping.

The faceless man remained a mystery, as did Brenda Carter, the woman who owned the construction company we believed to be his shell company. When the case replayed in my mind, these two suspects remained blurred images—shadows drifting in and out of the unsolved puzzle. Perhaps after Henry's arrest, the completion of his case had allowed my mind to rest. But now, the whispers that taunted me were growing louder.

My fellow FBI officers had assured me Skylar was safe, that whoever was on the yacht had no reason to harm her. The mystery man and Brenda Carter had gotten away with enough cash to keep them well off for some time. They wouldn't risk their money or being captured to get revenge for Henry's arrest. I'd promised Skylar that she was free to live her life. Yet, the loose ends of the case dangled, teasing me, never allowing me to tie them into a neat bow. But in truth, more than loose ends kept my mind from letting the case go. My torment didn't stem from the ones that got away; instead, it came from the one I allowed to walk away.

As I got out of bed, the weight of the past months settled on my shoulders. The burden aged me beyond my forty years. My life was flying by in a gust of mundaneness. Knowing I wouldn't see Skylar or hear her voice again blotted the color out of my days. My future resembled a coloring sheet. All the correct lines were there, yet reality paled in comparison to my imagination.

Standing over my bathroom sink, I shook off the gloomy feelings, as I did every day, so I could focus on the current possibilities. I let the water run until it reached its peak coldness and splashed it over my face. The water dripped off the five o'clock shadow I didn't care to shave. After throwing on a fresh T-shirt, I texted, *I'll pick you up in ten.*

Meghan Ambers—I've known her for years, but when I went through the training to become a special agent, she took over some of my past cases as the forensic accountant. The move made our paths cross more frequently, making this night harder to avoid. As I walked out the door, I envisioned Meghan, flustered and excited, putting on her final touches. We had been at the cusp of possibility several times before, and I'd always backed away. Meghan was never one to mince words. It was obvious what she wanted, but I knew once I crossed that line with her, things would never be the same between us.

Women like Liz, Skylar's flirtatious coworker at McClurry and Associates, promised half the male population a good time. The memory of Skylar's snide comments played in my mind. Liz was clearly not a friend but a wasp, swooping through the accounting firm's office to find her next victim. Skylar insisted it would be her, and after witnessing their interactions, I couldn't argue. But then Liz's sting was nothing more than her conversation laced with poison that would leave an allergic lump in Skylar's day.

I had no desire to have a physical relationship with Liz, even if it could be guilt-free. Liz would enjoy the one night together more than I would, and her attention would drift to someone else before she had her blouse buttoned. Meghan was another story. A one-night stand with her meant feelings of guilt and regret; she wouldn't move on with ease. Maybe if I faked my emotions long enough, I could create a reality from imagination. Meghan was attractive, smart, and kind. But I felt nothing for her besides friendship. Maybe that wasn't so bad. After all, there could be truth in the opinion that long-lasting relationships didn't begin with fireworks. Heated romance fizzled with the passing of time. Friendship needed to be the primary lasting fuel. Yes, Meghan was precisely the type of woman I needed. If only I wanted her as well.

I pulled into Meghan's driveway. The small, one-story home with clay-colored stucco sides sat on the postage-stamp-sized yard as proof the FBI should raise the salaries of its employees. Before I could step out of my truck, Meghan, with a glow of a high schooler sneaking out of her parents' home, bounded out of her front door. Her smile screamed out the possibilities that raced through her mind. Her purse, no doubt, contained a handful of Trojans. Did she think we would end up parked behind some thick Floridian bush and intertwined like teenagers? Again, the question nagged at me. Would I let the relationship go there? The calls would begin then, texts every other hour. Sweat beaded on my forehead. Who cared? She had to know that a one-night stand didn't commit me for life, didn't she?

I walked around the truck to open her door. Meghan stood a full foot shorter than me, with brown, shoulder-length hair and crystal blue eyes. Some of my colleagues would bust on me, when Meghan strolled by, about how well we complemented each other, me with my brown hair and brown eyes. After almost two decades of working side by side with special agents, I had grown accustomed to the busting of balls that served as a reprieve from more serious matters.

Only Skylar's dark brown eyes and slight smile haunted me. Skylar's beauty hid behind her conservativeness, but once seen, it could never be unseen.

As I held the truck door open, Meghan stared up at me as if I held some answer. "No," I wanted to tell her, to warn her, "you won't find that here," but something about the way her eyes lit up made my day just a bit less dismal.

"I like the scruff." Her fingers briefly touched my cheek.

"Thanks. It's nice to know I don't have to waste all that time shaving." She met my remark with a smile as she climbed inside the cab.

Did she know Skylar had sat there once, forever ago it seemed? But somehow, when I was alone on the road, I still felt her there. To be truthful, I felt her everywhere. "I'm so glad you called," Meghan said.

"Me, too. I needed to get out." I closed the door and headed to the driver's side. A large black dog watched me from

Meghan's front window; the animal's stare warned me not to screw with his master. For some reason, I felt myself nod in understanding, but not necessarily agreement. Placing the truck in reverse and laying my arm across the seatback, I started down the driveway. Again, Meghan's smile loomed between us. How could she be that excited about me?

"What do you think of Beaches in St. Augustine? There's usually music on Friday nights."

"Sounds perfect," she chimed.

Being our first dinner together, instead of guessing at her favorite type of music, I switched on a popular local station that played the familiar everyday hits. I much preferred the songs that resonated with the few, the tunes that weren't victims of the repetitive playing that weakened their power to be treasures. Regardless, I needed to cut through the uncomfortable silence as quickly as possible.

Meghan's scrambling thoughts were almost audible. Finally, she nudged my shoulder. "I heard them singing your praises again about your last case."

"Oh, is that why you said yes to a drink?" I said, expressing a playfulness I didn't feel.

"Of course. I'm always on the lookout for the next up-and-coming special agent to sink my teeth into."

I smiled at her, only long enough to see her eyes glistening with joy. Meghan was the opposite of Liz. I was the only one receiving the vibe screaming "I'm a sure thing," which was precisely the reason I couldn't let a relationship happen. Or shouldn't.

The drive down A1A, with its swaying palm trees and ocean views, didn't disappoint. We pulled into the Beaches parking lot with enough time to get settled in with a drink before the sun sank over the Intracoastal. After what seemed a lengthy amount of time, the bartender, a young woman, took our orders: Landshark for me and a Miller Lite for Meghan. After a long, hard swallow, I was ready for the painful small talk and able to face her.

"How are your recent cases going?" she asked.

I was thankful that the band, Overboard, filled in the lulls in our conversation. Even though I didn't want to deal with small talk, I feared a night of awkward silence more than trying to communicate over the music. The one perk to being out with another special agent was I could speak about cases without worrying about sharing classified information.

"The recent cases are not quite as interesting as the last one," I said.

"You got used to all that excitement and forgot how daunting the daily paperwork can be."

"The paperwork definitely found me, but I'm meeting with Ryan on Monday. He's going to brief me on something he said would be of interest to me. At least they are keeping me local. I was expecting to up and move after Henry's case."

She nodded while taking a long swig of her beer, leaving glistening moisture on her lips. Ryan Nelson was the head honcho, the senior supervisory special agent, at our field office. Retirement loomed in his future, and although he could still give a decent chase if needed, he was getting a bit thick in the middle. He commanded the office with fairness and confidence. We had become accustomed to his traits, and no one desired the inevitable change.

"And yours cases?" I asked.

"Tons of fun," she said with sarcasm. I sensed her annoyance with trying to talk above the other discussions and the band. Her gaze strayed to the beach area next to the bar. The tide was out, leaving room for the few people—children and one couple—to find solace.

"Want to get out of the crowd?" Meghan tilted her head toward the beachy area.

I nodded and followed her lead. Thoughts of Skylar kept creeping in despite my efforts to push her into the recesses of my mind where she belonged. How long would it be before I could live in the moment again, not feel like I had one foot in the past and one in a future that would never happen? Even though I'd never shortened her name to Sky, I could not hear the common everyday word without thinking about her or see the sunset without reliving our moment on the pier. The universe seemed to be mocking me with reminders, but why?

Meghan cleared her throat and repeated the words I had apparently not heard the first time. "I said, the sunset is beautiful, isn't it?"

"Yes, it is." I glanced at the sip left in the bottom of my bottle. The crowded bar, offering me refuge, called to me from a distance.

"Now that we're alone, do you want to tell me about the case that made you choose to go from forensic accountant to special agent?" she said with another smile. "My hours of paper shuffling aren't leading me anywhere, so I need to live vicariously through you."

Meghan was also a forensic accountant. It was one more reason she felt bonded to me.

"The case got a bit more hands-on, I guess. Being out there, with the other special agents, well, I guess you could say it gave me the bug. I can still do some accounting work, but it's more fun with a gun and a badge." I smiled, and this time I almost meant it.

The times I'd spent with Skylar, unable to be the man I'd needed to be, had changed me. When Adam had gone missing, she'd been afraid to stay in her home. When we traveled to the Netherlands to rescue him, I had only a pen in my pocket. I had no further choice but to allow other men to become the heroes of her story. The feeling of inferiority I experienced was enough to make me pack my bags and head to Quantico to begin my fifteen weeks of training. If there ever is a next time, I'll be ready.

"I heard you got to travel to the Netherlands. Impressive. Tell me about it."

The memories hit me like a wall; visions exploded in my mind. The sensation of Skylar's hand in mine was as real as the sand under my feet. Then the memory of Adam appearing from the building washed the warmth away like a cool breeze.

"Don't want to talk about it?" Meghan continued.

"No, it's fine. It's good, I mean." I paused, trying to figure out where to start. Was there a way to tell the story while omitting the details I didn't want to share? "Skylar's boss at McClurry and Associates, Bruce, got involved with a client who had many offshore accounts, money laundering scams, and shell companies. You know, all the typical criminal activities that catch our eye. The client, Henry Davis, bought hotels up and down the east coast. He even had some in the Bahamas and the Netherlands. He got tipped off somehow that the authorities were getting suspicious about his business dealings. That's when he decided to try to pin a portion of his earnings and activities on someone else. At first, Bruce only completed inaccurate tax forms, and that worked for a while.

"A woman named Skylar worked at the office. Bruce asked her to work on a special case. He and Henry planned on using

Skylar as a scapegoat. Since Henry was never able to complete his plan, we cannot be sure what his full intentions for Skylar might have been. At least, it doesn't matter now."

"Why her?" Meghan was obviously unaware she had wandered into troublesome waters.

"Word has it they sensed she had a thing for me." I chuckled despite myself.

"Did she?"

"I don't know, but their tactic worked. Henry and Bruce sent us on accounts out of town and were able to get some compromising photographs." Meghan's face creased with concern at the mention of the pictures. For both our sakes, I added, "They were nothing, but enough to make Skylar nervous. She's not married, not yet anyway, but she's involved with someone, has been for a long time. They recently got engaged, though. Anyway, she got nervous when Henry threatened her, and she signed a false Report of Foreign Bank and Financial Accounts."

"Those FBARs have a lot of people sweating lately."

"Yes, they do." I let a couple holding hands and rubbing shoulders pass by. We both watched them—me hoping Meghan didn't get the idea that at any moment, I would reach out to grab her hand. I continued, hoping to push any such notions out of her mind. "Once Skylar committed her first crime for them, they had her trapped. That's why she then opened the offshore accounts for them, bought Bitcoin, pretty much helped them hide all their money."

"Bruce and Henry's money?"

"Not so much Bruce's. Henry's."

"What was Bruce getting out of all this?" Meghan asked.

"As I said, we ended Henry's plan, so some things went unanswered."

"Didn't Bruce end up shooting himself before Henry even went to jail?"

"Yes. That was unfortunate. Bruce wasn't a terrible person. He got in over his head. Like Skylar." It was the most I had spoken of Skylar in some time, and her name was both comforting and painful on my lips. I was touching her, yet at the same time, trying to breathe life into something already dead.

"What are the other loose ends?"

"There was another person. He was on the yacht they used for the drug deal, but he sold it before we could find him. It was originally owned by Henry, so the discovery didn't get us anywhere. We have recorded conversations between a man we believe to be this suspect and Henry. There was also a woman, Brenda Carter, who owned the shell companies. Skylar opened a good deal of accounts in her name. Brenda holds a large sum of money in them."

"Is Skylar nervous about those people still being out there?"

I swallowed the last of my warm beer. "I think Skylar's fine. We suspect the man and Brenda are hiding out in the Netherlands. We're watching the accounts, but they remain quiet. It doesn't surprise me. They were stashing money in many places. Whoever was on the yacht must have enough to tide them over until they feel things have quieted down. The case is stagnant until they either use the money or someone decides to come out from under his or her rock. They kept their finances separate enough that when we arrested Henry, the other two main characters remained out of FBI reach because they couldn't be tracked down through Henry's finances."

"Pretty trusting, don't you think?"

"What do you mean?"

"Criminals don't trust each other that much, do they?"

Meghan said. "They either had a solid deal in place or a relationship strong enough that they didn't think the other would screw them out of their share."

"Agreed."

"Blood."

"Excuse me?"

"I'll bet they're related."

Energy rushed through me that had nothing to do with the investigator's blood coursing through my veins. The reason had everything to do with the door to Skylar that had just creaked open. We could trace Henry's relatives. So easy. The idea was so evident that if I had not been so excited, I would have been embarrassed.

"Yeah, we've been looking into relatives. So far, nothing," I lied. As I contemplated ways that Meghan could figure out my lie, the buzzer in my pocket went off, signaling our table was ready.

Moments after we placed our order, Meghan circled back to Skylar.

"I almost feel bad for her."

"For who?"

"For the woman with the crush on you. How unfortunate that her feelings led to an FBI investigation."

Meghan's smile tested me; I'd either protect Skylar or mock her. On the first day of the investigation, I'd seen Skylar. I'd viewed her with FBI eyes, and nothing more. As they'd paid me to do, I'd studied everyone. Again, I tried to pinpoint the moment something had shifted inside of me, the moment I'd confused the line between investigator and friend. Is that what I would call it? I couldn't, though. I couldn't find the moment because there wasn't only one. Instead, it had been every one of them. Each time I'd come in contact, the shield had been chipped away at until nothing had protected me.

"Skylar has nothing to be ashamed of," I said.

Meghan didn't mention Skylar again.

It was easy to avoid crossing a line in a public place, but when later that evening, she invited me back to her house, things became trickier. We entered her home, neat and tidy, not too feminine, but warm. She went straight to the fridge and opened two beers without first asking if I wanted one. Maybe she felt the drink bought her some time.

"So why are you still single?" For the first time since someone had asked me that question, my mind did not revert to Emily. She was the first woman I can say that I loved. I lost her to drugs in a meaningless binge, and she became the reason I went into the FBI. Skylar had pushed her to the recesses of my mind, where Emily deserved to be for many years before I was willing to forget her.

"Good question. I'll let you answer it first."

"My husband, ex-husband, couldn't stand being the spouse of someone working with the FBI. It appealed to him in the beginning, but the novelty wore off before too long." Never taking her eyes off mine, Meghan raised the bottle to her mouth. Slowly, softly, it grazed her lips. "Your turn."

"It's possible that I'm not a long-term-relationship kind of guy."

She smiled, taking a step toward me. "Or could it be that you haven't met the right person at the right moment."

"I guess anything is possible." I swallowed hard as her hand slipped into mine.

"Want a tour?"

Without waiting for an answer, she led me down a hallway. Her bed loomed in the distance. Meghan's hand slipped from mine as she entered her room and turned to face me. Nothing good could come of this. I needed to end her attempt at seduction before it began, but my mind began to drift, envisioning us wrapped up together, despite the consequences. I stood in the doorway of her bedroom, watching. As if I had bought tickets to a show, she unbuttoned the top button of her blouse, her gaze never leaving mine. It was nothing more than a means to an end. The act was a way to erase an emptiness, like eating a roast beef sandwich to end hunger pangs, when what I craved was a ribeye. Her fingers reached the second button. A small smile hinted at the corners of her lips.

I imagined watching the blouse drift to the floor, her hands reaching behind her to unclasp her bra. In my mind, I moved closer to her. My fingers traveled up her rib cage, feeling her skin react to my touch, enjoying the small bumps that surfaced as she came alive. My hand grazed her breasts as I explored her body, touching her neck, making her feel beautiful and vulnerable at the same time. She arched at my touch, and our mouths found each other. Except, I reminded myself, this wouldn't be a simple act she'd soon forget. It came with ties and emotions; emotions I couldn't share, at least not now.

"Meghan, I'm sorry, but I'd better get going." I could almost hear the screech of the imaginary record playing in the background of her mind. Anguish replaced the playfulness in her eyes. It was better to hurt her now than after the fact. "I'm sorry," I said again, taking a step closer to her until she stood within reach. "You deserve someone who is completely present," I said as I fastened the button of her blouse, "and it's not me. Not right now." I kissed her forehead as some sort of token consolation prize and turned to leave.

"Brent." I paused at the sound of my name but did not look back. "Is there a chance? Maybe? Sometime in the future?"

"I'd like to think there's always a chance." I headed toward the door. She didn't need to know the chance I referred to had nothing to do with her.

CHAPTER 3

Skylar

Journal Entry

THE SOUND OF the waves outside my window must have plagued me in my sleep and dared me to come back to the sea. My mind knew better. It would not let the events of the evening settle into an innocent memory without a fight. The fear and adrenaline of the evening blended into a vison where reality won, and the false euphoria was swept away.

I was in my backyard planting flowers when I noticed a small lake forming behind me. A childlike excitement intoxicated me as the cool water splashed across the manicured grass and slapped at my ankles. I playfully kicked back at the waves, as if they were friends coming to play. A smile naively spread across my face, and I ventured a step farther into the growing swells. The waves responded with increasing intensity, until my light-hearted laugh caught in my throat. I glanced back at my home; the waves were beginning to slam against the siding. A small uprooted daisy floated by me in the sea foam. Looking down, I didn't see the monstrous wave approaching. Unable to brace myself, my body hurdled toward my home until I felt the force of our collision. The sound of shattering windowpanes jolted me awake.

Over and over in my research, I'd found that dreams about waves dealt with emotional turbulence and uncertainty. Never had I felt so uncertain, or had I experienced such emotional turbulence, outside of the period following the loss of my parents—a time that I seldom revisit. Even writing about my parents' death reminds me of how the floors of my world swayed as my aunt relayed the news. Adam grounded me in still waters, making me forget the turbulence. But sometimes, storms find you even when you're trying to hide. The rumblings come slowly, beckoning you out of your shelter and awing you with the tempest's power. Would I recognize when the power was becoming lethal, or would I still be staring at it when, with unforgiving force, a tsunami slammed into me?

Current events, they were the waves I had dared to dip a toe in, forgetting how unexpectedly those very waves could become the enemy and destroy everything. My dream reminded me that there are some waters we are not intended to ever dabble in.

I wanted, I truly desired, to never step foot in them again. But that's the funny thing about life. It doesn't always go as planned.

CHAPTER 4

Brent

HENRY'S CASE DRIFTED to the bottom of the loose-ends-and-all files stacked on my office desk. The last bit of steam danced above my coffee cup, and I could hear someone in the distance refilling the pot I'd left empty. I tapped on the keyboard, bringing my computer to life as I gave one last glance at the stagnant files lying to the side.

The case rarely had enough fuel to ignite the attention I desired to give it. I kept one eye open for any incident that would warrant attention, hoping to see some action, but nothing revealed itself. Solving crime is a great deal like popping the head of an ugly pimple. For a moment, you feel successful, even a bit like you have won. That is, until you realize underneath the skin of that particular crime, a million other bacteria have scurried in to fill the gap. It's never as easy as taking out the headpin. While we waited for the next round, other crimes demanded our energy. The remaining bacteria would become active enough to make their infection rise to the surface, and we would be ready. But today, I was in the mood to dig, even if it was premature.

Henry remained a wealthy man by anyone's standard. He came from money and had the know-how to build an even greater empire. The hotels were legitimate money. Henry managed to keep the drug money separate by having it laundered through the construction company owned by Brenda Carter. But there was something missing—something that kept me awake at night.

Fortunately, and unfortunately, money makes a person a bit more intriguing to the press. Due to that fact, I immediately hit on an article written about five years before Henry's fall from grace.

The Rise, Fall, and Rise of Henry Davis
Hillary Bridges

Henry Davis. You might not know his name, but you have probably stayed in one of his hotels. He has built a small empire of budget-friendly to high-end properties. Henry is now one of the wealthiest men in the Jacksonville area, although his empire stretches far wider than our community. His life is a story of going from riches to rags and back to riches, and it can inspire each of us. It's about knowing how to get back up after you've fallen, but for Henry, the fall was so treacherous it would have crippled most of us. I sat down with him in a conference room of one of his hotels—the same hotel he'd inherited from his father, the last life preserver thrown out to him and his younger brother, Nick.

Nick. There he was, like a coiled snake under a bush and prepared to strike if discovered. Yet, up to this point, his silence and perfect record had made him undetectable to the FBI. I knew where my next search would begin.

When I was assigned to conduct Henry Davis' interview, I knew little about him. He entered the conference room, and I felt as if I was looking at the end of a long story where Henry stood victorious. His frame filled the doorframe, which he stood in for a moment, possibly to size me up. Was I worthy of his time? I didn't feel put off by the gesture, but his demeanor demanded respect. And I immediately felt obligated to give it. His Brioni suit was tailored to his impressive frame, and although I feared direct eye contact, I eventually did meet his gaze. He was already watching me, waiting, and for a moment, I forgot my purpose.

Gathering my thoughts, I reminded myself of the backstory Henry had offered beforehand. Perhaps he knew how intimidating his presence could be, and this offering was an attempt to give me an image to calm my nerves at this moment. At about the age of ten, Henry had realized for the first time how privileged he was, even among the privileged. Around that age, he also learned that he should never take it for granted. He rode out across the ocean on a yacht that, at times, served as his school. A tutor worked with the Henry and Nick while dolphins swam without care beside the boat. It was a perk their father had earned from his business ventures.

Hillary: (I cleared my throat.) Let's start at the beginning. Your mother? Do you have any recollections of your biological mother?

Henry: I have no memories of her. To me, it's as if she never existed. My first memories only include my father, brother, and me. My father was a businessman, so he was often busy or traveling, but when he was home, he was quite attentive. He wasn't the type of father to throw a ball back and forth. Even when my brother and I were very young, we discussed stocks and business.

Hillary: So, your father is why you love business?

Henry: Don't most young boys want to follow in their father's footsteps?

Hillary: Many, yes. And what influence, if any, did your stepmother have on you?

Henry was silent for a moment.

Henry: She never influenced me. Not in the ways a mother should.

Hillary: How old were you when they married?

Henry: I was about seven. My father took his yacht out on a business venture. I refer to the trip as Odysseus sailing to Troy. I don't know what happened on that trip, but I picture Blair as one of the sirens that tempted

Odysseus. My father never saw her like that, but she came home with him, and nothing was ever the same. I don't remember their dating phase, or what made him fall in love with my her. Lord knows, I never quite figured that out.

Hillary: It doesn't seem like you hold her in very high regard.

Henry's voice stayed steady and calm, as if he told his story as a bystander of a film. His lack of emotion spoke volumes.

Henry: She was very impersonal. I suppose if Nick and I had fallen overboard, she would have thrown us a floatation device of some sort, but CPR would have been out of the question.

Hillary: I'm not quite sure how to respond to that.

Henry: My stepmother would always lie in a lounge chair, watching us. I never quite figured out how to discern the look on her face. I can best describe it as her studying my brother and me and wondering how on earth we came into her life. Her expression was not one of adornment that a mother or even stepmother might show. Instead, it was as if she was watching a man in a speedo prance across their club's private beach while smoking a joint. You know, like she was asking herself: Who the hell let him in here?

A surprised chuckle floated from Henry. He paused, composed himself again.

Henry: That's what I always imagined went through her mind whenever she saw us.

Hillary: I've seen pictures of your stepmother. I'd be lying if I said she was not beautiful.

Henry: Beauty is a funny thing, is it not?

He let the silence settle between us before he continued.

Henry: We're drawn to it, empowered by it, blinded by it. It's a powerful quality that no one teaches us to fear. But her beauty alone didn't make Blair dangerous. Some people are black holes that will never have enough. They continue to suck in everything around them. The people left in her presence after my father died found themselves scrambling to get back what she absorbed into her nothingness.

Hillary: (I allowed us both time to take a drink of water before continuing.) That gets us to the fall. Are you ready to speak about it?

Henry gave me a look that suggested he was almost offended I believed life could have touched him in any way.

Henry: When I was twelve, my father passed away suddenly from a massive heart attack. He died in his home office. Our nanny kept us upstairs and tried to entertain us through the sounds of sirens outside. We knew, not everything, but we knew life as we'd known it was over. It took my stepmother three years to drain the accounts; three years to lose the yacht, the hotels, our home. Or, at least, that's the story. She was still doing well for herself the last I heard.

Nick and I went to live with our aunt and uncle we had met once. They were friendly and cold at the same time. We squeezed into their modest home on the Florida Panhandle, but then, to some, the residence wasn't considered mediocre. As you know, wealth is relative. We may have looked like an average middle-class family, but to us, we were living in poverty.

Hillary: Did you always know about the hotel, the one your father left to you and your brother?

Henry: No, but we knew he'd left us something, and we would find out what that was only after graduating from a four-year college. My brother graduated a year after me. That's when the executor of my father's will informed us about the hotel.

Hillary: Was it what you expected? Were you excited about your inheritance?

Henry: I didn't know what to expect, but I was far from excited at the time. In hindsight, my father gave us much more than money; he gave us possibilities. In time, I became confident that I could do something with my inheritance. After five years, I was able to buy Nick out of his share, and the rest is history.

Hillary: And where is Nick today?

Henry: Let's just say, we went our separate ways.

Hillary: Would you like to elaborate?

Henry: As I said, we went our separate ways.

My interview with Henry Davis ended on that final note, leaving me wondering about the secrets that would remain safely hidden from the public.

Nick Davis—he was out there somewhere, and he held the key to the only door back to Skylar. One way or the other, Nick was about to get to know me.

CHAPTER 5

Skylar

Journal Entry

I RAN TO MY *vehicle through an empty parking garage. Over the concrete walls, I could see a tsunami closing in on me. My car would serve as little refuse from a wave of that magnitude, but it was my only chance. The sound of trees cracking and structures crumbling to the ground drew closer. My heart raced as my fingers searched through my purse for the keys. After precious moments, I found them and frantically hit the unlock button. The wave was on top of the garage as I climbed inside the car, started the ignition, and headed toward the exit.*

The crashing sounds became louder as the wave appeared in my rearview mirror. Within seconds, my vehicle lifted and swayed in the water. The next thing I knew, a surge of rushing water pummeled into the rear of my vehicle. With violent force, the car was pushed down the declining paths of the parking garage. The walls loomed in front of me as I barreled toward them on what felt like a waterslide. I tried to steer around the corners, yet I had no control over the car's direction. Each time, the vehicle somehow turned at the last second until the final wall loomed ahead, leaving me no time to react. That's when my brain knew to jump ship and woke me with a start.

Without the help of Google, I'd translated my dream to mean I was overwhelmed and unhappy.

The tsunami represented a tidal wave of fear and emotions I had no clue how to deal with. Not to mention, life was pushing me along my path, and no matter how hard I tried to steer myself in the right direction, I lacked the control to do so.

CHAPTER 6

Brent

ONLY WHEN I reached Ryan's office Monday morning did I recall what he had said earlier. He was going to brief me on something that might be of interest to me. With piqued curiosity, I entered his office, giving only a gentle knock to gain his attention. He looked up, set his readers down on his desk, and motioned me in.

"Good morning, Brent."

"Morning, Ryan. You have me curious. What does this case involve?"

"A gentlemen's club and unexplained money. Suspected drug deals. You know, the basics."

"Okay, but what makes this one so interesting?"

"We have reason to believe there was a drug mule involved."

"What club?"

"The Full Moon," Ryan replied.

I nodded once, encouraging him to continue.

"The drug mule's name was Bruce McClurry."

Skylar's old boss, the one responsible for trapping her in Henry's web of crimes. The light went on. Henry's case was back on the top of the pile, and the road to Skylar opened before me. "So that's how Bruce was profiting from working with Henry. Now it makes sense why he stuck with him. How'd you find out?"

"Some suspicious accounts have come to our attention, but Bruce lived a modest lifestyle, apart from his expensive car. I guess he was saving up for something."

"Yeah, for something he could never buy."

Ryan rested his hands behind his head as he leaned back in his chair. "And that was?"

"His ex-wife. She left him for a wealthy CEO. Bruce never got over it."

Ryan nodded. "Oh, the age-old problem. Damn women." He turned his attention to the folder on his desk. "After some more digging, we found he'd frequented The Full Moon a bit too often. He would go in, sit in the same spot, have one beer, and leave. Our source tells us that Bruce never paid much attention to the women there. We're not sure that Bruce had anything to do with the club itself, but that's where he delivered his drugs."

What a bizarre and bitter beast love twisted into at times. Bruce's obsession with getting Chrissy back ultimately destroyed him. I pictured him at the bar, slumped over his beer, unaware of the temptations lurking all around him. We were not all that different, Bruce and I. We'd both been overtaken with the same blinding force. I wanted to tell myself I wouldn't let it destroy me, yet I wondered.

"This is what we know. The club is successful, but not enough to explain the lifestyle of one of the owners, Abigail Carswell. She's living well beyond her means. Because of your forensic accounting background, you'll be reviewing the bar's expenses while also doing investigative work." Ryan slid me some papers, which I glanced at before returning my attention to him. "Stay away from the bar for now in case someone might recognize you. We're hoping that the rodents return to their nest before too long. We need to identify the mystery man from Henry's case. For now, you focus on the books, and I'll let you know the next step."

"The mystery man, I have reason to believe, is Henry's brother, Nick. He disappeared after college."

"You got anything on him besides the fact that he disappeared?"

"I'm afraid nothing besides a feeling."

"Explain."

"The level of trust between the partners makes me suspicious. I also uncovered an old interview with Henry that discusses a brother."

Ryan sized me up for a moment before nodding. "I'll want to see that article. Let me know if you find evidence to support your suspicions. In the meantime, look over the club's accounts and get back to me."

"Will do."

At any given time, there could be forty active cases, each with its own share of paperwork, on our squad's plate. The paperwork was a part of the job I couldn't avoid even if I carried a gun, which for the most part, would remain unused. The gun-wielding, busting-through-door moments were few and far between. At least now, I was ready for wherever the case led me.

I left the office, knowing it was only a matter of time before Skylar and I would cross paths again. The surge of adrenaline, mixed with the realization that I could no longer assume Skylar was safe, terrified me. Because of that, despite what Ryan had said, my search needed to stray from analyzing accounts to finding Nick Davis.

Cynthia, our intelligence analyst, was the heart of the

squad. She supplied us with morning doughnuts and emanated positivity, which was why I seldom failed to visit her at some point in the day. Not only did Cynthia ease any tension in the air, she latched onto projects with the ferocity of a dog seeking the squeaky part hidden inside its chew toy. She never let up until she could place the little plastic organ at our feet with a mixed look of pride and *what else do you have for me?* Everyone in the office liked and respected her, yet I sensed when she left for the evening, her nights were quiet and lonely.

"Good morning, Cynthia." She was in her early thirties; still young. She was attractive in a neutral sort of way, blending into the background for the most part. My feelings for her never wavered beyond friendship, and from her behavior, I would say she felt the same about me.

She swiveled in her chair to greet me with her infectious air. "Good morning Brent. What can I do for you today?"

"I need you to do a little background investigation for me on a Nick Davis." I filled her in as I scanned the doughnut box and settled on a frosted maple treat.

"On it." She swiveled back to her screens.

"You're the best," I said through a mouthful of doughnut.

With purpose, I strolled down the hallway and began reviewing Abigail's accounts. Awaiting Cynthia's results preoccupied my mind, yet the results never came. All day, I had resisted the urge to pressure her for updates, knowing she was not one to hold back. When the clock struck five, I closed my files and headed home, planning on attempting my investigation off the clock.

As on most days, I entered my apartment with the air of the past ten hours stuck to me the way the aroma of cooked fish seeps into one's clothes. Energy from the people I'd encountered throughout the day sank into the small, one-bedroom apartment, settling in as unwanted guests, tossing their feet up on the furniture. To show some power over them, I spread out on my couch with my microwaved meal and pretended I didn't sense their presence, but I did. They were always there, impossible to shut out. After an hour of mindlessly flipping through the channels, I shut off the television and went to bed.

I scanned my bedroom, which was stale and uninviting—just like my personal life. Almost every item served a purpose. No frills, just function. My job occupied my days and nights. Distractions, I told myself, were unnecessary at best. Flipping open my computer, I began searching for what I could. I planned on savoring each piece of information as if it were a swig of expensive bourbon. As I'd suspected, what I discovered failed to whet my palette. Henry's words about them going their separate ways kept playing in my mind. Why?

Secrets didn't often hide between the covers of magazines, especially if the person of interest enjoyed his or her privacy. If Meghan guessed correctly, and Nick was the man from the yacht, it would make sense that Nick had disappeared to the Netherlands—a whole other world of logistics we would need to deal with eventually. Fortunately, there existed a Legal Attaché, aka Legat, in the U.S. embassy in the Hague, Netherlands. One consolation remained. Nick might not be anywhere near Skylar.

I thought back to the conversation we had listened in on while investigating Henry.

"He won't take care of this for us. I thought you said you had it under control. I didn't agree to murder," the mysterious voice said.

"Don't start having morals now. The matter can't wait until I get there," Henry answered.

"I wasn't planning on adding murder to my rap sheet. I sell drugs. I don't like to get my hands that kind of bloody."

"Just because you aren't pulling the trigger doesn't mean your hands aren't already bloody," Henry said.

"I don't want this traced back to me."

On the other end of the line had been a man with a clean record and a determination to keep it that way. He'd walked away with an untold amount of money and, most likely, a new identity. He had maintained his clean slate. What reason would he have to come back to risk all that? Something told me he didn't care much about avenging his brother. After all, they'd known their risk when they'd begun selling drugs.

My many years as a forensic accountant did not diminish the fact that I was still new to my job as a special agent. Even though I had gained my colleagues' confidence in my abilities, I was still an amateur, capable of negating all I'd accomplished thus far. I wanted to maintain my squad's level of respect as much as I desired to see Skylar again. No, I wouldn't let my deep-rooted need to see Skylar blind me. I told myself this knowing that the mind can be a very dishonest organ. I promised myself to do everything in my power to focus on the facts, even if they didn't lead me back to some unfulfilled fantasy.

Sleep threatened my eyes, and the unfulfilled fantasies I'd pledged to ignore called to me. My lucid brain began transforming the words on the computer into the fiction of dreamland until I succumbed to sleep, waking only once in the night to close my laptop and place it on the nightstand next to me.

My office was not much larger than the cubicles at McClurry's, but it allowed some privacy. Taking advantage of the lack of prying eyes, I scanned some more until I gave up. Putting

Nick and Skylar out of my mind, I pulled out my highlighter and, in what seemed an archaic fashion, marked the numbers on Abigail's accounts that gave me pause. Red flags, frantically waving at me, jumped off the page.

Cynthia appeared at my office door. She wore an expression I rarely saw on her: defeat.

"Nothing," she said.

Maybe my investigative skills were better than I thought. She went on to fill me in on how she'd had to finally accept her results.

Oddly, or maybe not so oddly, after the deal with the hotel, Nick Davis had disappeared. He didn't have a record, so there'd never be any prints, absolutely nothing in our database. According to the cyber world, Nick Davis had ceased to exist within six months of graduating from Florida State University. Cynthia could not uncover anything through the Combined DNA Index System or CODIS either. As suspected, up to the disappearance, at least, Nick Davis had never left DNA at a crime scene—that we were aware of anyway. Before Cynthia could turn and walk back out my door, I made a promise to myself and Skylar. Nick's spotless record was about to get dirty.

The next day, I had the pleasure of meeting Abigail Carswell. Ryan had me go to her house without Meghan, hoping that I could win Abigail's trust. Thoughts of the illegal money screamed at me as I pulled into the driveway of her prominent multimillion-dollar home on the St. Johns River. A red convertible Jaguar sat in front of a three-car garage. Somehow, I knew the vehicle was hers and that leaving such a masterpiece outside the garage was a choice. Illegally earned money or not, she had used her wealth to buy a sweet car. The home's brick exterior matched many in the neighborhood, making hers blend in with the crowd, but if her community was as I expected it to be, her profession was no secret.

Before I could reach the looming wooden doors, one swung open. Ms. Carswell stood in front of me—her forehead unnaturally smooth from injected poisons that melded with her DNA. One thing was for certain, her Devil-Wears-Prada persona was going to have a tough time in the prison system.

Abigail wore a tailored dress that somehow passed as casual even though the price tag must have said otherwise. Her French manicured hand shook as she reached out to shake mine. Being caught in the auditor's headlights was obviously uncomfortable for this otherwise confident-looking woman.

I introduced myself as Jake Fisher, a new accountant from the accounting firm that prepared her tax forms. My invented identity would prevent anyone linked to the case from being aware of the FBI's interest.

"Come in, Mr. Fisher." She welcomed me into the grand foyer where an obnoxious staircase began its ascent. "I've set out a small breakfast tray."

"Thank you." The impressive portraits and elegant furniture said anything but gentlemen's club. She guided me to her screened-in area at the back of her house. A ceiling fan spun over the outside living room positioned next to the stone and wood kitchen area. Did anyone ever swim in her glistening pool, or was it was only for show? An underprivileged family would be happy to inhabit only this part of her house. They wouldn't care to even enter the confines, except for the occasional visit to the bathroom.

She motioned me to a seat without saying a word. While she poured the coffee, I settled myself in, taking in more of her audacious lifestyle.

"Coffee?" came the obvious question.

"Please."

She placed it in front of me before pouring herself one. Then she took a seat while tucking her dress underneath her.

"So." She crossed her legs as if the conversation would be more comfortable that way. "I'm assuming you're here to ask some questions about my accounts."

"Yes. There do seem to be some, how do I put this, discrepancies."

"Are you sure?" She leaned forward, tucking a wisp of hair behind her ear. Was she trying to come on to me? I already lacked respect for her but found myself almost rooting for her not to be that dumb.

"I'm very sure." I handed her some of the paperwork I had highlighted.

"I'm not understanding," she said with a gentle flip of her hair.

"Well, let me explain. This number is what we are showing for revenue from the gentlemen's club."

"Could we just call it a club? Gentlemen's clubs have such an inappropriate connotation to them."

"Do you have strippers at your club?"

"Well, yes."

"Then it's a gentlemen's club, but if you would like me to refer to it as a club, then I will."

"Thank you."

"As you can see, this is your revenue. It's not that shabby. Still, we need to explain some of the purchases and monthly payments." I showed her the second sheet. We spent some time reviewing the columns as if it could change the obvious. I sat back and lifted the coffee to my lips. The steam prevented me from taking a sip.

"I'm sorry. I need to change the settings on that machine. The coffee is scalding."

"No worries," I put the cup down before I blistered myself.

Tucking the strand back behind her ear again, Abigail returned her attention to the papers. She offered me a nervous smile, as if she hoped I couldn't tell she was illiterate when it came to tax forms.

"Let me help you understand," I offered, to end the awkward moment. Carefully, I went over each number representing income, and then I did the same for her expenses—mortgage, car payments, trips. "Are you understanding the concern?"

Abigail stared down at the sheet as if she had no clue where the money had magically appeared from. I couldn't quite decide if she was that ignorant or if she were smart enough to play dumb, but still too stupid to realize her deception wouldn't work. Either way, her intelligence was questionable. "This is where we should start. I need you to see if you can find any other way to explain your economic status. Do you think if I check back with you in a few days, we can have an honest conversation about your finances and get some things in order?"

"I'll try. I'll talk to some people at our club and see if I'm missing something."

"That would be a good idea. The IRS does like us to account for our earnings."

"Oh, of course. Maybe I've just been a bit disorganized. How many days?"

"How about if I come back in three days? Same time?"

"Okay. I'm sure this will all work out, Mr. Fisher."

"Let's hope so."

The weekend came, and I couldn't resist hopping on my

motorcycle and letting it take me wherever it chose. Memories lingered within its metal frame as well. Before long, my bike settled into a parking spot at a diner I had once frequented with Skylar. What were the chances of running into her? Slim, but sometimes fate worked with a person if he or she were willing to help it a bit.

As I approached the door, I almost bumped into Patty, the secretary from McClurry & Associates.

"Brent! Oh, my goodness, it's so nice to see you." Her pleasure seemed genuine, and we gave each other a quick embrace.

"So, how's everyone in the office?" I asked. "Have things quieted down?"

"It's back to the same old daily grind. That's the weird thing about life, isn't it? Even after a tragedy like ours, life keeps on rolling forward."

I pictured the office, the crime scene tape, Bruce's funeral, seeing Skylar wearing her engagement ring for the first time.

"Yes, but how would we survive if we couldn't put things in the past?"

"I guess we wouldn't, would we?" Patty adjusted her purse strap. "Will you be coming to the wedding next weekend?" An uncomfortable look shadowed her face. "Oh, I'm sorry. I shouldn't ask such things not knowing who received invitations." That was the Patty I remembered—always in search of the next possibility of drama and with eyes on everything. Yes, her mention of the wedding had caused an overwhelming sourness to permeate my stomach, but not because of her pettiness. Instead, it was the fact Skylar's wedding was going to happen, and there was nothing I could do to stop it.

"That's quite all right. I was only a temp. I'm used to being viewed as an outsider in the office."

"No one thought of you as an outsider. Once people go through what we went through together, we become like family. It's only a small wedding," she said, a tone of pity heavy in her voice. "Otherwise, I'm sure she would have invited you."

Of course, it would be a small wedding. I was somewhat surprised Skylar and Adam didn't elope versus plan an event at all.

"Well, have a great time. Tell everyone I said hello."

One beneficial aspect of a gossiper is that when you wanted information to spread, you could rest assured that it would. Because of that very fact, a piece of me would ripple through Patty and touch Skylar. Problem was, I would never know in what way.

"I'll say hello for you. The office staff will be happy to hear you're still local."

"Just here on a ride, actually." I had no idea why those words had left my mouth. Could it be that the words were my attempt to feel untouchable? They failed. Something inside me broke as the future I'd dreamed of with Skylar drifted a million miles away.

Almost home, I passed an ABC liquor store and sensed my bike lean in that direction. Why not? I walked out with a bottle of Angel's Envy and secured it in my bike's side bag. The news of Skylar's upcoming wedding would go down smoother with liquid, and tonight's liquid of choice was bourbon. Some evenings, drowning in my sorrow seemed like a necessary escape from reality, yet it was a rare occasion I allowed it.

Scanning Netflix, I settled on the next episode of *Ozark*. It was always interesting, trying to anticipate the next demon to crawl out of the darkness. The waters in that town ran very deep and dark. By about the third episode and halfway into the bottle of Angel's Envy, the plot was too complicated for me to follow. My thoughts drifted into the world only discovered while my mind was tainted by alcohol. Knowing I shouldn't, I took one more swig. I would regret it in the morning, but the sorrow within me still breathed, and I'd hear its last breath before I slept.

In my drunken stupor, life's borders almost became tangible. They were glass borders where unattainable futures were visible. I reached for them, but my fingers slammed against the partitions. I called out through them, yet no one could hear. From my entrapment, I watched as each person walked away, leaving me alone. For a moment, only Skylar remained, but then she turned her back to me and disappeared from my view. Was my destiny to be banging forever on the invisible walls between reality and happiness?

Once again, I picked up my phone, as if I could make a text appear from Skylar. Nothing. I fumbled with the phone until I found the last words sent between us. Through the months, I'd seen Skylar's name drift from the first on my history to where I had to scroll for many pages before finding it. The strand of messages was a treasure at the bottom of the sea. When I clicked on the last one, I pretended it was possible to erase the time between the day she'd sent it to now. That somehow, I could erase the memories she was making daily with Adam, the wedding plans, the honeymoon. I tossed my phone to the other end of the couch.

Could it be that complete happiness was not attainable for me? We can say we found true love, but as many learn, that feeling ebbs with time. If I was honest with myself, I hadn't been as in love with Emily as my memory wanted me to believe.

But could I say the same about Skylar? Could my feelings for her be protected from their fall from grace because I'd never known her faults? Was she moody and distant when she returned from work? Did she cook chicken breasts until they dried to strands of unflavored jerky?

Was there even such a thing as chicken jerky? Probably not, because it wouldn't be any good. Chicken should never be cooked to that degree. My few failed attempts at grilling had proved the fact to me. I took another swig of bourbon and contemplated overcooked chicken, because the thought entertained my blissfully blurry mind. One more swig. I let it settle on my tongue. Life was a bit like chicken—too easy to overcook and dangerous if not heated through. There was only a tiny moment where poultry was healthy and flavorful; the perfect grilling time. Even when you cooked it to that exact temperature and tried to savor that precisely-timed chicken, you realized it was bland as shit. You'd been too worried about timing that you'd forgotten the marinade or panko coating that gave it any flavor whatsoever. Yes, life was like a frigging chicken breast. Just too damn hard to make it worth digesting.

As I attempted to set my glass down, it banged against the coffee table. My head spun. Soon I would regret drowning my sorrows. Throw in the fact that I had just experienced a whole life analogy having to do with chicken breast, and it was evidently time to go to bed. If I fell asleep fast enough, I could escape the total bed spins I felt coming on.

My phone buzzed. The screen lit up, and I considered walking away from it until I saw the name—Skylar.

More than anything, I wanted not to feel drunk anymore. My heart raced, pumping my alcohol-ridden blood into each crevice of my mind. The message disappeared, and I fumbled with the damn password on my phone. Finally, the screen opened.

"Brent, I know it's been a long time, but I had to text you. Someone is watching me."

I cursed the half empty bottle of bourbon in front of me for three reasons. One, I wanted to feel the moment, to savor it. I had waited too long to hear from Skylar, and now her words sloshed in my polluted brain. Two, she needed me, and I couldn't drive. I couldn't even trust my words to travel unobscured. Three, my drunk hands had to rely on autocorrect, and I'd had too many bad experiences with that. Carefully, I began to type.

*What are you taking—*Delete. *What are you talking about?*

There's a car I keep seeing, at the office, and the coffee shop. I'm almost positive it passed by my house tonight.

Skylar, we need to talk. I believe I texted. *Let's meet tomorrow. I'll come to you.*

Can you come to our house? Adam will be here all day tomorrow.

My fingers hovered over the buttons as if someone had stomped on them, and I wasn't quite sure they still worked. *Yes.*

What time?

I was an outsider, banging on the glass. The only way in was to wait for someone to open the door.

Whenever you want me.

Skylar didn't immediately reply. What was going through her mind? The commitments on her calendar? The idea of wanting me? I waited, knowing I would read into every word of her reply.

Sorry, I had to double-check with Adam. Can you be here at noon?

I typed yes and shut the phone off. Skylar's words were far too clear to need deciphering.

CHAPTER 7

Skylar

Journal Entry

THE WAVES SOFTLY *lashed against the beach, as if tired from a day of hard play. I could see him waiting for me amongst the crowd, and I drifted toward him. An ocean breeze floated through the crowd, before gliding gently across my skin. The faces of the people around me lacked detail and had no real meaning in my life, except the one face that I focused on. He was painfully familiar, as if he was a lost friend. As I approached him, I'd felt the pain soften. Feelings of peace and happiness soon danced in the currents of the air that encircled me.*

The sand beneath my feet grounded me, yet my senses were numb to its warmth and softness. My focus rested on my contented feeling, the contours of the man's face, and one other detail—the color of our clothes. The man wore a black, button-up shirt, and I wore a black dress. Both articles of clothing were beachy, despite the color. I smiled up at the man who returned my gesture with a warm smile of his own. The indistinct people on the beach surrounded us, making us the center of attention. It was our wedding, and nothing I'd ever experienced felt so right.

The desire to crawl back into the feeling the dream had created was as strong as the pull toward a down comforter on a cold winter night. When I saw him waiting for me on the beach, I felt complete. The fading vision left a feeling of contentment— a feeling both powerful and soft.

The quick glimpse of the event left me longing for more, yet as much as I tried to force myself back in, I could not reenter the dream.

Still, I could not help but question the importance of the color that had seemed so prominent. I Googled dreams and colors. Black represents the unknown or danger. It can also, among a large handful of other things, mean potential or possibilities. Even Google has no idea if my current situation is dangerous or full of potential. Where were the prophetic dreams, the ones that gave directives? Where were the dreams telling me what path to follow? I would listen. If the sign were clear enough, I would take the leap. I think.

CHAPTER 8

Brent

AS NOVEMBER LOOMED on the horizon, the Florida air finally cooled into the seventies—another perfect motorcycle day. The entire time I rode, I tried to distance myself from the emotions within me. *It's just another case*, I told myself over and over again, yet the sourness in the pit of my stomach and my rapid heartbeat reminded me otherwise.

I pulled into Adam and Skylar's driveway. Both cars sat side by side, and I saw Ted staring out the window. The yellow Labrador's head disappeared, I'm sure to alert his masters of my presence. Before I had a chance to ring the doorbell, Skylar opened the door.

"Thank you for coming." She rushed toward me and embraced me. How come when you finally get the moment, the one that's gone through your mind a million times, it's over before your body has had a chance to absorb it? My mind had been much more patient with its fantasies, allowing time for hugs to linger and my fingers to feel the warmth of her skin. Oddly, the sensation of Adam's callused palm in mine continued to scratch at my senses long after the handshake ended.

We stepped inside the kitchen. "Why don't we start from the beginning?" I tried to sound more professional than I felt.

"I brewed coffee," Skylar said. "Come and have a seat. Is...."

"French vanilla is perfect," I said with a private smile, hoping she would remember the familiarity of the break room forever ago. She turned toward the counter. Her expression remained hidden, holding onto to its secrets.

Adam motioned for me to take a spot at the kitchen table. He sat in the chair I had once, for a moment at least, filled.

"Skylar said the vehicle's a black BMW. I took her by the dealership yesterday so I could get more detail. From her best guess, it's a 320i or a 328i sedan."

"Nice work. I'm assuming you haven't seen the license plate."

"You're assuming correctly," Adam replied as Skylar, with a shaking hand, placed the steaming cup of coffee in front of me. What was the cause of her shakiness? Was it the black BMW or the fact I sat at her kitchen table?

Skylar pulled the chair out to have a seat, making a scraping sound that alerted Ted. His head jerked up, and then, when he sensed the danger had passed, nestled on his paws again. Once seated, Skylar rested her head in her hands, to avoid eye contact, I presumed.

"Skylar, where did you see the car the first time? What made you notice it?"

Finally, she lifted her head, and her eyes met mine. My breath caught. Thankfully, it was her time to speak. I became lost in her gaze, and for a moment, everything around us paused.

"I was walking to my car to go to lunch, and I noticed the BMW because it wasn't parked. It was just sitting there."

I tried to focus on what she was saying, but instead, I found myself watching her lips part to form the words. The actual words were a side note. I cleared my throat, bringing me back to the kitchen, the cabinets, the chair beneath me. "Was anyone with you?"

"No, I was alone."

Skylar, the loner; the one who stood apart. It all came rushing back to me again.

"You were alone." I pulled a small notebook from my pocket and wrote down what I knew so far. "What happened next?"

"Nothing, really. I kept a close watch on the car as I unlocked my own. I couldn't see inside the BMW because the windows were tinted, and then he sped off."

"So, how do you know the person was male?"

"I'm not sure." She paused. "I guess I don't, but it seemed like a male silhouette."

I jotted some gibberish down. "And then when did you next see the car?" I was in a trance, going through the motions, saying words only to hear her response. Was Adam still at the table? I looked his way once. He stared at me and through me. Could he read my mind? It was probably best if I cleared it.

"I was at the coffee shop, and about to step off the curb, when the BMW blew past me—way too close for comfort. I saw the silhouette through the window. I'm almost positive it was a man, but maybe I thought that because of how he, or she, was driving." Skylar rubbed her hands on her jeans. Her palms must be sweating. "Again, I was too shaken to think of looking at the license plate."

"Last night, you saw the BMW again?"

"Yes. I had just pulled into my driveway and was locking my car when he drove by slowly. This time I did try to get the license plate, but I couldn't see it well enough."

The room became silent. Adam and Skylar expected a solution that I was not prepared to give.

I glanced over my notebook and nodded, at what I'm not sure. "You've given me some good information to go on. I'll let you two get back to your day, and I'll handle it from here. From what I've heard, it's going to be a busy weekend for the two of you. I guess I should have said congratulations or something."

Their blank stares said it all. They had no idea what I was referring to. After a glance at each other, Adam said, "Excuse me?"

"The wedding?"

"Oh." Skylar chuckled. "Can you believe Liz is getting married? It'll be interesting to see how long her marriage lasts."

"Liz," I said to myself more than anyone else.

"Who did you think?" Skylar looked me straight on.

My feelings of embarrassment fought with my feelings of relief. I successfully hid which emotion won by keeping a straight face as I locked eyes with her. "I, well, I thought it was your wedding."

"We have a couple of months left before that." Adam reached for Skylar's hand. "After so many years together, I think a couple more months won't change a thing."

Without permission, words that had no business in the conversation barged in anyway. "It's amazing what can happen in a couple of months," I said.

Before either of them could respond, I stood, shook their hands, assured them I was there to help, and headed to the door. I could only hope Skylar had heard me loud and clear. I hadn't given up yet.

Since it was the weekend, I waited until Monday to contact Cynthia, who immediately began the search for the suspected vehicle. She first ruled out any BMW 320i or 328i that might have once belonged to Henry. The search then focused on recently purchased or rented sedans fitting the description. As luck would have it, there was not one BMW 320i or 328i car rental at any of the local agencies. Next stop, the dealerships.

Wanting to be as hands-on with the case as possible, I drove out to Atlantic Boulevard and decided to browse the area. So many of the sedans had similar appearances, I couldn't rule out the chance the vehicle Skylar had seen could be one of many different models. As I'd expected, a salesman—a man in his forties, dressed in khakis and the company shirt—soon approached me. He had a welcoming face. His expression said *I could drink a beer with you.* The next minute, the same look could talk you into purchasing a car for twice the amount you wanted to spend.

Jerry introduced himself, and after some small talk, I got to the point. "I'm interested in the BMW 320i or 328i. You sell many of them?"

"They're pretty popular. Want to take a look? The 328i has some extra features that will run you about five grand more, but you may find them well worth it." He took a couple of steps in the direction of the sedans.

"Actually, I'm more interested in any recent sales. Any that stand out." I flashed my badge with enough indifference to keep the situation light. After all, at this point, I didn't have much to go on.

He eyed me up and down. I've found there are a few different types of people when it comes to drama. There are the ones who clam up. There are the ones who give sheepish answers afraid they might incriminate themselves somehow. Then there are the ones who become so excited about the suspicious activity they become overinvolved. As luck would have it, the car salesman was a mix of the latter two. Once he was sure I had no intention of purchasing anything, his attitude shifted from salesman to buddy, making me believe we'd get along fine.

"Funny you ask. Someone did buy one—a 320i—in cash about a month ago."

"Have many customers come in and paid for a car outright?"

"More often than you might think. The Dave Ramsey craze of never having loans has some merit. Must be nice to be able to slap down thirty or forty-thousand, sometimes a great deal more, without a second thought." Jerry paused. "But not cash. That's what made this sale stand out. We get checks, but not a lot of cash transactions. Did think it was a bit weird. Kind of made things feel shady, but money is money. She wanted the car that day."

"She?"

"Yeah." He looked around, "Quite a hot little number, too. There was a bit of talk after she left, I can assure you—the legs and the briefcase of cash made her hard not to notice. Not a deal any of us will soon forget."

"Can you describe her?"

"Before I do, want to tell me why you're asking?" The hint of excitement in his eyes highlighted the fact he wanted to entertain himself, rather than ease fears he might have of saying too much.

"I have my reasons for asking, but for now, I'd like to keep it to two guys talking in a parking lot, if that's okay."

Jerry glanced around the lot again, contemplating, I presume, what could be so wrong about sharing a little information. "I guess there's no harm in that. She a criminal?"

"That's what we're trying to figure out before we take matters any further." Luckily, my vague answers said enough, and Jerry's trusting nature worked to my benefit.

"She was blonde—not bleach, more of a golden blond— maybe 5'7", but that's a guess. Model thin with…. She was well-endowed, put it that way."

"You happen to remember what her name was?" I held my breath. We might have our first real lead on Brenda Carter, the woman who possessed much of the money but was more of a ghost than a human.

"Let me see. Was it Tammy? No, something with a T." Jerry rubbed his forehead, as if the small massage would loosen the information lodged within. "Tori. Definitely Tori."

"Tori? Are you one-hundred percent sure?"

"I'm sure that was it." A family walked by, and Jerry reached into his pocket. Handing me his business card, he said, "Here's my number. Not to be rude, but I should get back to work. If you give me a call tonight, I'll give you the VIN if that helps. Brent, correct?"

"Yes, it's Brent. And yes, I would love the VIN."

CHAPTER 9

Skylar

Journal Entry

THE DECISIONS ARE getting more complicated. But then, am I making decisions or reacting to circumstances? I can't be sure anymore. Would I choose to drown if I had an anchor tied to my ankle? But was that the situation I was in, or was I merely deciding to dive deeper into the murky waters?

I can't sleep. Well, that's not exactly true. My exhausted brain falls into the unconscious state of sleep within minutes, but too often wakes to the images it has produced.

The office was quiet, or at least I was unaware of the rhythmic normal sounds: fingers on keyboards, pages rolling off the printer, and chairs wheeling around in my coworkers' cubicles. My eyes were focused on the documents before me. I stared intently at Henry's name as I tried to make sense of the numbers that didn't add up.

Something caught my eye, and I leaned in closer to better see it. At first, it looked like a smudge, and then it moved. I jolted upright as the blemish increased in size and headed toward me. From the blurry image, a spider took form and then another and another. They scrambled toward me at lightning speed. Before I'd released the scream that formed in my throat, my subconscious mind unclenched its fists on my thoughts and allowed me to resurface.

My anxieties are apparent; hundreds of them spanning across everything that I do, creeping in and out on legs that scurry into the crevices of my brain. The anxiety explanation was too predictable, too straightforward; to be honest, to warrant my investigation. However, the Google interpretation I couldn't explain was that dreaming about bugs could also represent sexual thoughts. I should just leave that interpretation alone, and not try to figure out how a black spider could have anything to do with sex. Except I can't. Instead, I envision the creature scurrying about, carrying with it unwanted thoughts. One minute it's only one distracting thought, and the next moment a web is spun, becoming more substantial than I should ever allow.

Was I in this web due to my own actions or because fate brought me to this point? If it was fate, then I couldn't be blamed, right? If I didn't have a choice, I could someday enjoy the rewards without the feelings of guilt. Was it possible I wanted the anchor to pull me under the water's surface into the unknown?

CHAPTER 10

Brent

OUR SQUAD—A FAMILY within the FBI—met with Ryan first thing Monday morning. There were five of us in all: Gabe Kemp, Chris Bailey, Roger Hall, Meghan Ambers, and I. During our briefing, we informed each other of any developments in the multiple cases we juggled. My run-ins with Meghan had become more comfortable since our dinner together. I still refused to refer to it as a date.

With my colleagues sitting around the office table, I briefed Ryan on the red flags from Abigail's accounts.

"Hmm."

I wasn't quite sure how to read his response. Ryan was hard to figure out—quiet and watchful one moment and friendly the next. Today would be one of those quiet days.

Ryan took off his readers, placed them on his desk, and then leaned back, "Anything else?"

After clearing my throat to remove any unwanted hints of unprofessionalism, I jumped in. "Skylar texted me the other night." As I'd expected, the elbow nudging and under-the-breath comments began. Meghan remained silent.

Luckily for me, to the other agents, the feelings Skylar had for me appeared one-sided. A piece of me felt guilty for this fact, as the men's jokes and taunts circled the office. The agents harassed me with comments about my effect on women. I was the one who had cracked the case because I'd molded Skylar in my knowing hands. What none of them guessed was that I'd been the one spinning on the potter's wheel. Each time a piece of her had pressed back on me, she'd changed me. And when the wheel had stopped spinning, I'd known I'd never be the slab of clay I'd been before she'd touched me. It felt almost unfair, as if I laughed at her feelings and left her sitting out there alone to face my colleagues' jokes, but what choice did I have?

"And," Ryan said, unmoved by the banter.

"She believes she is being followed. She gave a description of the vehicle. After visiting the BMW dealership, I found that someone recently purchased a 320i sedan in cash. I'm looking into the car's owner, but I do know it's a female named Tori."

"I'll get someone else to watch over Skylar's house and workplace. Not you, Brent. They'll recognize you right away. Stay low key."

"She's pretty frightened right now." I heard my concern in my voice before Ryan's expression confirmed it.

"Brent, I'm going to ask you once. Is this case going to get too complicated for you?" The question hung in the air, thick to the point of suffocating.

"I assure you, I'm completely capable of working this case."

Ryan studied me carefully and then released an exasperated breath. "Very well. We'll meet back in a couple of days. Roger, you and Gabe are on watch—Skylar's home, work, wherever she goes, make sure someone is covering her at all times." They nodded.

We all dismissed at the same time. Meghan timed her departure perfectly with mine, leaving the two of us alone at the tail of the crowd.

"So, Skylar's reaching out to you. Could what they say about her interest in you be true?"

"I was the one she knew best from the case. It makes sense for her to reach out to me."

"Well, either way, at least she has good taste." Meghan patted my back and turned down the hallway to her office.

The encounter left me annoyed. Life would be more comfortable if Ryan hadn't placed Meghan on our squad but trying to prevent the move would have created an awkwardness that I'd chosen to avoid.

Before heading out to meet Abigail for the second time, I stopped by to see Cynthia. As I approached her, I once again noticed how unnoticeable her appearance was—mousy, thin, brown hair; brown eyes. On top of that, she often chose to wear glasses instead of contacts.

Cynthia's whole being went into befriending every computer system known to man so she could find any piece of information that could assist us in our jobs. She couldn't be bothered with such trivial things as makeup and hairstyles. I rather liked her for it.

A bit like an excited puppy sniffing out a treat in my pocket, Cynthia looked up. "What do you have for me?"

"A VIN."

"Are you serious? A VIN? Child's play."

"That's why I love you." Cynthia lifted her hands and gave an expression saying, *How can you not?*

"It only takes minutes to tell you who owns the vehicle."

"I have to run. Plus, once you find the owner, I need you to find out what you can about them."

"At least that's a bit more interesting."

"Thanks, Cynthia. You're the best."

"I know," she replied with a hint of amusement in her voice. Then she disappeared into the cyber world again. I knew I would hear from her shortly.

I pulled up to Abigail's home. Abigail met me at the door. She was wringing her hands and noticeably uncomfortable.

"We have to talk," she said. She led me down the hallway and to her lanai overlooking the water. After motioning for me to have a seat, she did as well. "I have to tell you where the money is coming from, but I'm afraid you will judge me."

"I'm your accountant, not your judge." At least she was admitting things weren't adding up.

She wrung her hands some more. "There's a man. I don't want to give his name, but he's quite well-known in the area. We're, how should I put it, friends."

I resisted cutting to the chase and blurting out, "You have a sugar daddy." Instead, I allowed her a bit of undeserved self-respect.

"I do have money, which I inherited from my dear Uncle Andrew. He didn't have children." She paused as though wondering if she should say something. "Anyway, he left some inheritance to his nieces. And I do have an income from the club. But I know, there might be a discrepancy. I just don't know how to claim that money from my friend without causing a big scandal."

"There's a lot of extra money, Ms. Carswell."

"The friend, the one I don't want to mention, well, we have been quite close for a long time." She looked me square in the eye long enough for me to get her meaning, "He would have married me, I'm quite sure, but in the beginning, this man had to care about appearances. I wasn't always the person you see before you. He had to choose—his future with his trophy wife who could move him up in the ranks, or me. He would have eventually hated me. I didn't want that. I love him too much for that to happen." She stared at her hands. "So we came up with a plan. I would be here for him, sort of a secret second wife, and he would accomplish his goals."

She studied me a moment, waiting for me to say something.

"Well, Ms. Carswell, as I said, I'm nobody's judge. Love is a funny thing, I guess."

"I've sometimes thought about ending it—the relationship, the checks—but the thing is, love is love. As you said, it's a funny thing, and I can't seem to move on without him. He's stuck like glue to something inside of me. I know you might think I only care about the money, but that's not it, truly. I accept it because it binds us, but I could find someone else." She wiped away a tear that had escaped down her cheek. "I know I deserve someone's full attention, but I care more about his partial attention. I can't give it up."

Now she was crying. Crap. I awkwardly rubbed her back as I wondered how to get out of the situation. That's when I noticed she had shifted toward me, her thigh now pressed against mine. As I tried to move my arm, her head fell to my shoulder, where the tears began to wet my shirt.

"Please tell me you understand. Haven't you ever just needed love?"

Her body inched even closer, and her hand slid over my shirt across my chest. Sweat beaded on my forehead. No way in all hell was I traveling down that road. The doorbell rang then. Abigail seemed unmoved by the visitor and remained curled into me. The door opened even though no one had answered it, and I heard the sound of a woman's high-heeled shoes clicking down the hallway toward us. Before I knew it, a human Barbie doll stood in the doorway.

"Am I interrupting anything?" she asked with a sly smile.

"No. I was just leaving." I didn't need to be introduced to the mysterious woman joining our party. I smoothed my shirt and reached out to shake Abigail's hand. "I'll be in touch. I'll show myself out."

I couldn't get out of there fast enough. Still baffled by what had just happened, I hurried across the driveway, but stopped in my tracks.

Sitting in the driveway was a BMW 320i. What were the chances?

My phone rang. "What did you find, Cynthia?"

"Plenty. The car belongs to a Tori Carswell." *Sisters.* It appeared that they both had the same disastrous taste in men. I stopped myself. I was making too many presumptions. There was no proof the black car following Skylar was someone involved with Nick or Henry. No proof, either, that the sedan purchased by Tori was, in fact, the same vehicle following Skylar.

"Okay, so besides a name, what do you have for me?"

"Now, I've heard you can make some good money stripping but buying a car with forty-five thousand dollars in cash? That might be a stretch when it comes to a good week at work."

"Tori's a stripper?"

"That she is." Cynthia said.

"Now, now. Maybe we have a thrifty stripper who has saved for years for her BMW."

"Unlikely. She has several drug possession charges against her, and a charge against her for a small brawl that happened at her place of employment. She doesn't seem like the smart thrifty sort of girl, but I could be wrong."

"I see your point. So, where did the money come from?"

"Here's where it gets interesting."

My ears perked up. I was ready for the piece of information that would bring it all together.

A loud rap sounded on my window. Startled, I dropped my phone.

Tori Carswell stood beside my truck. Her bosom stared me in the eyes, which come to find out was a much more pleasant view than the glare she gave me over her Ray-Bans.

She banged on the glass again. "Roll down the damn window."

CHAPTER 11

Skylar

Journal Entry

THE ROOM *WAS* hot and stale. Light filtered through the window and glistened off dust specks that floated in the air. Around me, my classmates' sleepy faces stared forward at the teacher who sat at his desk. He wore a white button-up shirt. The sleeves were rolled up, most likely due to the uncomfortable temperature. We sat in silence except for the teacher's thick finger, tapping out a hypnotic rhythm. A pendulum on his desk demanded my attention. The sound that lulled me now emanated from the colliding silver balls. I remained entranced until the tick-tick became so loud and fast that I awoke in a sweat. In the darkness of my bedroom, the ceiling fan clicked rhythmically, bringing the strange teacher and his pendulum into reality.

I find it strange how we depend on the rhythm of familiarity to lull us into false securities. The fan was one of the rhythmic noises in my life. Others sounds in my life were Ted barking at the doorbell, the alarm clock going off each morning, the tapping of my fingers on my keyboard. In a sense, these sounds have become my life's heartbeat.

I need to find the heartbeat I once knew, to remember the rhythmic melody of the past, no matter how badly the memories sting. I should never have let the memories become buried, as if they themselves were corpses that would rot in time. All I can do now is to bring them to life once again within the pages of this journal, one memory at a time.

When I was growing up, my parents had a grandfather clock in the foyer. The piece was old and hardly what most would consider a prized possession. But my parents did. To them, the ticking away of the moments of their lives wasn't a threat, but a reminder that life wasn't permanent. My dad, on the way out the door, would walk by the clock, pat the side of it as if he touched an old man's shoulder, and say, "I hear you mate. I hear you." I would giggle, and my dad would smile down at me, knowing his weirdness entertained my young self.

But my dream hadn't warned or reminded me of the passing of time. Instead, it warned me of the rumors and lies surrounding me.

Was the dream warning me of Henry's lies or my own?

CHAPTER 12

Brent

WHOA, LADY! I have no idea what you're talking about." I opened the truck door and stood to bring the conversation with Tori to an eye-level exchange.

"Don't play dumb with me. I know men, and I believe my sister. She's in there crying right now."

"I'm her accountant! I'm only here to file her tax forms."

"Oh, right! Until you notice something a little shady, and then you try to use it to earn yourself a sick bonus."

I dismissed her accusation with a wave of my hand. "No offense, but you're both crazy." I got back into my truck. "Your sister was the one who sat next to me and decided to have a meltdown on my shoulder. I just sat there and tried to be polite." I started the ignition but was unable to drown out her voice bellowing at me through the glass.

"Do you expect me to believe a stranger over my sister? I saw how you tried to get the hell out of there when I walked in."

I put up my hand. "This conversation is over."

"You're right. I am done talking with you. The next conversation I have will be with your boss. Stay away from us, and if you know what's best for you, you should be wrapping things up all nice and tidy when you get back to the office."

There were a million things I wanted to say, and not one

of them led down a path without repercussions. I settled with rolling down my window and calmly saying, "It's been interesting meeting you, Tori."

I backed my truck away. My last glance behind me revealed a bewildered look on Tori's face as, I'm sure, she pondered the fact I knew her name. In my opinion, her expression added more weight to my black sedan theory.

After a bit of fumbling, I found my phone and switched it over to Bluetooth. "Did you get all that?"

"She was screaming, so yes." Pressing concern crept into Cynthia's tone. "Brent, what the heck was that about?"

"Little Ms. Carswell wants her sugar daddy to remain a secret, so she's getting creative."

"Did I hear you say Tori?"

"Yes, you did."

"The sedan Tori?"

"I believe so, but to be sure, run this plate." I told her the license plate number before it disappeared from my mind. I waited, envisioning Cynthia pushing up her glasses and typing away on the computer.

"You're correct. The vehicle belongs to Tori Carswell."

"To clarify, we know that for some odd reason, Tori bought a BMW in Jacksonville, with cash, that matches the description of the one following Skylar. But why in hell would Tori be following Skylar?"

"I believe that's where you come in. Just tell me what I can do to help."

"Will do, Cynthia. Thanks as always."

"You know I love it. And by the way, I recorded Tori's rant. I'm not sure if the recording will be of any use to you, but know it exists if needed."

"You're the best. I wish you could have had a camera in the house instead. Let's hope my encounter with Abigail won't come to anything."

"I've got your back, Brent."

The call ended and. After a deep breath that was not able to erase the nightmare scenarios going through my mind, I settled on the next level of therapy and gave my steering wheel a small beating while yelling profanities into the empty air.

Later that night, Cynthia phoned. She should have been home, not still stuck in the office, but then maybe that's where she felt most at home.

"Sorry, but I couldn't let the whole situation go," she started.

"You're forgiven. So, what did you find?"

"Abigail Carswell's high school boyfriend."

"Go on."

"Governor McGregor. You know, the one running for reelection; the one with the pictures of his beautiful wife and two young kids plastered all over the flyers in my mailbox."

I let out a laugh. Yes, I knew the one—always in a suit. The governor's idea of dressing down was rolling up his sleeves to make it appear he was ready to get down to business. I thought of Abigail, attractive with an edge of trash in her makeup applied a bit too thickly. His wife, the public one, seemed a picture of class. What was her name? Anna, I believed. She knew how to play the part, something Abigail would fail at miserably. Both the governor and Abigail were forty, or at least, closing in on it quickly. "Well, well. I can see why they want their relationship kept quiet.

"As you may know, Governor McGregor's family were

ranchers; very successful ranchers at that," Cynthia said. "His governor's salary pales in comparison to his ranching income, not to mention the handsome inheritance from his father."

"I guess he can afford two wives. Either way, my job isn't to ruin the governor for having a mistress. His relationship with Abigail is none of my business, in my opinion, as long as what he's doing with the taxpayers' money is legit—and I have reason to believe it isn't." I pondered the facts for a moment. "There must be some way this information will prove beneficial."

"If there is, I'll find it. And if not, ruling something out counts for progress as well," Cynthia said, reassuring me. "Good night, Brent."

"Good night, Cynthia. Go do something fun now."

"Silly Brent. This is my fun."

"I know," I said into the quiet phone. Cynthia was already gone, most likely typing away, trying to find answers to the next mystery circling in her mind.

Regardless of Tori's threats, my work with Abigail was far from finished. I needed to find something besides an affair to keep me on Abigail's case, and I sensed if I kept digging, I would discover what I needed. As much as a governor's secret mistress made for a great headline, it did not warrant FBI interference. Since I could not meet Abigail at her club or in the privacy of her home again, I arranged to meet at a restaurant.

By the time she arrived, I was seated in a back booth where we would not be overheard. I intended to leave the restaurant with two problems solved. As per Ryan's suggestion and approval, I had a bug placed inside my phone. The bug allowed Meghan, sitting in a car outside, to record any pertinent information. We hoped to absolve me from any creepy accountant lawsuits.

Knowing Meghan was listening and recording everything was both reassuring and awkward.

Abigail entered, still wearing her Hollywood sunglasses despite the darkness of the restaurant. I rose and greeted her with a professional handshake.

"Good afternoon," I said. "It's nice to see you again."

She removed her sunglasses, revealing the aftermath of a good cry.

"Oh, Jake, I'm so sorry about my sister. She can be so protective sometimes."

We both slid into our booth seats.

"Yes, that was rather surprising, I must say. But what would make…. Tori is her name, correct? What would make her think I'd acted inappropriately?"

"My sister and I, well, let's just say, we've run into a lot of characters in our day. When she saw me crying, she just assumed, I guess."

"You didn't say anything to make her believe I was acting inappropriate?"

"Oh, no. Why would I? You were only acting as any gentleman would have in the situation. You listened to a girl and her sob story."

Mission one accomplished, even though I doubted her innocence in her sister's reaction. A moot point, so I moved on to business. "Let's get back to your tax issue. I have no desire to drag anyone through the mud, but we need to deal with the donations, as I'll call them."

"But how? His family can't know. I can't tell you everything, but this has to be kept very quiet."

"I'm assuming your benefactor is a person of some importance. He must also have an abundance of money to have kept up with your lifestyle all these years." I paused to let her squirm. "Let's cut to the chase and admit he's some sort of public figure."

She nodded and dried her eyes. "I do get money from being a part-owner in the club."

"Can I ask, why did you invest in a gentlemen's club?"

"Timing, I guess. When I got my uncle's inheritance, some acquaintances had heard of the club. They needed investors; I needed to have a job, so to speak. Well, I don't do much of anything, to be honest." She looked at her hands, gripped together. "I never went to college, and the other owners, they know the business end. It's nice, feeling a part of a business."

"And you trust them."

"For the most part. I can't say I would know if they were stealing from me. I make some money, and they do the work. It's a good system. At least, it's been good to me."

I drew a deep breath. This lady was probably being robbed blind on a daily basis and could care less.

"Anything else I should know? This boyfriend of yours, is he on the up and up?"

"Oh yes. I'm his only vice."

"Well, I wouldn't think he could afford two of you." We both chuckled. "If that's true, he may need to fess up, a bit anyway, not to the affair, but about the money. You need to speak with your mystery man. See what you can come up with because there's a good amount of money the IRS will want accounted for, and they don't care about reputations."

"I have no idea how to do this. You have to help me."

The waitress arrived with our lunches—burger and fries for me, house salad with balsamic for her that she would pick at, at best. The conversation ceased, giving me time to think, while the waitress searched the tables nearby for a full ketchup container.

"What do you have in savings again?" I asked.

"A couple of hundred thousand."

"Perhaps your boyfriend had an interest in your company."

"Oh, he wouldn't want to be associated with my club."

"Okay, then," I paused and thought on the issue some more. "I've read about some complaints from the locals. The building is in desperate need of repairs, correct?"

"I guess," she answered nervously. "I mean, yes, but Cory and Brad, they don't care much about appearances. They keep their costs low."

"What if you could get some of the people off your back by fixing the place up a bit, maybe improving the clientele?"

"Cory and Brad tried to get a loan. They couldn't."

"But what if you could? What if you did? Maybe this friend of yours had reasons to clean up the area—make some people happy." The place looked like a run-down biker bar in the middle of an otherwise decent area; not a classy location but decent. I couldn't tell her I knew who her boyfriend was, but it was possible, if only slightly, that the facelift could appease some folks. "You said your friend wouldn't want to be associated with it. Maybe he was trying to help you clean it up some, make the premises a bit classier. If that's the case, maybe people would believe the reasoning."

It would appear to her that I was offering genuine help, but the truth was, I just wanted to get to Nick, and I was getting impatient.

"I need that money."

"For what? More Botox?"

"Excuse me! That's insulting."

"It's called honesty. And, let's face it, it's time someone starts speaking the truth. You have enough money. Even if you tone down your lifestyle a bit, you're still doing better than most." Abigail fidgeted with her napkin. Apparently, losing her possessions was more frightening than losing her morals. "Even if your relationship ends, you are a part-owner in your club. Start thinking like a businesswoman; make the club into a joint that brings in better clientele."

"They would never allow me to make drastic changes. I stay quiet, and all runs smoothly."

"Invest the money, and then let them buy you out. Start over. Get away from the gentlemen's club."

"That's not as easy as you might think—changing everything."

"Abigail, you're on the radar. Things are going to change. Take some control."

Abigail searched the restaurant; for what, I'm not sure. "You know, most of the people who come into the club are no more than sad souls looking for a little excitement. Some are out for a rare night of entertainment—bachelor parties, guys' weekends."

"And what about the ones who don't fit that mold?"

"They're not quite as easy to clean up."

"Want to elaborate?"

"Better I leave it there. Back to saving me."

I studied her for a moment before concluding she would not be revealing any Nick details even if pressed. "Whoever 'loaned' you the money," I said, making quotation marks, "might be a businessman wanting to clean up the area a bit. Maybe you went to him with a proposal. He liked the idea of cleaning up the clientele that frequents the establishment at this point, so he agreed. You use the money appropriately and start paying it back. He looks solid, and you make something of yourself; become something other than a kept woman."

"Again, that's insulting."

"Again, it's honest. Right now, you're both in trouble with the IRS. I'm not here to save you. You do know that, don't you? I'm doing you a favor, giving you some suggestions—off the record, so to speak. It won't be easy, but you and your friend," I said, making quotation marks with my fingers, "will need to work out all the details. And Abigail, who knows. You might even like the new you."

Abigail pondered my idea. I could almost see her envisioning a new her. "This change, it's overwhelming. How do I even begin?"

"You need an overwhelming change. You're in deep shit, the two of you."

"And this will work?"

"I can't promise it will. You have some work cut out for you; I'm not going to lie. But it's a hole you dug. I'm only giving you a possible out." Abigail buried her face in her hands. "And you know, he can still give you a gift here and there, if he keeps it under fifteen thousand dollars."

"Or maybe I could stop needing them." She lifted her face and gave a small smile.

"Even better."

Abigail's hand reached across the table and rubbed the back of mine. "You're a good man, Jake."

Trying not to be insulting, I eased away from her. "And a taken one."

"I'm sorry. I didn't see a wedding band."

"Some bands are invisible." I took one last bite and waved for the waitress.

I lay in bed that night thinking about possibilities. Not one piece of me was interested in Abigail, despite her beauty. Yet, the fact I'd sat across the table from a beautiful woman and told her I was taken baffled me. Why should I care if word got back to Skylar about me having a scandalous affair? Every night she shared her bed with Adam, never thinking back to me, never giving any hope to me that maybe, just maybe, my holding out would bring her back. Yet still, I held on to the belief. If a window opened, I wanted her to know I thought she was worth waiting for. I didn't want another hurdle, another layer to our story. I wanted her.

CHAPTER 13

Skylar

Journal Entry

MY CELL PHONE *rang with a faraway sound, as if muffled by a pillow. Frantically, I yanked back the covers and tossed the bedding to the side. The demanding device was nowhere to be found. I jumped from the bed and searched the room, including my suitcase and under the bed. Pausing and giving one final listen, I heard a faint ring coming from the closet. Digging through my shoes, I saw the lit-up screen, and answered the call before the ringing stopped.*

"Hello. Hello," I yelled.

Through the static, I heard the familiar voice of a man, but I couldn't decipher a word he said. As if my life depended on the conversation, I pressed the phone as tightly to my ear as possible.

"You have to listen to me," he said.

"I'm trying."

Before I could comprehend his words—and trust me, I wanted to understand him more than anything—the hotel phone woke me. On the other end of the line, Adam's voice reminded me that my reality was anything but blissful.

Connections are difficult for me. Why, I can't be sure, but when I attempt to self-analyze myself, it comes down to my parents' way of life. They created a bubble around us, but it wasn't a negative wall. Inside the bubble, life was secure to the point of being blissful. The deep-rooted feeling spread out to their view of everything—the world, bosses, coworkers. And then they left the bubble, and I viewed the world through a translucent barrier that blurred over time. The wall remained, but my perception became tainted, untrusting. I didn't know how to be happy without my parents, to fit into a world where so much negativity resonated in the atmosphere. I didn't know how to translate it into the language my mother and father had spoken. I was alone, and no one could understand how lost I had become.

For the most part, I believed I didn't care. After all, how many confidants did I need in my life? Adam joined me in my bubble, albeit a different bubble. The critical world had seeped in, penetrating me, overwhelming me, changing me. Connecting didn't come naturally, and once I'd found my person, I'd had no need to try any longer.

Until now.

CHAPTER 14

Brent

DAYS PASSED. ROGER and Gabe were unable to catch the BMW anywhere near Skylar. In fact, there'd been no sighting of it whatsoever. The following Saturday, I decided it was my duty to touch base with Skylar and, of course, Adam. I was expected at their place at noon and found myself pulling into a Wawa gas station in Jacksonville at eleven-thirty. Liz's wedding would be later that evening, and for a moment, I was close to disappointed that I had not received an invite.

As I watched the pump numbers circle past the thirty-dollar mark, I allowed myself a brief fantasy. I stole Skylar away from Adam and danced across the dance floor, letting words I hadn't decided on drift to her ear, still warm from my breath. Her face brightened, and I wondered what my whispered words might have been.

The gas pump clicked off at forty-six dollars, and the vision faded. I needed to watch myself, my fantasies. My mind had the capability of creating memories that were vivid enough they could fool my brain into thinking they were real. My actual experiences were tainted with the many imagined ones, and I feared my pain and sense of loss might only be the effect of an over-active imagination. But then I remembered sitting on the beach together. I pictured her crying on my shoulder in the back of the cab. I could still feel her body pressed against mine as she clung to me from the back of my motorcycle. No, the pain would be there with or without my imagination.

I pulled up to an empty spot in front of the Wawa. Wandering the aisles, I settled on an iced tea and a power bar, rather than one of their surprisingly good gas station sandwiches. I strolled to my truck, trying to waste the extra minutes. Each visit, each chance granted to me, seemed to hold too much significance. Would it be five times, ten times, before Skylar became a married woman, forever closing the door on my chances with her? What could happen in those visits with her that hadn't happened in our months together that could change her mind? Maybe nothing. The clock showed eleven forty-five. Time to make the last stretch to her neighborhood.

When I pulled in, all was quiet. Even Ted hid from view. Skylar's car sat in the driveway. I assumed Adam's car was in the garage. I stepped out of the truck, and from behind the house, Ted shot into view. His happy face beamed as he ran innocently at me, a new playmate. I bent to rub his head. His panting almost drowned out the sound of footsteps behind him.

"Ted, get down. Sorry about that. We don't quite have him trained yet."

I wiped the bit of drool off my hand as I stood.

"What's the fun in being too well-trained?"

Her expression radiated peace in a way I didn't witness in at McClurry's. I didn't often get to see her in blue jeans, standing in her yard, being Skylar, the Skylar I didn't know well enough. I didn't want to ever leave. I wanted to belong right there beside her.

"Unfortunately for me, but fortunately for Ted, I have no clue how to make him understand my perfectionism."

"No worries. Dogs try to remind us how to live and love as if we were kids. That's their job," I said.

"He's a pretty smart dog." She bent down to pet him again. "Adam had to run to the store. He should be back at any moment. Do you want to come in?"

"Sure." I followed her, too closely, but not on purpose. I couldn't explain the draw to be near her. Despite knowing the lines of personal space, they often became blurred when I was near her. I gravitated, without permission, across the boundaries to be in her orbit.

She wore her hair up in a messy ponytail, strands spilling out and brushing her neck. I wanted my hand to graze by them, to feel the softness, as I pulled her closer, letting our lips touch. I became lost in my thoughts again, and her words became inaudible despite my being aware she was talking.

"I asked if you would like a glass of water."

"Oh, yes. Thanks." Skylar went to the cupboard for a glass and filled it with ice. "Liz's wedding is tonight, correct?"

"Yes," Skylar said over the clanking of the ice machine. "I'm making a polite appearance and getting out of there as soon as possible."

"Don't you want to stick around and get some tips for your big day? When is that, by the way?"

She kept her back to me, letting the water fill the glass. Some thought on her mind, though, seemed heavy in the air.

"The wedding's in a couple of months," she said with the resolved expression she had used often in the past. "We were working on invitations last night. Adam thought maybe you would like to come."

My heart sank. For a moment, I thought it might not beat again.

"Would you like to?" she asked. "I mean, I don't want to make you feel obligated."

"Why do you think I'd feel obligated?"

"Well, because you only worked at McClurry and Associates a short time, and…." Avoiding my gaze, she handed me the glass. "I don't know if you consider me a friend, if…well, it's hard to put a label on it."

"Yes, it is, isn't it? Friend, I mean. It doesn't quite sum things up between us, does it?"

"Would you want to be at my wedding? You won't insult me if you say no."

"How about you send the invitation, and I'll see if I'm free? I'll have to drum up a date. It's no fun attending a wedding alone." I hated going there, but reactions could be very telling, and I needed to see hers.

"Oh, yes, of course. I wouldn't expect you to come alone." Somehow, we had not moved since she'd handed me my water, which left a small space between us, allowing me to study her face with each word spoken. "So, are you seeing anyone?" she asked. "You must be, of course. Why wouldn't you be?"

"Are you talking to me or yourself?" I said with a knowing smile. She was rambling, obviously uncomfortable. A good sign. "No, I'm not seeing anyone. Not really. Just a date here and there."

"Oh, why not? You could have your pick of women, I'm sure."

"Are you?"

Skylar blushed, "The ladies at the office all seemed to go out of their way to talk to you."

"I wasn't interested in any of them." I took a drink of water and set the glass on the counter behind her, letting my arm graze her. "I would think you knew that."

The door creaked open, and Skylar spun around to face Adam. Fortunately, he bent over to pet Ted, making it impossible for him to witness Skylar's expression, the one that had ignited me and would have infuriated him.

Adam approached with his hand out in greeting. "It's nice to see you again, Brent. Any luck?"

"Well, possibly. A woman bought a BMW fitting the description from a Jacksonville dealership. A couple of things make us think she might be connected. First, she paid in cash, enough cash that she shouldn't have access to on her own, but we haven't found her connection to the case yet. The cash makes the transaction a bit harder to track down, but I am quite sure someone bought the vehicle for her. Following you may be part of the payment."

"You said a couple things. What's the other?" Skylar asked.

"We're following up on some other details, but it's probably best I leave it at that for now. I promise to let you know whatever I can."

"Okay," she said with a hint of disappointment in her voice. "You said a woman bought the car, but I could have sworn I saw a male profile. The windows were tinted. I have could been wrong."

"I know you're concerned. Special agents are watching out for you."

"Not you?"

I tried to hide my pleasure at her concerned tone. "No. The woman who bought the car knows who I am. If the driver of the car sees me watching over you, it would give up my cover as an accountant. Trust me, though, the other agents will tell me everything that happens almost as it happens. I won't be very far away at any time."

Adam moved closer to Skylar and placed his hand on her lower back; laying claim.

"Thank you, Brent. I mean it. I appreciate everything." Skylar's sincerity caught me off guard. The world, including Adam, faded away, and I stood alone with her, wanting so much more than she was willing to give.

"Let me walk you out." Adam's voice interrupted my thoughts as if he could read them. I had only just arrived it seemed, but the trip had been far from a waste. I would have traveled much farther for a second alone with her.

"Sounds good." I approached Skylar, and we awkwardly decided on a hug over the professional handshake. "Don't worry. We'll keep you safe."

"I believe you."

Adam stood with the door open, waiting for me. I followed him out to my truck, not sure of what the conversation would be, part of me ready for anything.

"Now, I need you to be honest with me." The pause made my breath hitch. Maybe Adam could read my thoughts. "Is Skylar safe? I can take her away for a while if you think she is in any danger."

Could I genuinely say she was one-hundred-percent safe? Would it be a good idea for her to go away? I hoped I could answer honestly. "For now, let's just keep our eyes open. We still don't know of any reason why she would be in danger. Revenge doesn't seem like enough incentive to get caught, and we don't even know for sure if someone connected to Henry is following her. I'll let you know if things change."

Adam shook my hand. "Thanks, Brent. It's good to know you've got our backs." His hand stayed locked with mine, a more prolonged and firmer shake than was necessary, warning me without words.

Did I feel like a traitor? Yes. But I couldn't force Skylar to love me over Adam. If it happened, then it was meant to be, even if I helped things out just a bit. "Of course, I'm happy to do whatever is needed."

As I backed down the driveway, Adam watched, hands in his pockets, hiding the fists that stood ready if needed.

CHAPTER 15

Skylar

Journal Entry

I DIDN'T NEED MY alarm to wake me. Instead, another vivid dream, a dream that began so pleasantly, startled me out of my sleep.

I sat at my kitchen table eating bacon, one of my all-time favorite foods. Ted, whimpering for a taste, sat next to me. I wouldn't share, though. Instead, I looked into his sweet, desperate eyes and continued to shovel the calorie-free dream bacon into my mouth. As dreams go, I couldn't complain. Until I took another bite, and the bacon tasted of death. The putrid taste jolted me from my sleep.

The staples of our life—shelter, water, and even bacon—should never be taken for granted. That's what Google told me my dream was telling me. Kind of humorous that dreams of bacon can represent the staples in one's life, yet it made sense. I also found it a bit wicked that my mind would take one of my favorite staples and taint it with rottenness. All the facets of my life were becoming corrupted by the rotten fruit in the bowl. Isn't it why we flip our strawberry cartons over when we are selecting our purchase? We know that no matter how fresh and delicious looking the top ones appear, their time is short-lived if somewhere on the bottom hides even one strawberry that harbors the infectious beginnings of decay.

The rottenness within me—the consequences of my decisions—is seeping into the parts of my life that I loved. How long would it be until my choices destroyed everything?

CHAPTER 16

Brent

SOMETIMES, AMID A backdrop of meaningless sights and sounds, some item or word jumps out, as if it was a piece of gold in a jewelry box of silver. In my opinion, there's but one reason for the strange occurrence, and that is, to make me take notice of it. As I drove down the interstate leading to my home, the notion of hidden messages plagued my mind. Like an animal circling the house before a storm, something scratched at the surface of my consciousness. I was far from a professional when it came to understanding the secret, silent language that animals responded to naturally, but I knew something was speaking to me.

A now-retired agent had often told us his scars would itch before a rainstorm, insistent in the belief of a connection between nature and living creatures. The other agents and I would exchange private glances while keeping one eye on the clouds. Some swore he'd been a quack, but when the rain hammered down later in the day, I wondered: Could there be a sixth sense, a plan, a predestined outcome? And if this were the case, shouldn't I be heeding it?

Watching the world through the windshield of my truck, a chunk of gold stood out against the silver backdrop over and over again. I thought nothing of the sign for Uncle Gene's Soul and Seafood Restaurant, except for the fact that I'd noticed it. Next, an advertisement for Monkey's Uncle Tavern caught my eye. I shook it off. Shortly after that, I passed a billboard where Uncle Sam pointed at me, demanding I take heed. I began to wonder why I was so aware of the appearances of uncles but continued to shake it off. What finally clinched it for me was when I heard Uncle Kraker on the radio singing the lyrics to *It's Good To Be Me*. I could not deny it any longer. Something begged for my attention.

I needed to find more details on the uncle that had left his inheritance to Abigail. Abigail had referred to him as Uncle Andrew. I decided to try the last name Carswell. The universe might be going to make things easy on me since it had, after all, pointed me in that direction. Adrenaline raced through my body at the lead, as if I was a hunting dog that had picked up the scent of a deer in the drifting breeze. My heart raced, and my muscles took in the extra hormones, making me ready to pounce. In this case, I needed to perform one task, and it did not include pouncing. I dialed the number for Cynthia. It rang twice before she picked up.

"Cynthia at your service," she said with cheery familiarity.

"I have a feeling about something. I need you to check it out."

"Gladly. What do you have?"

"Abigail Carswell had an uncle she referred to as Uncle Andrew. He died maybe seven years ago. Could you find out everything there is to know about him?"

"Want to tell me what you're thinking?"

"I'll fill you in later. See what you can find out." My answer sounded more professional than confessing, *I heard Uncle Kracker on the radio, and now I'm pretty sure the uncle is somehow involved.*

"There's a good chance I'm sending you on a meaningless mission."

"There are no meaningless missions. If this one doesn't go anywhere, it means we ruled something out."

I could already hear Cynthia's fingers typing away on her computer keyboard. "You're already at work, aren't you?" I asked, amused.

"Every time you call, it's like Christmas morning, and I just received a new puzzle piece."

Cynthia always had a way to remind me why I loved my job. "Well, let's hope I'm on to something that fits."

Once in my office, I tried to shift my thoughts from unexplained suspicions to the myriad of paperwork awaiting me. Somewhere in the transition, my mind settled on Skylar, as it often did. What was the addiction I had for her? Why her? Skylar was like the forgotten child in the back of the room. The other students chattered away, ignoring her quietness, mistaking it for blandness. Yet, if given a moment of attention, she would shine brighter than any of them. Only she didn't know this about herself. But I knew. I wanted to be the one to solve her riddle, to give her the attention she demanded, to be the rain when she was ready to drink. In the moments—on the beach, on the pier, in the break room—when our eyes had met, I'd seen her—the real her. Because of those times, I knew she was worth my time and patience.

My thoughts about Skylar drifted in and out, both fueling and distracting me. I managed to be productive despite my wandering mind and left the office by five o'clock.

In the quiet of my apartment, I became intent on learning why Skylar found security in her safe ways. A vague memory of her mentioning her parents and her upbringing came back to me. I kicked myself for not having paid closer attention to what she'd said. What I could remember was that her parents had been adventurous and free-spirited. That part stuck out since Skylar had seemed to create a world of routines.

As I opened the last IPA hiding in my fridge, my cell phone vibrated under the pile of junk mail I had tossed on the counter. Before I finished my greeting, Cynthia jumped right into the conversation.

"There was a man named Andrew Carswell; he died eight years ago. A good deal of suspicion surrounded his death. He was well-off but not rich by some people's standards, but he left Abigail half a million. He also left her sister, Tori, the same amount—pretty much his life's savings, including equity."

"Well, then, I guess Tori may have had enough money to buy her car outright."

"But why cash? She hid something by doing that. Not to mention, there's no evidence of any withdrawals from her accounts. The money didn't come from her uncle."

"It would appear that way." A million questions ran through my mind. "You said the uncle died suspiciously. Give me details."

"They found his body in a park at night. He had died of a heart attack."

"What makes that so suspicious?"

"According to sources, it was quite out of character for him to go to the park at all, let alone, to go at night. He was out to dinner with a client. The client reported that Andrew Carswell received a phone call and then became on edge. He finished the dinner in a rush and excused himself. Within a few hours, a passerby found his body. There weren't any signs of a struggle, and he still had his wallet on him. The only missing item was his phone. There were no witnesses. No evidence of foul play. Eventually, the police dropped the case."

"Not one lead?"

"There was one. His son."

"His son? Abigail said he didn't have children."

"Tell his son that. His name is Patrick Carswell. The client, who knew Mr. Carswell was struggling with issues pertaining to his son, suspected Patrick had something to do with the phone call. There wasn't any evidence to back his theory since it was only a hunch.

"And how did Patrick act during the investigation?"

"He was very cooperative and emotional. The notes paint a picture of a distraught son, even though he admitted to having a rather strained relationship with his father. The relationship was bad enough that his father didn't leave him any inheritance."

"That must have stung."

"I'd imagine it did. At one point, the officer heard him mumble, 'I'm sorry,' through his sobs, but further questioning didn't lead anywhere. They let Patrick go to wallow in his guilt for whatever troubled him."

"Find out more about Patrick and get back to me."

"On it."

Meanwhile, I Googled Patrick Carswell. The search results showed a coach for some college football team, a hockey player, and an immigration and customs enforcement officer. Besides that, I couldn't find anything to excite me, so I closed the computer and let the cold beer penetrate my mood. Glancing around the atmosphere of my dismal apartment—the bare walls, the bland color, the lifeless décor—slammed into me like a fist. Who was I kidding? I was boring as shit as well. A picture of Skylar nestled up with Adam, Ted curled up at their feet, obtrusively entered my mind. What did adventure matter, when I had no one to share it with at the end of the day?

Monday morning, I headed straight to Cynthia's desk, hoping for some more insight before meeting with Ryan again. She swiveled in her chair as I approached, apparently alerted of my presence by a passing greeting in the hallway. Her face lit up like a teenager with a secret.

"So, the brother who was left high and dry is a transportation security officer at the airport."

"Interesting," I replied.

"Didn't Skylar get through the checkpoints with the help of a transportation security officer looking the other way?"

"That she did."

The memory of being frustrated as she'd stubbornly headed toward the longer line flooded my mind. At the time, I thought she was trying to avoid me. Later, she confessed the real reason. Henry had his people at the airport, turning a blind eye to the large amount of cash she'd carried through security.

"Do you have a picture?" Cynthia proudly waved her hand toward the computer screen. A man with light brown hair and blue eyes smiled back, in an impatient 'get this over with' sort of way. A look more suitable for a teenager than the nearly thirty-year-old I guessed him to be.

"Does this man match up with the description Skylar gave you?" she asked.

Due to the passing of time, the details were a bit hazy. I had a professional duty to reach out to Skylar to double-check the facts. Beyond any excitement about a possible lead, I again found the potential contact with her empowering.

"I think so, but I'm going to double-check. But what are the chances?"

"I've found that one way or the other the pieces find the right boxes. Life's a puzzle begging to be solved, Brent."

I met her gaze. "You really believe that, don't you, Cynthia?"

"I think that secretly, we all do. That's what makes us so impatient and frustrated sometimes. We were born with a desire to figure things out. It's a balance between listening, waiting, and doing."

"Ask any investigator; not all mysteries end up solved in the end."

"The end is relative. If you try your best and the mystery goes unsolved, then there must be a sequel to the story that we can only hope we're around to read." She passed me a picture of Patrick without glancing away.

As she'd spoken, Cynthia's eyes had glistened. Who was I to wreck her enthusiasm with my doubts? Doubts about killers never getting caught, drug deals never being busted, love stories never being realized. I liked the optimism bursting through and didn't want to wreck it. After all, hadn't I heard my hints from beyond when I'd allowed myself to listen? Only I wasn't brave enough to admit to my peculiarities.

Like a parent watching a child listen for the jingling of Christmas bells, I nodded and turned away. Maybe Cynthia was right. Some stories could be novellas, and some could be series where many of the characters came and went. But the stories all eventually had their intended endings.

"You'll see, Brent Foster." Her voice followed me as I headed down the hallway. "The pieces will come together when it's time."

"Shut the door," Ryan said as I entered. "We may have a problem."

There went the feeling of blissfulness. Why did the moments have to pass so quickly? "What problem?"

"Some things happened this morning."

Fear for Skylar pounded on my chest like an unwelcome visitor demanding acknowledgment. I refused to let it barge its way into my consciousness.

"We have reason to believe there was a falling out between the mysterious man and Brenda Carter."

My heart calmed. I could handle this problem; I was quite sure.

"Why? What happened?"

"A recorded phone call from the prison that took place between Henry and another man, William. William was trying to find a way to get the passwords to some of Brenda's accounts for Henry. Brenda either changed the passwords or Henry had not memorized them and no longer has access to them."

I let out a small chuckle. "Those damn passwords will get you every time."

"Never fails. In this case, it's a good thing, at least. But the interesting part is that this William guy is not going to Brenda. Since only Brenda seems to have the passwords, there is no reason to freeze the accounts at this time. If she makes a move, it may help us to locate her."

"This was a good sign; they're getting restless. Someone's going to make a move, and we'll be there to catch him—or her."

"What I need from you, Brent, is a detailed report of each account, every name on it, and the last time there was activity."

"On it."

I left the office on a mission that was pretty routine and not pressing until a thought crossed my mind. The idea in itself was nothing miraculous, and honestly, I should have thought to check on it long before that moment. But for whatever reason, the black cloud that had hidden it from my view slid to the side, making the nothingness transform. After a bit of searching in the rubbish of information, I discovered what I sought—the info that placed Brenda Carter in a conundrum.

At one fateful moment of her life, she had met a dangerous man: Nick, the beneficiary of every account we're aware of at present. Brenda Carter needed to be willing to share passwords, or Henry would help Nick get the money by less pleasant means. The plan was yet another way that Henry had stashed his money, as he'd known prison was a real possibility in his future. He'd trusted that whatever money went to Nick, would, in time, become his again.

Within moments, I was sharing this information with Ryan.

"Henry's brother? That's exactly the evidence we needed to prove that he's involved. As far as we know, though, he's still hiding out in the Netherlands."

"Well, if you can't find Nick, someone better find this Brenda Carter lady. She might be realizing her head has become a very expensive trophy. Maybe she'll be willing to talk now."

CHAPTER 17

Skylar

Journal Entry

MY ONLY FOCUS *was on the hand I held. I knew the man, and in my waking hours I would have been aware of the fact I shouldn't be holding his hand. But I wasn't awake, and my mind allowed me a moment that reality could not. Only the image of our fingers locked together and the feeling of completeness the bond created within me stood out in the dream. I wanted to stay in the warmth of the moment forever, where everything felt good and right. The vision was the most intimate one I've experienced because the man touched places I've let very few people explore. Somewhere in my alternate world, his hand is still wrapped around mine.*

Dreams slip away, though, and give way to reality. And hands drift apart when the deeds they have done are revealed. Who would be there for me in the end? Who would hold my hand when they knew the truth?

∽ও∾

My parents walked on either side of me—my hands clasped theirs. I wore a yellow sundress. I remember that at the young age of four, I believed if they swung me high enough, I would blend in with the sun.

They were laughing; they were always laughing. As my parents prepared for the next lift-off— counting three, two, one—they smiled above me at each other, and the sun made halos around their heads.

Peace wrapped around me like a blanket, and I laughed in as light-hearted and free a manner as they did. The best part of it all was that this image wasn't a dream of warm hands gripping mine. It was a memory—one of the best.

CHAPTER 18

Brent

PATIENCE, I TOLD myself. Savor the moment, the time before outcomes become sealed into existence—before they become a memory. Earlier, I'd reported to Ryan my suspicions about Patrick being the TSA officer who had helped Henry. The conversation had led to this moment—me preparing to reach out to Skylar to positively identify Patrick.

I scrolled the texts that had become the record of our relationship. Every word was still there, impossible for me to delete.

Are you available? We need to talk, I texted.

The image of Skylar, in her cubicle at work, materialized like a ghost of the past. "Look at your phone, Skylar," I begged the air. The text message bubbles appeared.

I can meet for lunch at the diner across the street. Give me half an hour.

Deep breath. The line between feeling passionate and being a fool was very thin. I had to be careful. It would take me at least a half-hour to get to the diner, so I started the ignition. Before I could put my truck in reverse, I noticed a burgundy SUV with tinted windows parked in the row behind me. Why did it demand my attention? Who knows? Maybe special agents developed secret spy powers over time, or perhaps tinted windows simply required a second look. Not wanting Henry's acquaintance, or some pleasant elderly woman for all I knew, to realize my suspicions, I kept a casual speed. Sure enough, as I began my turn onto the street, the SUV eased out of its parking spot. Adjusting my pace to catch the approaching red light, I slowed to a stop and glanced back in the rearview mirror. The SUV was two cars behind me. Assuming whoever tracked me was already well aware of where Skylar worked, I didn't divert my path.

For twenty minutes, the vehicle kept a safe distance until I was about to pull into the diner parking lot. The turn to the diner was at a light which would be changing to red on my approach. There were no cars between the SUV and mine. I waited until the last possible moment to get into the turning lane, forcing the driver to either make a last-minute switch of lanes or pull up next to me at the light. The plan came together perfectly—the SUV stopped alongside me—leaving only the problem of the right on red law. I would only have a moment before sitting at the light became awkward. I glanced for oncoming traffic behind me. I had a minute. I then fixed my sight on the vehicle and what I could make out through the tinted windows. There was one silhouette—the driver. From what I could tell, the person wore a baseball hat, and although I couldn't be sure, I believed it to be a man behind the wheel. I took a moment more to study the hazy shape before I became almost certain the person stared right back at me.

Before I could make my turn, the light turned green. The SUV accelerated fast enough to make a sound that was only decibels below that of a squeal, but not quick enough to prevent me from seeing part of the license plate—KVC. At least, that's what I believed it to be. The rest remained hidden by the car following the SUV. As soon as I parked my vehicle, I scribbled down the few letters I'd seen and was about to call Cynthia. That's when I saw Skylar. She stood on the walkway in front of the entrance; her warm expression called to me. The license plate could wait. I stepped out of the truck; my legs moved forward; my mind sped ahead. In the twenty paces it took me to reach her, I somehow managed to pull myself together. When I hugged her in greeting, I was able to present myself as an FBI agent and not a fumbling teenager.

"It's great to see you, Brent," Skylar said mid-embrace, which I noticed lingered longer than was cordial but less than 'let's find a hotel.' I'd take it for the moment.

"Great to see you too, Skylar." Opening the restaurant door, I motioned for her to enter before me.

We reached the hostess station. "Table for two, please," I said.

The waitress led the way to the table. My hand found the small of Skylar's back, guiding her despite the fact she didn't need it.

We sat across from each other in a booth. Skylar sighed and her shoulders relaxed. The tension visibly lifted from her body.

"So, how was Liz's wedding?" I asked.

"Oh, yes, the wedding. It was nice. Liz actually looked— how do I explain? —not Liz like. Happy, and I dare say, classy."

The waitress walked by, delivering food to the nearby table where a young boy, approaching a sound resembling a scream, scrambled to get out of his seat. The mother coaxed him back. "I see your food coming," she said in her mom voice. The clinking of silverware followed, and the temper tantrum subsided. My attention returned to Skylar who had also been distracted by the commotion.

"Classy. Wow. Was that a compliment?"

"I recognize the rarity, but I've been working on some things."

"Really? What made you feel you needed to change?"

"Recent events. Feeling petrified and alone. The moment, afraid for my life, that I held a kitchen knife and realized only two people in the world would care if I disappeared."

"I'm hoping I was one of the two."

Skylar's expression became flustered; she knew she had revealed too much. Then her features softened. "Am I presuming too much?"

"You know that answer."

The corners of her lips hinted at a smile. She quickly looked away from me to straighten the napkin on her lap.

"I know you'll look even classier at your wedding, and I have to hope you're genuinely happy."

She opened her mouth to say something, but the waitress interrupted. We ordered and I tried to brush the waitress away, but the moment was too fleeting, and whatever had hovered on Skylar's lips would remain a mystery.

"So, about Henry?" she began.

"Yes, about Henry. That's what we're here for." I pulled the photo of Patrick out of my folder and slid it across the table. "Look familiar?"

"Yes, that's the TSA officer. The one Henry told me to look for at the airport. Are you onto something?"

"We've got some leads."

"Care to elaborate?"

"Sometimes it's safer not to know everything. I hope you understand."

Skylar adjusted the napkin on her lap. Again, I assumed

she was avoiding eye contact. "Too many things are a mystery sometimes," she murmured.

Our gazes locked, searching for responses we weren't allowed to give. The intimacy forced a barrier inside of me to crumble. Words I didn't expect poured out. "Ever feel you're in a situation for a reason—a reason that somehow feels, I don't know, crucial maybe?"

"Go on," Skylar said, encouraging what could very well be my demise.

"Okay, well, sometimes, it's like events have led me right here. It's like each moment is pivotal, and I'm petrified I'm going to let something slip away that I'll always regret." I paused, but Skylar didn't speak, forcing me to continue, dropping bait until it became appealing. "Do you sometimes feel like the universe is telling you something, telling us something?" What man tries to win a woman over by speaking of the universe and its workings in his life? Not me. Not generally, anyway.

Skylar stared at me like I had two heads. The silent pause lasted only a moment, but it stretched out to an eternity of possible outcomes.

"Every day lately."

She'd saved me, allowing me to breathe again. We were officially weird together.

"Thank you," I said.

"For what?"

"For not leaving me out there on that one." I let out the breath I'd been holding. "Listen, Skylar." I shook my head and laughed.

"What? Why are you laughing?"

"Because I'm trying to say something, to tell you something, but I don't know how to do it."

"Brent, it's only you and me. You can say almost anything."

"It's the 'almost' that gets me; the invisible line I don't want to cross."

"I want to hear what you're thinking."

"You asked for it." I inhaled deeply, preparing myself. "Why do you think we ended up right back here, like the case never ended?"

"Because the case never completely did end."

She had a point, but not the one I was trying to get at. "Or it's because the universe likes to nudge people, Skylar."

"Agreed."

"Sometimes, when I'm investigating cases, there are facts, important facts. We need those facts to solve the cases because, in this world, facts are what count. We understand what we can touch and feel and prove without a doubt. Sometimes though, before you get to the facts you can prove, there are the intangible factors, the gut feelings. It becomes like a language we need to decipher. It's the messages in the wind, so to speak." I paused, allowing my words to settle in like testers to tell me if I should continue. Skylar, engrossed—or entertained at least—studied me. "It's a secret language that can be harder to learn than Japanese if you ask me, but I have faith in it. I always have."

She laughed. "I only know English."

"Yes, because if you want to learn another language, you need to set aside time to study it, to be open to learning it, at least." I paused. "The sad truth is that we expect to just magically know the most important language without putting in any effort."

Skylar was quiet, I hoped that no matter how she processed my words, the outcome would be favorable for me.

"I used to have dreams. I still do. I once believed that they were trying to tell me things, lead me in another direction."

I would have given anything to know her dreams, but I had a feeling she wouldn't share them. "Maybe they were trying to nudge you. Did you listen to them?" It was the closest I could come to knowing what secret thoughts drifted through her mind while she slept.

"No, I didn't." Skylar's gaze rested on something, or maybe nothing, that existed on the other side of the window. Her focus came back to me. "And how about you, Brent? How is the universe nudging you?"

"It brought me back here, which, by the way, makes it a beautiful language in my book."

I let the words linger between us like a flame in the darkness, hoping and praying she wouldn't blow the flame out and still hoping she remained true to herself.

"Perhaps, it is." The flame brightened. "But then it is a language far more confusing than any other to decipher."

We stared at each other for a moment. My mind was frozen, unable to decide where to go next.

"Do you ever read poetry, Brent?" My face must have answered her question because she laughed. "It takes work. Sometimes it appears to be nothing more than rambling phrases leading you nowhere, but that's the beauty in it. There's often secret depth to those phrases and when you get it, well, it's like crashing through a glass pane and seeing something new even though it was clearly in front of you the whole time."

My mouth started to move, and even I was curious as to what it would say. With perfect timing, the young girl serving our meals approached, saving me. My burger wouldn't come anywhere near to satisfying the hunger inside of me.

I lifted my drink. "To learning new languages."

Skylar clicked my glass. "To new languages."

The waitress, who should have been on her way, lingered until we both paused and gave her our attention. After an awkward moment, she reached into the pocket of her apron and pulled out a note.

"A man asked me to give you this." The waitress timidly reached out her hand.

"Thank you," I replied, but she had already turned on her heel and headed back to the kitchen. I unfolded the small piece of paper and saw one short sentence scribbled on it. I read it in silence. *You should have followed me.* My mind scrambled to make sense of the words, and then I remembered the SUV that had kept pace with me as I'd approached the diner. Whoever had been in the vehicle had been staring back at me.

CHAPTER 19

Skylar

Journal Entry

SOMETHING SHIFTED IN *my mouth. I sprinted to the bathroom mirror and studied my reflection. One of my front teeth was missing. Suddenly, many of my teeth slid out of place and then fell from the sockets into the sink. I knew if a tooth was returned to its rightful place, it might retake like an uprooted plant. One by one, I forced each tooth back into its hole. The mission was futile. For each tooth I replaced, another one fell into the sink. With each clink on the porcelain, panic filled me. The final clink jolted me from my sleep.*

Our sleeping minds create a mysterious state of existence, allowing us to enter a new realm of being. What was more real? Obviously, my teeth were intact when I woke. That part is not the reality I question. The part I ponder is our ability to see the unseen when our eyes are open, and the sights and sounds are stimulating our minds before us. All the stimulus leaves our brain continually trying to form responses to the situations, leaving it overwhelmed.

But when we sleep—when all else shuts down—is that when our brain finally interprets our circumstances correctly?

If so, should I regret what I'd chosen to share when confronted by the FBI?

There were a million ways the people in my life could be deceiving me, and I wondered about all of them. Did he wonder as well? Who were we in reality? When all the walls came down, and we stood metaphorically naked in front of each other, who would we see standing before us? Would we like that person? Would we like ourselves?

Sometimes, before bed, I would watch my mother's image in the mirror as she washed her face and put on her layer of face cream. She would hum along with some song playing in her mind. When my mother finished, she would smile down at me, lift my chin and say, "Time for bed, beautiful." And I believed that I was beautiful. In her eyes, it seemed, I was everything she wanted me to be, a miniature version of herself gaining color and life with each day. Until she wasn't there, and I froze in a phase of transformation.

The outer layers of the flower bud sealed the contents tightly within it before I truly got to see what could have been. What would I see if someone could help me unclench the fist that had taken hold of me? I wasn't sure what was worse—to find the contented place of nothingness and remain there; or to always feel a determination for more pecking at my insides. I wanted to run, run a million miles, to bust through a wall. Yet, even as I stood at the precipice of becoming, I was too afraid to jump.

CHAPTER 20

Brent

ISCANNED THE RESTAURANT but saw nothing suspicious. Coworkers conversed, moms tried to settle their children, but no one appeared mysterious.

"Excuse me, Skylar." Quite aware of her bewildered stare, I rose from my seat.

As I stood in the middle of the diner parking lot, only a lingering memory caught my attention. Bruce, many months ago, had confronted Skylar and fessed up to some of his misdeeds. Had he known then that he would soon take his life? A gentle breeze swept by me, touching my skin like a ghost, and I wondered for a moment if Bruce was telling me yes. He had already given up on happiness ever settling in his corner of the world. I felt the hairs on my arms rise, and then gently fall as the memory floated away on the tail end of the wind.

Skylar approached me from behind.

"What is it, Brent?"

"I'm not sure," I answered, no longer positive if I was talking about the breeze or the note anymore. "I probably need to get back to the office." After a friendly hug goodbye, I turned back to my truck.

"Hey, Brent."

"Yeah?"

"Next one's on you."

"Excuse me?"

"You left me with the bill." I began to apologize, but she raised her hand to stop me. "No worries. It just means there'll be a next time," she said with a hint of playfulness in her eyes I would lock in my memory for days, maybe years to come. Keeping an eye on my surroundings, I hopped in my truck and found the license plate number I had written down. It remained in the cup holder where I'd left it. It could wait until I returned to the district office and spoke with Cynthia.

I drove in silence, reliving the conversation I'd had with Skylar, cementing every word into a mental photo album of memories I could revisit at will. Was I crazy for trying to change the direction of her life? Should I just let go and watch where our lives fell as if we were Plinko chips predestined to meet a particular ending? Was stressing about our path merely a waste of time and energy?

As I approached the office, my thoughts drifted away from Skylar and back to the many cases awaiting my attention. The loose ends associated with Henry's case wagged their fingers in my face. There was more of a connection somewhere in the characters.

I concocted a whiteboard in my brain and listed the cast members of the most recent mystery. Henry and Nick, brothers who for some reason, seemed to have gone their separate ways, but in reality, their ties might have only become too dark to stay in the open. Then there was the elusive Brenda Carter, who held a great deal of their money. Could she be the missing stepmother the boys had parted ways with years ago? Whoever this Brenda was, if that was her real name, she'd been close enough to them at some point to make Nick the beneficiary.

When Henry had taken part in the interview, he hadn't been fond of his stepmother. But things could have changed, or could she have had a better relationship with Nick?

How did pampered Abigail, a part-owner of a gentlemen's club and mistress of the governor, fit into the plot? And her sister, Tori, the not-so-classy stripper? She was willing to follow Skylar around in her car paid for in cash. Patrick, the transportation security officer, had been shunned by his very father, the late Andrew Carswell, who'd left each of his nieces a large sum of money. Had Andrew known his son was shady enough to be paid to look the other way at the airport security checkpoint, but not enough of a criminal to have a record? And let's not forget Governor McGregor, the man who was such an ideal family man he'd decided he should have two—or at least two 'wives.'

My imaginary whiteboard clouded my concentration as I headed into my office. I walked like a mindless robot, knowing a route due to programming. I could have walked over a misplaced piece of furniture without acknowledging it, apart from a small stumble. Lines appeared and disappeared between characters. Mentally, I tested connections that made sense one minute and faded the next as if written in disappearing ink. Nothing was sticking.

"Brent." The sound of my name broke through from another dimension, bursting the bubble I had formed around myself. "Brent." And then it popped, my mental investigation temporarily delayed. I turned to see Meghan racing down the hallway toward me. "Are you trying to avoid me?" She grinned while speaking, but I knew the question was not all in jest.

"Never." I returned her expression, but as always, with a bit of hesitation, not wanting it to say too much.

"I spoke with Ryan this morning. He thinks I should travel with you more often. Roger and Gabe are busy protecting Skylar, which leaves Bailey or me to do some of the investigative work with you. You got me."

"Great," I replied, feeling the tension in my jaw. That would mean I could be sitting at a table with Meghan and Skylar, not to mention Adam. As an agent, though, that shouldn't bother me in the least.

"What's on the afternoon agenda?"

"I have a few things I need to research from the office today. I'll get back to you tomorrow."

"Maybe we can grab dinner and go over where things stand with the case."

"It's pretty much what I've gone over in the briefings, but…" I paused, wondering if my aloofness was professional or not. "Sure, dinner it is. I'll swing by your office when I'm done here today."

"Great. See you then."

I stopped by Cynthia's office to give her the license plate number only to find that she had taken a few days off to visit her family. The license information could wait. I had more pressing items on my plate. I needed to rule out whether or not Brenda Carter was an alias for Henry and Nick's stepmother.

Hours sped by as I lost myself in the world of computers. I didn't hear Meghan enter, and was only alerted to her presence when her arm brushed against mine as she slid down to be eye level with my computer.

"Any luck with the research?"

Fortunately, the research she saw on my computer involved what I'd planned on sharing with her over dinner, but I was still annoyed by the intrusion. I wondered if she sensed the stiffness of my posture or noticed my tightened jaw as I faked being cordial.

"Not much luck yet. Henry's stepmother's name was Blair Davis. Her maiden name was Kessler. She came from a family of modest means and was a good fifteen years younger than Henry's father. Pretty much, she struck gold due to her youth and good looks. According to an interview I read awhile back, there seemed to be no love lost between her and Henry. He and his brother were probably a burden that she needed to bear if she wanted to keep her rich husband."

"What's making you interested in her all of a sudden?"

"I'm just ruling her out. We still haven't found Brenda Carter. You were right when you thought the one partner would be related. We're pretty sure that's Nick. I just want to see where the stepmother disappeared to after losing most of their money."

"She lost it?"

"That's what Henry said in an interview. Maybe she just hid it from them." I closed up my computer and turned my chair toward Meghan, who became uncomfortably close with the change in position. She laughed slightly, as though realizing she'd been guilty of creating the proximity between us, before standing and taking a step back. I stood, trying to ignore the awkwardness.

"So, where do you think we should eat?"

"Someplace close. I might come back to the office."

"Well, it is a working dinner."

"Yes, it will be that."

To give Meghan credit, she was as professional as any person in the office, except for when it came to me, and even then, she never crossed a line. She only flirted with it. How could I judge her? I knew the adrenaline that raced within her when she came around me. I understood how the forces of those hormones could overpower even the sanest person, making them behave like a high schooler with a crush. Her infatuation did not create a cockiness inside of me; instead, it made me feel foolish for my pulls and distractions. What an unfair, mixed-up world existed due to those often-misplaced desires. I stuffed some work papers into my bag. I was determined to make it through dinner, neither leading Meghan on nor pushing her away. But I knew the boundary was too thin for even the most skilled not to stumble across since each step would be scrutinized by a judge hoping for failure. Crossing the line would allow Meghan a closeness that would only lead to pain. I wouldn't let a bad choice on my part hurt her in that way.

Later that night, when I entered my apartment, exhaustion from the strain of keeping our conversation from becoming personal overwhelmed me, yet sleep eluded me. I turned and saw the nightstand clock glare 3:45 in the morning. Insomnia seemed to be a part of the profession. Each spiraling thought, begging for attention, knocked against my consciousness. Each victim waited for answers and closure. Each criminal slithered out of his hole, doing in the darkness what he didn't dare do in the daylight. Yet, my watchful eyes became blinded with tired eyelids. I pushed the thoughts and images from my mind. Finally, without warning, my brain slipped into a place that lies between reality and dreams.

My imaginary whiteboard appeared like a cloud but with emerging faces. Hidden strands attached them somehow to the middle of the thick white blanket. With unnerving smiles, the faces peered out at me. Skylar was in the center of the cloud, playing some pivotal role, holding everything together. Rain began to drip at a steady pace. I became mesmerized by each droplet, as if they were grains of sand dropping through the hourglass and landing with an ever-increasing sound of warning.

I woke, sweating, from the dream. The piece I was missing, the invisible bond, begged me to see it. In my subconscious thoughts, it had felt almost tangible. But as the dream faded, so did my certainty that the one piece would make everything fall into place.

The following day, in partial disguises with bandanas and dark glasses that would remain on while we were inside the bar, Meghan and I approached The Full Moon. Meghan wore a dark wig and black tank with a tight-fitting pair of jeans. I tried to brush off the tender memory of me readjusting her wig after it had become stuck inside her helmet. The unsettling part was that I knew Meghan had not forgotten that moment.

In my pocket, I held an old photograph of Nick, taken back before he disappeared to where we assumed was the Netherlands. The connections the brothers had in the country—the hotels, the yacht business, the bank accounts—were too undeniable for us to discount the possibility, at least. Tori's car was nowhere in sight. With Tori elsewhere, we had time to investigate without another psychotic episode ensuing.

I opened the door, and the smell of smoke hit me. As I moved farther inside the dark bar area, I saw a few lost souls sitting on the red leather seats surrounding a runway lit by laser lights. Because I'm male, and by nature visual stimuli are a strong driving force for the male gender, I also noticed the young women dancing around the poles. They wore string bikini bottoms and nothing on their top halves. Dollar bills were already tucked in the sides of their garments.

Remembering rule one of undercover work, we acted like we fit in to make people more open to conversation. I went to the bar, ordered a couple of draft beers, and swiveled around to watch the performance. Meghan mimicked my behavior. Watching the half-naked women dancing with Meghan pulled up close to my side was about as awkward of a moment I wished ever to experience.

It was still early, and a somewhat eerie air lingered in the darkness, as if, without the darkness of night, the bar was not capable of hiding its sins.

"Business always slow this time of day?" I asked the bartender.

He didn't bother looking up from rinsing a glass. "Yup."

I took a swig, let the bond from our initial conversation settle over him. "What's there to do around here?"

"I can't help you there," the bartender answered. A man at the end of the bar waved his credit card. Addressing the other patron, the bartender asked, "You starting a tab?"

"Yeah, I'll take a Bud," he answered and then turned to watch the ladies while waiting for his frosty mug to appear before him. I studied him until my attempts at being observant became a bit too obvious. The man faced me and gave me an irritated once-over. Nodding casually, I returned my attention to the women performing.

I sat my nearly empty mug on the bar. My desire to fit in might have been a bit too enthusiastic. Meghan's look reminded me to slow down, which I planned to do right after the next drink.

"Need another?" the bartender asked.

"Yeah, that would be great."

"What brings you to Jacksonville?"

"Business."

"You in sales?" he asked, with no apparent interest.

"No." I paused before continuing, not wanting to scare the bartender off. "I'm looking for an old friend, Nick Davis. I've heard he hangs out here."

The bartender froze for a moment, towel still stuffed in the mug, and then calmly continued his drying. "Never heard of him."

The tension in his voice spoke volumes. "As I said, I'm just looking for an old friend." I slid the picture of Nick across the bar. "Maybe this would help jog your memory."

The man reached in his pocket and pulled out a pair of readers. I took this as a good sign he was going to give his act a bit of effort.

His glance went from the picture to me and back again. "What did you say your name was?"

"I didn't."

He eyed me carefully. "Could be one of our patrons, but this would have to be an old picture."

"Yes, it is."

The bartender handed back the photo. "What the hell. I don't like the guy anyway. There's a man who looks similar. I believe his name's Nick."

"How sure are you?"

"Pretty certain. He's been getting a few private dances with one of my girls. As I said, looks a bit aged from that picture."

"What girl?"

"Tori. Tori Carswell. To tell you the truth, I'm not thrilled about their relationship."

"Why do you say that?"

"Well, to begin with, the girls aren't supposed to have

relationships with the patrons, but I'm almost positive I saw her get into a car with him at the end of one of her shifts. She denied it, but I assured her I was watching her closely. I've found mixing business with pleasure just leads to problems in the workplace."

"When's her next shift?"

"She'll be here tonight. And if your next question is, when does he come in, usually Friday evenings around ten."

I put my money down on the counter. "Thanks for saving me the time of asking."

"No problem. I might not be so forthcoming with everyone, but that girl has an attitude. I would need a good reason to get rid of her, though. Tori's the sister of one of the owners. Don't much care for her either, to be honest."

I nodded. "I'll see if I can give you a reason." I couldn't care less about Tori losing her job or not, but I was determined to keep my new friend on ally status.

As Meghan and I walked back to my motorcycle, my phone rang. Ryan was wasting no time on retrieving the details of my mid-day strip joint visit.

"What do you have for me?"

"The bartender confirmed that Nick is in the States. He shows up on Fridays evenings around ten, and even better, he usually spends extra time with our friend Tori."

"Perfect. We have the connection. Roger is sitting outside a coffee shop as we speak. Tori decided to get her afternoon caffeine across the street from where Skylar works. Tori's driving the black sedan."

"Well, at least some of the pieces are coming together perfectly. But why do they care about Skylar?"

"That's the question, isn't it? And unfortunately, we have

nothing to bring Nick in on yet. We can't prove he was the one driving the yacht. We can't prove he was the other person on the phone, discussing the kidnapping. We can't even prove that he is the one paying Tori to follow Skylar. At this point, we have nothing on him."

"I told Skylar I believed she was safe. I'm not sure I believe it myself anymore."

"I can't assure you that she is, Brent. We're keeping a close eye on her. Right now, that's all we can do, short of having her and Adam disappear for a while."

"Do you think that's necessary?"

"Not yet. Let's try to get some evidence against Nick. I'll do what needs to be done before Friday. Maybe we can get him to stumble."

As much as the possibility warranted excitement, something inside me knew better.

I helped Meghan adjust her helmet before I climbed on my bike.

"Nice work in there. You seemed almost like a natural. You frequent those places often?" she asked playfully.

"Only when I can't avoid it."

She slid on behind me and wrapped her arms around my waist, yet I felt only the emptiness that the wrong hands upon your skin could create.

Ten-thirty sharp, having given the players time to have arrived at the club, I hunkered down in our surveillance van. Gabe, Meghan, Bailey, and I covered our positions while Roger entered the club to do the dirty work. He had a look that would fit into the club surroundings the best. The voices were hard to make out through the music and occasional catcalls. Besides the initial check-in, Roger remained silent. The suspense started to build. My foot tapped against the van floor until Gabe's gaze traveled from my foot up to my face. I took the hint. Finally, I heard Roger put in his order.

"Jack and Coke."

Then nothing but the background noise and the occasional click of ice on glass. I looked at my watch. Roger had entered the bar ten minutes ago, and so far, I had only found out his drink of choice.

"This seat taken?"

I heard a man's faint voice. "It's all yours."

"Is it always this crowded in here?"

"Are there naked women in gentlemen's clubs?" The voice behind the words sounded unwelcoming. If not for the investigation, Roger likely would have moved on to another seat. Only a desperate soul subjected himself to more rejection.

I pictured the nodded touché in Roger's silence. There was another clink of ice against glass. Surveillance sometimes resembled a blind date on *America's Got Talent*, that is, if they allowed picking up women as actual talent. Even though we couldn't hear our audience in the background, we knew we were being judged by our abilities. At the moment, we all had our hands hovering over our X buttons while we banked on Roger's inability to conjure up anything worthwhile. Had Nick been a woman staring up at Roger's strong jawline and five o'clock shadow, Roger would probably have had much more luck winning his trust.

By the whooping sounds and change of music, I assumed a new dancer had stepped on stage. "Now, here comes a hot one," Roger said. "She might be worthy of a private dance."

The lack of response suggested a tension in the air, and as

usual, our heart rates all increased as if we were a unit, connected through sound waves.

"She's taken for the night."

Tori. I glanced at my colleagues, and judging by their expressions, they'd assumed the same.

"My apologies. I'll catch up with her another night."

More silence. "Suit yourself." There was a shuffle of chairs. Damnit. Roger had lost him.

"Hold on; there are plenty of women here. I'm not looking to cause problems," Roger said. "Sorry, I didn't catch your name."

"I didn't give it to you," Nick replied with ice in his tone, "and like I said, suit yourself."

I heard another clink of ice and then what I imagined to be Roger's glass being set on the bar. A moment later, the squeak of a door, and the sounds of cheering and music became muffled.

"I'm not sure what else I'm going to get from him tonight. I'll hang out a bit and observe." Roger had apparently gone into the bathroom to fill us in on what we already knew was his failed attempt to get information. "Were you able to hear any of that?"

The door squeaked again, followed by a voice that sounded identical to the man from the bar. "You talking to yourself, or can I assume we're not really alone in here?"

My heart sped up, ready for action.

"Excuse me?" Roger was trying to buy two seconds of time to ponder an answer.

"You're either talking to yourself, or you have some reason to have people outside listening to your conversation. So? Which one is it?" There was an eerie amusement in his voice.

"I'm afraid I have to disappoint you. I'm just a guy trying to pump myself up with a little private mirror talk. I usually don't get caught. I'm a bit embarrassed, but what can I say? Naked women can make a man nervous."

The idea that Roger, with his muscular frame, strong jawline, and full head of hair, needed a pep talk was far from believable, and the silence proved it. I braced myself for an intervention.

"So did the pep talk work?"

"Not tonight. Now, I'm heading home to my cheating wife and clinging to the shred of morals that are preventing me from enjoying this evening any further. If you'll excuse me."

I heard the bathroom door and followed the sounds of the bar through the mic until Roger appeared in the light of the doorway and headed to his car. We stayed parked as he drove away, and within moments, Nick stood in that very doorway and glanced around the parking lot. His gaze rested on the van. The world stopped. A million possibilities of unfavorable responses froze in the air, only to melt away like snowflakes when Nick let the door close between us.

CHAPTER 21

Skylar

Journal Entry

I WALKED ALONG THE *paths of my college campus, going somewhere. I recognized the buildings, but suddenly, nothing made sense. What class was I going to? Had I even set foot in the classroom this year? Another realization hit me from nowhere; the final exam was today. I searched my bag for my schedule, hoping it would reveal where I should be heading. Frantically, I pulled out all of my books, realizing I didn't recognize any of them. The paper was nowhere. My mind in my dream reality drifted as if I were on drugs. I couldn't capture my thoughts or recollections.*

I walked, hoping something would rekindle a memory but nothing came to me. Finally, I saw a blond, curly-haired friend I hadn't thought about in years. I ran toward her, but she kept getting farther away until she disappeared into the crowd. I stopped in my tracks, waiting for clarity, until reality brought me back.

Did I feel incapable, as Google suggested? Emphatically, yes.

CHAPTER 22

Brent

THE NIGHT OF the failed undercover assignment, Nick Davis had stood in the doorway of the bar —a smaller, less intimidating version of Henry. We hadn't been able to get enough evidence to bring him in, so we'd had to allow the door, momentarily at least, to close between us. If he had resurfaced in the United States for the purpose of collecting his money, then we could assume Brenda Carter was somewhere in the country as well.

In the first round of the investigation, Brenda's construction company, Construction with Care, had been scrutinized, but the probing into her accounts was never completed due to the fact that we were still searching for her. The company had appeared legit in the way that they took in money for construction jobs to be completed mainly in Henry's hotels, not only in the Jacksonville area ones, but in the many hotels he owned. The problems with the company's legitimacy emerged as the investigation dug deeper and the details became less than impressive, at least from law enforcement's standards. At the time, the investigation had focused more on Henry's crime of smuggling in the drugs than taking down the owner of the shell company. It was time to find Brenda Carter.

The FBI had moved in to seize and analyze the records

of Construction with Care. The problem was, when our squad returned to the company's office, it was boarded up. The firm was nothing more than a rented office space that apparently had no actual full-time construction employees. After questioning other construction companies in the area, we found that some of the construction workers would take on side jobs with Construction with Care every now and then. They informed us that most of the work was completed by illegal immigrants. Many only took on one or two jobs when work was slow, and most of them stated the atmosphere was weird and uncomfortable. Unless, they were desperate, they avoided doing business with them.

Since we didn't get very far with the employees, we began making our way down a list of Henry's hotels now run by a board of directors. Each hotel in our area had its own individual manager, and those managers became our targets for the coming days and even weeks if necessary. The first hotels targeted were the ones we suspected of having repair jobs completed in the past year or two and the ones that appeared in need of them.

This search turned out to be more telling than the construction company itself. Now that the head honcho was behind bars, disgruntled hotel managers were eager to talk. Boxes of receipts, photos, and bills started to pile up, meaning I'd have extremely long nights with Meghan. The disgruntled managers also shared that no one at the hotels had ever seen Brenda Carter. When they became frustrated with this issue or that, their calls were always redirected back to Henry, who had assured them the repairs would be dealt with shortly. Sometimes there was an attempt at following through and sometimes there was not. Not only had the managers never seen nor spoken with Brenda Carter, but when the language barrier was not a factor between the construction men and the disgruntled managers, they found that none of the men that had worked for Brenda Carter had ever seen her either.

The woman, Lisa Carter, who had appeared to be in charge of their small, nearly unfurnished office, had reported she was the granddaughter of Brenda Carter and that her grandmother was suffering with some illness or other. Lisa sent daily reassurances that she had things covered while her grandmother's health improved. Since the construction workers changed so frequently, no one seemed to catch on that Brenda had never returned from her absence except, maybe, the hotel managers. The special agents' search for a Lisa Carter that matched the given description could not turn up anyone. Lisa Carter did not exist beyond the alias the mysterious woman had created, which made our team concerned that Brenda Carter might have already met her fate. If the shell company was running fine without Brenda, and if Brenda had no one to notice she was not at the office, she could be floating in the ocean somewhere while Nick decided how best to collect his money without being accused of murder.

The search was expanded to include elderly women, missing persons, and obituaries. The name Brenda Carter proved to be a popular one, and many days in, the leads were still going nowhere. Lost in a world of corruption, I sat behind my desk. There were so many bills, so many payments made up front, and so many letters of complaint that had fallen on deaf ears. If only the managers had known that Henry didn't want the work completed. He only wanted it to appear that the work was being completed. His drug money was buried within Brenda's shell company and its main accomplishment had been to take in his dirty money and spit it out clean.

Henry's hotels could be found up and down the East coast

and even in the Bahamas. Yet, at its peak, Construction with Care had been a million-dollar company run from an office barely bigger than a cubicle, by a woman working under an alias.

A couple weeks into the investigation, our office received a call from one of the lucky managers that had actually had work completed in his hotel. One of the construction men had heard of the investigation and had come to him with a picture of Lisa Carter, and because I truly believed it was important to do so, I phoned Skylar.

As the phone rang, I held it tightly to my ear as if I'd capture more of the moment by doing so.

"Hello, Skylar Shaw speaking."

"Wow. Very formal." I tried to shake off the fear her coldness had created.

"Brent, I'm sorry. I was working and answered without even looking at the screen. It's good to hear from you. I hope it means you have some news."

"I have a picture I would like you and Adam to look at tonight. It's of a woman. I thought maybe Adam might know her."

"Why would Adam know her?" Skylar's voice was protective, and I shoved my resentful feelings to the side.

"Because of the case we believe Henry invented to get him fired. Did you forget about that already? It's possible the woman in the photo is one of the women who accused Adam of sexual harassment. At least, we want to rule it out."

"I've been trying to forget about that case. Thanks for the reminder." Somehow, I felt responsible for the tiredness in her voice.

"She worked for Henry, or at least for the shell company that is associated with his hotels."

"We'll both be home by six."

"I'll see you then."

"Brent, I actually have a crockpot meal that I wouldn't mind showing off. Would you like to stay for dinner?"

Sadly, my only chance to be near Skylar would involve sitting in the warmth of a home she'd created with another man. The idea stung, yet what choice did I have? "I'd love to."

After deciding not to bring Meghan along, I rolled into their driveway at six fifteen. Their cars sat side by side—a metallic couple representing their tastes and status. Both cars were well-kept, new, and conservative. I couldn't help but notice how my F150 loomed over his Nissan Altima. Ted, ready to greet me as if I were coming home, barked by the door. Adam stood at the entrance and gestured me in. The smells from the crockpot were inviting, and yet, somehow sour to my senses, reminding me that none of this belonged to me. Skylar's hair dripped out of her clip as she bent over the oven to pull out some warming rolls. After setting the rolls on her granite countertop, she approached me with her arms outstretched.

"Brent, thanks for coming. Perfect timing. Dinner is about to be served."

"Great."

"Can I pour you a class of cab?" Adam asked.

"Sure, that would be great. Thank you."

Skylar placed her pot roast in a serving dish and brought the dish to the table. Adam followed her with the rolls and wine glasses and began pouring the wine. They worked with synchronistic movements, making the dinner preparation more of a dance they had practiced for years. Suddenly, I felt like a wolf in sheep's clothing—a feeling that did not settle well.

Or worse yet, a salesman coming to their home and offering something to make them happier, healthier, or better in some way. In the warmth of their kitchen, I wondered if Adam was showing me, telling me: *This is what we have. Can you really give her something better?* I searched my mind like a salesman's briefcase, panicked because I wasn't sure I could offer her more. Who was I to make promises of a better tomorrow? In that moment, I knew there was a worse scenario than watching Skylar marry Adam: her marrying me and then living to regret it.

We sat in unison, and my hand went to the wine glass as if its contents could wash away my fears. I wouldn't push. I could just show her what I had to offer and let her know that it would come to her freely. Then, I would force myself to be happy for her and move on if it wasn't enough—if I wasn't enough. I took another long drink.

After the "nice meal, weather's a bit chilly" conversation, I decided to get to the point.

"Adam, I'm assuming Skylar told you about the picture I wanted to show you?"

"Yes, she mentioned it."

I reached into the pocket of my jacket and pulled out the four-by-six image of a blond woman in her thirties. I suspected she'd dress up very nicely, but this picture showed her in one of her more conservative roles. I slid the photo to Adam. He studied it while wiping his mouth with his napkin.

"Do you recognize her?" I asked.

"Her name was Rose. Let me think. Rose Mackenzie. That was definitely it. I found it rather odd that such a young woman was named Rose. Trust me, she wasn't wearing an outfit like that one when she came to my office. Although, she did dress in a way that turned heads."

"I'm sure she knows how to dress for each part she's playing," I added.

"So where does this connection get us?" Adam asked.

"This development is just one more baby step. Right now, we're just seeing who fits where in Henry's web."

"Please let your people know we're here to help. We are more than happy to answer questions from anybody."

He attempted to close the door to my connection.

Skylar glanced at Adam, and I was almost certain I saw panic in her expression. She took Adam's hand sitting on the table before looking back at me. "Brent, please know that it's much more comfortable to have someone we know working with us. I understand we'll most likely speak to other people as well, but we really appreciate your extra efforts in this case."

"Of course," Adam added before releasing her hand and going in for another bite of pot roast. He chewed it while keeping his eyes on me the whole time.

I took yet another sip of wine. "It's hard to let this one go, for some reason, but as I said, I won't be able to be the only one involved. That's for sure. You should feel comfortable, since you've both met the other agents. Well, you've met all but one—Special Agent Ambers." Meghan, being new to the squad, had not been involved with Henry's arrest. "She's been paired up with me a bit lately."

"A female agent?" I heard what I hoped to be a trace of concern in Skylar's voice.

"Yes. I believe you'll find her easy to talk to as well." An awkward silence settled over the table. "Can I help you clean up?"

"Oh, no, of course not. You're the guest," Skylar responded.

"Clean-up will fall on me, Brent. But thanks for offering," Adam replied.

"Well, then, I really do hate to have to run, but this is a crazy time right now, and I have tons of paperwork waiting for me."

"Let me walk you to the door," Skylar said standing from her chair. Adam stood as well and shook my hand firmly. At the door, Skylar quickly embraced me before I turned to go. As the door was closing, I heard her soft voice reaching out to me. "Good night, Brent." What were words anyway, but a vehicle to carry a feeling from one person to another. She could have said anything, and it wouldn't have mattered, because I heard the one thing I needed to hear in her voice—longing.

CHAPTER 23

Skylar

Journal Entry

A FROZEN RIVER SURROUNDED *me. Up ahead, I saw a group of people and realized they were my childhood family. I raced toward them. The experience of running across the slippery floor thrilled me. The white backdrop sparkled, and the crystal waters splashed up the sides of the ice. My heart raced as I closed in on my parents. Right before I reached them, the ice cracked, and I dropped into the freezing waters. I swam with stiffened arms to the underside of the hole and climbed out. Panicked, I scrambled toward my family while calling out that the ice was melting.*

Much of the ice around us disappeared before I could reach them, leaving only the shrinking island we stood upon. Below us, killer whales bumped into the underside of the island and, one by one, bounced each of us into the freezing water. Each time, whoever fell, scrambled back to safety. Imagined images of the unlucky victim being tossed around like a ball at SeaWorld haunted me. We stood in the center of our island, our hands clasped together, until a whale's head jarred into us, and I was jolted awake.

I wasn't surprised to find that dreaming of frozen water symbolizes feelings that one has turned off or won't let flow.

We were in Ocean City, Maryland. I was about ten, maybe twelve. People bustled along the boardwalk, drank drinks the size of their heads in the restaurants along the strip, rode the giant Ferris wheel to gain a view of the beach. Memories of the weekend had blurred in my mind through the years, but I remembered that for the first time, I'd seen a fortune teller at work on a client. The woman had wiped tears away from her cheek as the fortune teller, dressed in a flowing skirt, had flipped cards and whispered words I hadn't been able to hear.

I'd been licking an ice cream cone, engrossed more in watching them than in the enjoyment of the treat. I hadn't noticed that my parents were watching me until my mother put her hand on my shoulder. "Now why would she go and wreck the mystery?"

I looked at my mother, who was now only a half foot taller than me. "Don't you want to know your fortune? Aren't you curious?"

"That's not how it works, Skylar. Today's experiences teach you the lessons needed for tomorrow. You're not meant to know how hard the exam is until you've taken the class. You would quit. Once you prepare, it might still be tough, but you'll be more ready than you know. Let life happen. It's set up for study periods and test periods. If you go out of order, if you cheat, you aren't trusting the instructor. Nothing good comes from that."

I took another long lick of my ice cream and eyed the crying woman before turning away. Leaving my curiosity behind, I continued down the boardwalk with my parents and prepared for the tests to follow.

CHAPTER 24

Brent

WELL, IT'S ABOUT time," I said, entering Cynthia's office.

"Can't a girl take a few days off to visit her aging parents?" she replied with faked annoyance.

"Not in this line of work." I pulled a chair up next to her and took a swig of my coffee. "How was your visit?"

"Good, but it's a bit depressing watching what ten years does to a person. My youthful parents are starting to sound like a bitter elderly couple bickering over the need for hearing aids."

"It's good you got to see them."

"Yes, but bothersome too. I realize how much I'm missing and how fast time is flying by." She took a deep breath. "But on to better things. What did I miss?"

"I have a partial license plate, KVS, that belongs to a burgundy SUV."

"No make and model? You like to make it as challenging as possible, don't you?" she said teasingly.

"The SUV driver kept a good distance and then my view got blocked."

"Excuses," she said as she placed the doughnut box in front of me. I grabbed the one covered in chocolate. "I'll see what I can find. Anything else?"

After swallowing my mouthful of morning sugar, I replied, "I want to rule a few people out of the scenario. Could you try to find out who Nick and Henry's stepmother is and where she went after their father's death? According to an interview done with Henry, she blew a bunch of the money and their relationship was pretty rocky."

"On it. And what's on your agenda for the day?"

"More digging into Abigail's accounts and a few other details begging for my attention." I stood to leave.

"I hear Meghan is your sidekick now."

"Yes, she is."

"She thinks quite highly of you, it appears."

"I think you're right."

Cynthia paused, no doubt hoping for more information. I offered nothing.

"Not in the mood to share?"

"She's great, but I don't want to go there right now."

"It's hard to be in two places at once, isn't it?" she said with a knowing smile and the tenderness of an older sister, even though I had her by several years.

"I'll catch up with you later. Let me know what you find."

Abigail Carswell's accounts were clean apart from her hidden boyfriend. Her gentlemen's club had been used mainly as a meeting place and somewhere Bruce would unload drugs without the business owners even being aware of a drug mule in their midst. I couldn't even be sure how much Tori knew of the business. She could very well just be a woman willing to do some odd jobs—private dances and a little stalking—to cover the bills. But the construction company was a whole different story. Digging through the boxes of information was like cutting into the very heart of the scheme, except the body that should be encasing the heart was missing.

Brenda's accounts remained inactive. We could have them frozen, but we hoped they would lead us to her if she was still out there, or incriminate Nick, even though we had to assume Nick had enough money of his own to play with and he could go quite some time before ever needing to tap into that resource. As I studied the screen, a gentle knock on my door demanded my attention.

"We have the TSA agent who let Skylar through security," Roger said.

"Patrick?"

"Yeah. He's down the hall being questioned. Thought you might want to observe."

"Thanks, I do."

I entered the connecting room where I could observe the interrogation already in progress. It was easy to spot the real criminals compared to the imposters by how much sweat soaked through their shirts. Patrick was drowning in his making us aware of his guilt and his unpolished talents as a criminal. The Carswell family appeared to be the type that would jump on a speeding train heading for a brick wall if they thought it might earn them some easy cash— always the puppets, never the puppeteers. Not one of them had impressed me as having the intelligence to think through their actions. We liked the Patricks of the world. They crumbled easily.

"Patrick, I'm going to ask you again. Who was paying you to let Skylar through security with all the cash?" Gabe asked with a building intensity.

Patrick was silent for a moment, an action used, I believed, to imitate loyalty. He ran his fingers through his hair and then rubbed his forehead. "I wasn't getting paid."

"You're going to stick with that story then?" Gabe asked.

"No. I mean, it's more complicated than that." Patrick squirmed in his chair. He was sitting on the tip of an iceberg of sins that threatened to be exposed. "Tori introduced me to some guy. She'd met him at the club years ago. They have some weird stripper/client relationship. She refers to him as one of her special customers. I didn't care to know much about her life. We're not close."

"Why do it if you weren't getting paid?"

Patrick rested his head in his hands. "I had to," he whimpered.

Gabe studied him, probably deciding which path of crime he should continue to chase Patrick down. He chose to keep the momentum going by returning to the investigation dealing with Henry. "How long have you known Tori's customer?"

"Me? Not more than a few years, maybe. Tori, I think, has known him much longer. He's out of the country a lot, so I wouldn't really call it a relationship, but then again, I don't keep close tabs on my cousin." Gabe had guessed correctly. Patrick took a deep breath and appeared ready to talk again.

"Want to explain your falling out with your cousin?" Gabe apparently thought the falling out could be connected to the case.

"Not really. Just family crap." I couldn't be certain, but the layer of sweat might have thickened. Gabe watched him long enough to make Patrick uneasy. My colleague left whatever was behind Patrick's silence untouched again. There was a whole other trash can of rotting debris we weren't here to dig into at the moment.

"So, you went to the club, owned by your cousin Abigail, that employs her sister, Tori, who earns her living stripping. Classy bunch."

Patrick shrugged in a *what can I say, we're losers*, kind of way.

"What happened from there?"

"Nick and I talked for a bit, and he led me to believe it would be beneficial for me to help him out."

"Beneficial? How?"

Patrick avoided eye contact. "He said something about it being in my best interest."

"Want to explain further?"

Another shrug. "I took it as a threat. That's all I can say."

"It's best if you give more detailed answers, Patrick. Start helping yourself out."

I imagined Patrick had watched his share of crime shows, yet his failed attempt at mimicking the nonchalant criminal was uncomfortable to observe.

"Nick convinced me that following his orders was a good choice, put it that way." A few more moments passed in awkward silence. "So, if I talk, will I be protected?"

"What do you mean by protected?"

"Like not go to jail?"

"The judge generally looks favorably on individuals who help us get to the people we really want."

Patrick studied Gabe. After a long pause, Patrick said, "There was just something in his tone. I didn't trust him."

Apparently, my colleague had not instilled enough faith in the system for Patrick to delve further into his web of crime. Despite Gabe's efforts, from that point on, Patrick's answers only spun in circles.

Tori's turn came the next day. Again, I sat and observed from the other side of the glass. Her arms crossed, she remained cocky, chewing a piece of gum and glaring at the special agent.

"Tori, it says here you work at a gentlemen's club downtown. The Full Moon. Correct?"

"Yeah. So?" Tori obviously attempted to appear natural, yet at the same time, avoided eye contact. "You should check it out sometime." She failed miserably at portraying the sensual body language that, I'm sure, flowed easily during work hours.

"I think I'll pass," Gabe replied with enough disgust Tori's flirtatious tone should be laid to rest. "Do you recognize this man?" He slid the picture of Patrick across the table, testing her, since we were well-aware of the fact that she did.

"He's my cousin. I try not to associate with him too much."

"And what, may I ask, makes him so far below you that you can't speak with him?"

"Just family crap. Stuff your records won't show. Crimes that only break family laws, so you really don't need to know about them." Gabe let a moment of silence pass, allowing the nervousness to build within her. "Why am I here?" she asked.

Ryan slid the next picture across the table. Tori stared at the photo of Nick, but she remained silent.

"Our investigative team has uncovered a great deal of information, so you might want to answer honestly. It's the smarter way to go, Tori. I assure you."

"Then you know his name's Nick. He comes into the club sometimes. That's about all I can tell you."

"We hear he's a special client of yours. You spend a good deal of time giving him individual attention, so to speak."

"Whatever I do is legal. If he pays for a private dance, he gets it. End of story."

"Oh, but Tori, we both know that's not the end of the

story, don't we? We are also aware that Nick knows your cousin Patrick. Patrick has done a few unusual projects for him, hasn't he?"

"Nick and Patrick have never met. I think you're confusing Nick with his low-life brother, Henry. Henry's in jail already, so I guess your work here is done."

"Funny, that's not what Patrick told us."

"You talked to him?" I heard a hint of panic in her voice.

"Why does that upset you, Tori?"

"I'm not upset. Talk to him all you want."

"We intend to. So, what brought Nick back from the Netherlands?"

"Family. He wanted to be near his brother."

"I thought you said Henry was a low-life in jail."

"Just because I don't care for him doesn't mean Nick feels that way. They're family. He wanted to check in with him. That's not illegal."

Gabe leaned back and folded his arms over his middle while he watched her. Tori crossed and uncrossed her legs, checked her watch, and became increasingly uncomfortable.

"Are we almost done? I have a shift tonight and I need to rest beforehand."

Roger placed his folded hands on the table, a sign of his changing approach. "Tori, I'm not your enemy." She released a small grunt and looked away. "The problem is, we have some concerns, some very important concerns, about your friend Nick. If these concerns turn out to be warranted, I believe you could be in danger."

"Nick would never hurt me."

"Maybe not intentionally, but sometimes good people get caught in situations that are out of their control. They dangle a toe in the murky waters and the next thing they know they've fallen off the dock and are sinking in mud. We don't want that to happen to you. I want to help you, Tori, before you drown in sludge. Do you understand what I'm saying?"

"You want me to turn against my friends?"

"What makes him your friend? The fact that he buys you cars?"

"How do you know about that?"

And there we had it. One more piece had slipped into place.

"We always know more than you think, Tori. While you're not being placed under arrest today, it doesn't mean it's not going to happen tomorrow." Tori took a swig of water but was unable to regain her cocky composure.

"And Tori, it doesn't fare well to have restraining orders placed on you, either."

"What do you mean?"

"It means, you're not that great at discreetly following people." He paused again. "Would you like to share anything? Why is Nick having you follow Skylar Shaw?"

"I don't know what you're talking about."

"You're still going to play that game?"

Silence.

"I want you to take two steps away from the edge and see it for what it is. Save yourself before it's too late."

"Can I leave now?"

"You've always been free to go, Tori." Roger handed her his card. "Be smart. You're young, and you have no record. The world is yours. Keep it that way."

The endless papers, the ones that held the answer to the mystery, were sprawled out before me, yet somehow the mystery had nothing to do with illegal money and everything to do with something that had a much greater meaning to me. How could bank statements and receipts somehow reveal what lay in Skylar's heart? Maybe they couldn't. Maybe I would never really know her feelings.

On my drive home, I searched my mind for each moment that had given me hope, yet the realness of the moments would sometimes fade to nothingness. A sound of longing became nothing more than a tiredness in her voice. A lingering look became fear of her situation—a clinging to someone who may be able to help. I dug deeper and deeper into my box of memories for proof, but nothing added up to the reality I sought.

Songs from the radio filled my truck with heartache, as if they'd been written just for my situation, yet they hadn't. The words had been, in many ways, written over and over again in the lyrics for melodies that dated back to the beginning of music. That realization should have helped me feel less lonely; instead, it made me recognize I was only experiencing a pain that was so well known it bordered on mundane. And of all those songwriters, how many of them had been able to quench their love with the reality they'd dreamed of, and how many had lived on to feel an occasional tug at their heart until its final beat? I refused to be the sap that never let go of an unrequited love. I would allow myself this feeling up to her wedding day, and then I would move on and never look back. It was a promise I had to make to myself.

I reached my apartment after eight and threw the mail down on the counter before heading to the fridge for a beer. After cracking it open and taking a swallow that may have been a third of the bottle, I glanced down at the mail I had tossed aside. That's when I saw it. The white envelope with silver printed words stared up at me like the sad eyes of a dog begging for attention. I ignored it.

When I was only blocks from the office, the phone rang. Too agitated to take the time to look at the number, I answered with an abrupt, "Hello."

"Good morning." Her voice sounded soft and questioning. I'm sure she had never heard that tone directed at her, from me anyway.

"Skylar, sorry. Rough morning already."

A pause. "I wanted to…I was wondering. Did you get the invitation?"

My stomach burned, and the need for fresh air became overwhelming. "Yea, it came yesterday."

More silence. "I'm sorry."

Now I really needed air. I tried to think carefully how to continue. "What do you have to be sorry for? You asked me if I wanted an invite."

"I know. I just…I think maybe Adam was testing me. And maybe you."

Thankful I didn't have to focus on driving anymore, I pulled into my parking spot.

"Want to explain?"

"Do I really need to?"

"I would appreciate it."

"It's just…it's just that…I wouldn't be able to watch you marry someone else."

I lay my head on the steering wheel. Her words should have excited me; instead, my heart ached as if it were literally being ripped apart.

"Then you'll understand if I don't attend?"

"Brent, I want you to know that I love Adam. I really do, but I also want you to know that I have thought about you every day. I know it's wrong, and I'm terrible for even saying it, but I wanted you to know. It was very painful for me to see you drive away that day, and I think Adam sensed that."

Breathing went from difficult to impossible. "Skylar, are you ready to get married if your mind is still wondering? Don't you think that when it's time to get married, you should only be thinking of the one person waiting for you at the end of the aisle?"

"I shouldn't have said anything. I'll understand if you can't come. Bye, Brent."

"Skylar, wait." She'd already hung up. And after a moment, I let what I'd just discovered sink in. She loved me too. She just needed to realize how much.

CHAPTER 25

Skylar

Journal Entry

I STOOD IN *A field, and out of the grass arose an impossibly large group of balloons. The blue sky hid behind the array of colors clumped together and held by a hand slowly emerging from the ground below it. Even though my very brain was creating the image, I had no clue what was coming next. Who would have expected to see an enormous Superman balloon being lifted by all the other little ones? For a dream, it was quite an impressive, colorful sight, and I stood mesmerized by the image of the floating Superman until he'd drifted far enough into the distance that my brain became bored and brought me back to consciousness.*

Heights bring many emotions to the mind. We want to fly, to take off, to excel, and to reach the top. But that's not what my dream was telling me as the balloon rose to heights that were no longer attainable. Height here represented blighted hopes, the need to release feelings, to let people go. My dream was asking me to do the impossible.

Heights could also be terrifying. Being raised by my parents was much like being swept up in a giant parasail. The world below looked colorful and beautiful. Nothing was frightening… until something ripped the parasail open, forcing them to release their grip on me. As I spiraled to the water's surface below me, I watched them floating, arms outstretched. The world closed in on me, and what was once beautiful turned into a wall that I slammed into, alone. I often wondered what was more damaging to a soul—to experience the best of humanity and have it ripped away or to never know that such a heaven on earth ever existed.

CHAPTER 26

Brent

WE WERE CLOSING in. By the way he had disappeared again, Nick knew it. Ever since the night in the bar, no one had spotted him, and as expected, Tori had ceased following Skylar. Strangely though, we were alerted that Tori had been put on Henry's visitor list, the same Tori who had claimed complete disgust for the man. Did they really believe we weren't listening to their conversations? Brenda's accounts still sat dormant. Not a surprise. There were dumb criminals and completely stupid criminals. I wasn't quite sure if this trio fell into either category, except for the fact I found most criminals to be ignorant at some level.

Being dumb was also true when it came to love, as evidenced by the fact I was willing to act on the improbable, despite Adam finding out. The clock was ticking. The present moment, full of possibilities, would soon become the past, holding in its grasp regret and remorse or a sense of knowing that at least I had done all that I could. There would be no more regrets, no more what ifs.

The wedding was two months and two days away, but who was counting? After a few hours of looking over bank statements and receipts that were painting a dismal picture of Brenda Carter's business, I thought of the perfect text.

I have a proposition. My finger hovered over the send button like a diver on the high dive before I plunged into the depths of the unknown.

And what would that be? she replied.

Skylar opened the door and welcomed me in with her response. At least, a part of her wasn't ready to shut me out yet.

Meet me after work. One drink, maybe two, and I'll tell you.

Nothing. And then a bit more nothing. I stared at my phone, not breathing. And then the bubbles popped up on the screen. *Where?*

I released the breath I'd clung to and typed the name of a small pub nearby.

See you there, she replied.

The only chance I had at being focused was that my work meant Skylar's safety, so I threw myself into the tainted accounts and hoped to come out on the other side with the belief that the good guy always won in the end, unless of course, there were two good guys. Then it was inevitable. Someone's world would darken, despite the fact he didn't deserve it.

Just before seven, I finally pulled into the pub's parking lot. Her car was already there. I sat next to it in my truck for a moment and wondered if there was any feeling in the world more intoxicating than love. It was the root of all other feelings, feeding the limbs as they branched out to emotions that hardly resembled what fueled them at all. Anger, hatred, sadness, joy—they all circled back to the core emotion. Hate seeped into the crevices of souls when love failed them in one way or the another. From our first breaths, love is expected to nurture us. When it doesn't, and we watch others soak it in greedily, sadness builds. The sadness turns to bitterness, and from a soil that had awaited the seed that was never planted, where love was intended, hatred grows. We were born needing love much like we need oxygen, and when our source is extinguished, we suffocate in the darkness. But how can love not fail each of us at some time?

Skylar sat at a booth, a glass of wine already in her hand. The dim lighting softened her features, almost making me blind to the anxiety hiding behind her smile. Only when I approached the table did I remember I had not officially thought of the proposition. Skylar stood to greet me, embracing me with just enough warmth that an onlooker could not decipher the relationship between us. *No*, I told myself, *I knew the proposition, just not the words in which to express it.*

The waitress was there before I could settle into my seat. I ordered a lite beer in the hopes I would have time for several.

"So?" Skylar began.

I stalled. "So, what?"

She raised her eyebrow at me. "Seriously."

"First, let's have a drink and catch up. My colleagues are interviewing people. Making headway."

"That's great. I can't wait le.

 for this to finally be put to rest, and we can all move on with our lives."

Strike one. I wouldn't give up that easily.

"We'll all sleep easier; that's for sure. I still believe you're safe, but we're keeping a close eye on you to be sure. We think Nick has skipped town."

"Wait; I didn't know that you had located him."

"I'm catching you up. We also found out who was following you—a woman, Tori. I believe she'd be more likely to ask you to mud wrestle than to pull a gun on you."

"What?" Skylar asked with obvious amusement.

"She's a friend of Nick's, I would guess a close friend, and happens to be a stripper. She's also the cousin of the TSA officer Henry bribed."

"Seriously? Do you think she's done following me now?"

"I can't imagine she would be stupid enough to continue."

The waitress set my beer down in front of me, and the frothy head spilled over the sides of the glass. She nervously cleaned it up while apologizing. Little did she know, I welcomed every delay.

"To Henry and his brother, they were just toys; too ignorant to know they were being used to do some of the dirty work with little compensation."

"How about Brenda Carter? Any leads?"

"No. She's lying dormant right now. We're not sure that they're working together anymore. In fact…Actually, maybe it's best if I fill you in on all that when we know more." Disappointment shadowed Skylar's face as she lifted her glass to her lips. I'd suspected the not knowing would cause her concern but sharing everything wasn't appropriate. "I promise, I'll tell you more when the time comes."

"I understand." Her tone changed. "Was that enough small talk? Are you ready to tell me the proposition yet?" Skylar tucked a strand of hair behind her ear. The overhead light reflected off her diamond, and for a moment, made me question my decision to meet with her. The words stuck in my throat, and I looked up at Skylar. Her gaze locked with mine, which didn't help my nerves in the least.

I smiled, hoping she couldn't be mad at someone who was smiling at her. "Why don't you take one more big drink first?" She obliged, and I did the same. "I'm going to be honest with you, and I want you to hear me out."

"Okay." She sounded nervous. "I'm assuming this will have something to do with our conversation from the other day."

I took a breath. "I'm questioning some of your decisions."

She shook her head. "I'm sorry. I shouldn't have said the things I said to you. I wasn't trying to make you question my wedding." The defensiveness in her tone hadn't been there before. Maybe I should have brought note cards to help me through my proposition.

"Maybe that's not what I wanted to say."

"What are you trying to say, Brent?"

"I'm trying to say…." I was starting to doubt everything. Crap. How did she turn me into a blubbering idiot? I was an FBI special agent, damnit. "Do you know why we didn't arrest Nick the night we saw him in the bar?"

"I didn't know you saw him in the bar."

"That's where we officially found him, but that's not the point. Do you know why we didn't arrest him?"

"No."

"Because we hadn't gathered all the facts. When you're trying to make big decisions, like whether a man's guilty or not guilty, you need all the facts before deciding. If you only have some of the facts, or a one-sided account of the facts, what seems like the obvious answer could still be the wrong one."

"Go on."

"Do you remember when I said goodbye to you, and we said you had to follow the leads until they were taking you nowhere? Then, after that, you could move on to the next one?"

"Yes, I remember."

"It's still good to do that, as long as you don't shut out the chance of going back to the other ones." Skylar looked at me perplexed. My mind scrambled, trying to find words to clarify my thoughts. "There might be something important waiting to be discovered there. You have to be sure."

"What are you saying, Brent?"

"Have you ever watched those crime shows where they first tell all the details of a crime and you think he definitely murdered his wife or whomever?"

"Yes."

"You dare them in your mind to try to convince you otherwise because the facts are way too strong in one direction." I looked at Skylar who seemed to be listening attentively with a sprinkle of impatience. "Then they start looking at the defense side and everything you think was undeniable evidence becomes very gray."

"And your point is?"

"You haven't collected all the facts. You're not ready to make a decision yet."

"About Nick? Are we talking about the case?" She was trying to twist my words, to avoid having to respond to my proposition. I wouldn't give in yet.

"No, Skylar. We're talking about your life," I said a bit too emphatically before calming myself, "and your marriage."

I'd said it. Pretty well, I thought. Maybe not very romantically, but the reasoning sounded great to me.

"Are you telling me not to get married? Because you know the invitations have been sent? It's kind of happening."

"I'm telling you, Skylar, to open your mind up to the defense side. The side you pushed away because you thought you already had it all figured out. The judge has not banged the gavel yet, but when that day comes, I'm going to walk away and not look back. I promise both of us that, but until that day, I want you to open your mind up to other possibilities."

"So, what exactly is the proposition?"

"Give me a chance. I'm not asking you to sneak off to hotel rooms."

Skylar's shoulders drooped as she sat back into her chair. "Well, how kind of you."

"Skylar, I'm sorry. I'm not finding the right words." Skylar's gaze drifted away from me. "I'm not trying to offend you or steal you away from Adam."

"You're not? It sure sounds like you are."

"Well, yes, and no. I don't want to steal you away. I want you to decide if you want to walk away, but not until you've really thought about it, honestly, about both of us. I don't want you with me if I don't make you happy. I couldn't stand the thought of being one of your regrets. I care about you too much to ever be that to you."

Skylar took one last sip and straightened her spine. "I've heard what you have to say." And then she left without looking back.

When I walked in the door of my apartment, the pile of mail loomed in front of me. I tossed the day's delivery on top of the bills and junk mail, hoping to cover up the one thing I did not care to see, yet there it was, staring back at me and demanding a reply.

All right, Adam. If you want to test me, go ahead.

After shuffling through my junk drawer and resisting the urge to dump the potpourri of garbage on the floor, I discovered a pen.

Yes, Adam, I'll be at your wedding with a date of my own. That person was yet to be determined.

After watching you and Skylar exchange your vows, I'll graciously walk in line with your other attendees, shake your hand and kiss her farewell.

My actions would be so gentlemanly and rehearsed, Adam would not see any sort of emotional flinch. I'd pass the test with flying colors yet fail the course. Before I could come to my senses, I sealed the envelope and walked it out to my mailbox.

CHAPTER 27

Skylar

Journal Entry

MY DREAMS HAD been quiet for a while. I both enjoyed the silence and craved more dreams at the same time. I had grown to depend upon my nighttime sessions to feel connected to the world. Last night, they came back, along with all the torment they were capable of conjuring.

I woke to the shower running and sat up in my bed. Water seeped out from under the bathroom door. Something was wrong. My heart pounded a warning in my chest. Slowly, I walked to the door and tried to push it open. Something blocked me from being able to move the door more than a couple of inches. Through the crack, I saw Adam's hand lying palm side up on the floor. He was dead, and I bolted awake with a lingering, sick feeling in my soul.

Dreams of such nature can signify a change in feelings for a person. If that's true, if my feelings for him have faded, why do I feel so sad? Why do I feel like I killed him in some way? Forgive me.

My mother would sometimes speak in poems. Poems were to her what my dreams are to me—a mystical way to express everything inside of us with rhythm and color that everyday language can't replicate. The difference between my dreams and her poems was that her poems brought her such happiness. As she recited them, her face glowed, but my dreams continued to trouble me.

Sometimes, when I revisited some of the words she'd recited, it was as if I could find her there. If I spoke the words she'd once spoken, I saw her again, dancing in our kitchen to the rhythmic patterns depicting the bittersweet flavor of life. Maybe one of these times, I would be free enough to dance with her.

Sometimes, while she moved around the kitchen as if doing a dance, her bare feet tapping the linoleum, my mother mentioned her dreams as well. But usually she preferred to recite a poem, while occasionally interrupting herself by exclaiming how a cardinal had landed on her birdfeeder for the first time in forever. My father and I would exchange smiles, because she never quite got the connection that she had to remember to put food in the feeder if she wanted the constant companionship.

She'd always loved William Blake's *The Clod and the Pebble*. She would ask me, "Skylar, which one do you choose to be?"

"The pebble," I answered. I wanted her to see that I wasn't a wimpy girl who would allow some man to shape me. My mom wasn't strong in a business world sort of way, but she'd never doubted who she was and who she wanted to be. I thought surely, that was the answer she was looking for, but it wasn't.

She lifted my chin with her warm, soft hand and forced me to look her in the eyes. "No, Skylar, you need to be both. Be strong; hold onto the parts that should never change, but always allow for the potter's hands to mold you into something incredible. If you are only stone, when life finds your breaking point, you crack. If you are only clay, the wrong things can shape you into something ugly. Be both, Skylar. Remember to always be both.

"Is that the poet's interpretation?"

"That's what the poem says to me, and that's all that matters." Then she turned with a smile and continued to dance through her chores.

CHAPTER 28

Brent

OUR SQUAD MET in Ryan's office first thing the next morning for a briefing on the ongoing cases. Henry's still took precedent over the others, or at least, that was my perception. I took a seat off to the side, while everyone else filed into the room. Ryan stood before us, arms crossed in front of him, leaning back on his desk that created a makeshift chair.

"Brent, you first. Any major findings on Brenda's accounts?"

"Only that Construction with Care is one of the most illegitimate companies I've ever seen."

"I'd like you to get some more face to face time in Henry's hotels. Someone has to know something about this woman."

"I'll pick a few hotels to visit today."

"Meghan, you go with him."

"On it." Her reply sounded a bit too enthusiastic.

"Kemp, what did you get from the prison?" Ryan asked.

Kemp stood. "We have a recorded conversation between Tori and Henry at the jail." He hit the play button, and Henry's voice came alive in the room.

"Do you know where Brenda is?"

"Our mutual friend knows. He said it's best if he tells me that information later," Tori responded. "He assures me this will be easy."

"The official business of it is always easy. It's the aftermath that gets tricky. It's nearly impossible to trudge through the mud without leaving footprints."

"Huh." In my mind, Henry rolled his eyes at Tori's inability to decipher a rather weak analogy for committing a crime and not getting caught.

He took a deep breath, as though he tried to draw in patience he had never possessed. "Just do as you're told, and nothing else. Don't talk to anyone, including your sister."

"I would never tell her about this. She'd throw my ass out on the street. A bit self-righteous, if you ask me."

"Tori," Henry said with annoyance. "For God's sake, keep your mouth shut."

"You know they talked to Patrick?"

"What? Who did?"

"FBI, I believe."

"How do you know this?"

There was silence. Apparently, Tori had discovered that if she ratted on Patrick, she could easily slip and rat on herself as well. I waited, amused almost, to see how she would respond.

"He told me."

"I thought you didn't speak because of the uncle incident."

"The uncle incident," Tori repeated, obviously upset. "He was a good man. If it weren't for Patrick... He's to blame. He let the riffraff into our lives."

"Now look who's being self-righteous. Maybe Patrick opened the door, but you put the tea kettle on for them. You're why they stayed."

"I need to go."

"Does the truth sting a bit, Tori? Get off your pedestal."

"I'll tell Nick you send your regards." I heard the sound of her chair scrape across the floor.

"Tori." Henry scolded her with a whisper. I pictured him in his orange jumpsuit looking this way and that to see who was listening. Was Henry not aware that we already knew of Nick's part in his dealings? The line went dead then, and Ryan stopped the recording.

"The conversation obviously confirms that Brenda Carter is no longer an ally. If we can find her, she'll be the key witness we need. She knows all of them and will be more than willing to talk in order to save her life. Brent and Meghan, you know your job for the day. I want you two going to as many hotels as you can and digging up whatever information you're able to while looking into their accounts. Someone out there can lead us to Brenda."

"I'll get what I need from the office and head out," I said. "A few of the hotels actually had a decent number of repairs. I guess when the roof has a hole in it, you need to deal with the issue. We'll start by visiting them."

"Great. I expect a report in the morning."

"Will do."

"Kemp and Hall, let's get Patrick back in here tomorrow and rule out any other connection. They're covering something. It seems like more than the simple family feud Tori would like for us to believe it was."

In my office, I collected the paperwork for the accounts I would be visiting. From what we'd could gathered, Brenda Carter was the grandmother of the young woman who'd sat behind the desk of the tiny Construction with Care office, yet Brenda's age just didn't seem to fit the profile. Hopefully, my colleagues would find the lady who claimed to be the granddaughter, and when that happened, I was quite sure we would find some inaccuracies to her story. But today, my goal, with Meghan's help, was to find someone with the spark of information that would ignite the rather stale progression of a case that needed to end, not just for Skylar's sake, but also for the mysterious Brenda Carter. My hope was that we would find her before Nick and Henry added murder to their rap sheet. Brenda's Construction with Care business had made her a very wealthy woman who would most likely never get to enjoy her ill-earned gains.

A gentle knock made me look up from my desk. "I'm ready when you are," Megan said from the doorway.

With a final glance at my collection of papers, I stuffed them in my bag. "I'm set."

"I'm assuming no motorcycle ride today."

"You assumed correctly."

"It was surprisingly enjoyable," Meghan said as I passed through the doorway that she lingered in, making our paths uncomfortably close. "I wouldn't mind another ride sometime; maybe a leisurely ride, rather than an undercover adventure to a strip joint."

I continued down the hallway and toward the door. "What? Strip joints aren't your thing?"

"Not even if there were hot, young men breakdancing in thongs."

I let out a small laugh and looked down at her. "Well, we have that in common."

"Not to mention our addiction to days full of paperwork that lead to moments of somewhat scary excitement."

"Well, I can't promise that today's work will be either scary or exciting."

"Anything to get out of the office," she said.

As we traveled to the first hotel, I managed to escape any further conversation of a weekend motorcycle ride. Instead, I stuck with details pertaining to the case.

Finally, we pulled into the first hotel. Immediately, I noticed a few details that could be of interest to the case—first, the name, The Willow Tree. I might be stretching things a bit with my overactive imagination that had been consuming me these days, but what I knew about willow trees was that if a place seemed to collect too much water, this type of tree was the perfect one to plant. It absorbed the surplus liquid. I found it interesting because it was also the hotel that had absorbed the most of Henry's money. Willow trees were also not part of Florida's vegetation, so why the name for a Floridian hotel?

The second was that a maroon SUV with tinted windows was parked up front, in the manager's parking spot. The letters KVC stared back at me from the license plate. Cynthia had not gotten back to me, so I assumed I hadn't provided her with enough information to give me anything worth getting excited about. I scribbled down the full license plate number.

Meghan watched me intensely. "What do you see?"

"That SUV was following me the other day."

"Why would that be?"

"I'm not sure, but maybe you will get your excitement today."

When we entered the building, the man behind the counter first appeared startled. This reaction happened at times when I entered in FBI attire, but Meghan and I wore business clothes. Just as quickly, the man's expression eased into one I could only describe as relief. He appeared to know who I was before I even introduced myself. The man greeted me with a nod and a slight glance at the person standing with his back to us while trying to decide what flavor of beverage to purchase from the machine. For some reason, I understood the manager's silence and mannerisms to mean: Be quiet for a moment, or at least follow my lead.

"The restrooms are around the corner to your right," he said to the air, while he focused on some task at the counter.

I nodded, thinking it was best not to share the sound of my voice with the other patron, and then walked toward the restroom. Meghan stayed in the lobby. I heard the telltale sign of the selected beverage falling to the pick-up slot.

"Have a nice day, Mr. Davis," the manager said to the man who had purchased a beverage. A moment after, I heard the hotel doors slide shut.

I could only assume the man was Nick, but without being certain, Meghan and I had no choice but to let him walk out the door. We also still lacked the evidence needed to make any charges stick. Once in the bathroom, I quickly phoned Ryan and told him what had transpired, As I hung up, the door to the bathroom swung open and the manager entered.

"You found me. I was hoping you would."

For the first time, I took in the full picture of the man before me. His nametag read Evan; he was lanky and had the hands of a pianist, long slim fingers, although I didn't get the impression he played.

"Were you following me the other day?" I didn't bother mentioning the fact I had actually just stumbled onto him by luck.

"Not so much following you; rather, I was trying to make you follow me. Bring you back to the beehive so to speak."

"Why me?"

"Other managers said you had been at their hotels, checking

the books. I wasn't sure how long it would take for you to come here, or if you would come at all. I tried to be obvious enough to draw your attention."

"Why didn't you just call?" I asked, slightly irked by his game.

"I'm a family man; wife, kids, two dogs. If you came to me, I felt I had a better chance of keeping things that way. I don't trust the phones not to be tapped."

"Who are you so afraid of? Mr. Davis?"

"Well, there's him of course, but I'm more afraid of the people I don't know to fear, the ones who will share information, puncture a tire, whatever is asked of them just to earn cash. The ones who appear to be your friends and tempt you to show your allegiance is not to the Davis's."

"So, what do you have for me?"

"Room 432 may be of interest to you, for starters."

"Take me there."

"Not now. He's coming back. Just promise me, you'll keep me and my family safe."

"We'll talk to the people who can help you, but for now, I need to know everything you can tell me about Brenda Carter."

"Your people have asked this before."

"And I'm asking again. I need to see whatever work was completed, the payments made, any receipts you may have."

"I can do that. I've kept copies. Henry wanted all the information faxed to him and told me in a polite way that there was no need for me to deal with the bookkeeping for the construction, only for the other hotel business. Something told me it would be a good idea to keep track of those expenses anyway."

"Did the company actually complete the work?"

"Some of it, yes; the pressing stuff anyway. They fixed damage from leaking air conditioners or pipes, but instead of removing the rug like the bills say they did, they would take out only the damaged part and repair it with something they found to match it closely. Never looked the same, though. Even if it was the identical pattern, time had faded the rug, or use had darkened it. There was really no one to complain to since Henry owned the hotels, and he didn't care."

"Did Henry visit here often?"

"Just toward the end. He would come in with suitcases, yet never stay the night. We were never allowed to clean Room 432 or enter it."

"You never had any idea what was in the room?"

"I have my suspicions, but no. I'm assuming a man like Henry knows how to work cameras. I was pretty sure if I ever entered it, I wouldn't live to see the next day."

"When did Nick start coming?"

"Recently. What you heard me say to him today was just about the only words we've spoken besides me asking after him one time. I noticed he would come in and go to the elevators, yet never stop for a key or to check in or out. He told me he was Henry's brother and would be staying in the room sometimes. Once I knew who he was, I kept my distance."

"Probably best that you didn't approach him, but you should have contacted someone."

"That's easy for you to say. You're used to the dark world. It petrifies me."

"What about Brenda Carter? Has she ever been to the room?"

"I never saw Henry walk in with anyone, but that doesn't mean she wasn't there. They could have come in separately."

"Why don't you take me to where you keep your records? I'll see if there's anything I'm missing."

I followed him toward his office, motioned for Meghan to follow, and then we settled in at Evan's desk. Leaving the door open, Evan went back to the check-in counter. I heard him greet a few guests and check others in and out. I soon managed to block out the background noise while Meghan and I scanned the documents. Somewhere in the back of my mind, I may have heard the door to the reception area open, but what I heard more clearly was the silence. Evan, for some reason, said nothing to the newest guest. Possibly, someone left, but still, the manager normally wished them a good day as they departed. I paused in my work and listened intently to the lack of noise from the lobby until a voice broke through.

"I don't remember formally meeting you. It's Evan, correct?" I pictured the man speaking, eyeing Evan's name tag.

"You introduced yourself as Henry's brother some time ago. I'm sorry if I didn't return the introduction."

"Oh, yes. I remember the time." A tense pause. "When you addressed me a short time ago, I realized we seldom greet each other, especially by name. Odd, don't you think? I guess, it seemed out of character, but then again, maybe I should know the man who manages my hotel."

I pictured Nick, with an unspoken threat in his eyes, staring Evan down. The act of Evan swallowing hard was almost audible.

"My apologies if I've offended you in some way, sir."

"No apologies needed, Evan. You'll know if you've offended me. I'll make it quite clear."

I heard the door shut behind Nick. I could only hope Ryan was well on his way to having the search warrant in his hands.

After about an hour, Ryan, along with Roger, burst through the hotel doors with an authoritative air I felt through the walls. They introduced themselves in the unique way FBI agents do, and Meghan and I rose to greet them.

"Excuse me," Evan stuttered. "I'm not quite sure how I can help." The FBI raid needed to be convincing in case Nick or Henry had any witnesses in the lobby. Evan had to appear like an innocent party in the event.

"We need you to let us into Room 432."

The manager shook, and to be honest, I pitied him. Adrenaline was a very different drug to each person, as evidenced by my racing heart. I thrived on it.

The four of us walked to the elevator and did not utter a word until Evan opened the door. We walked in, opening bathroom doors, drawers, closets.

"Shit," Ryan said.

The room had been emptied.

CHAPTER 29

Skylar

Journal Entry

I ENTERED MY HOUSE, *yet it wasn't my house. I went down the hallway to my bedroom and saw a door I had never seen before. Thinking it must be a door for a linen closet, I opened it. Instead of towels, I found a staircase. Slowly, I walked up the stairs. I didn't experience an ounce of fear, only curiosity.*

When I reached the top, I found an immense area that seemed much bigger than the floor plan below. The rooms weren't completely finished, but I saw an area that would make an amazing living room. There was another cutout for a kitchen and many extra ones for bedrooms. My mind started spinning with all the ways I could decorate and furnish the area.

I woke invigorated and could not stop myself from mentally revisiting the mysterious rooms of my dream home. So much potential and possibility were contained in an area that was mine, yet still undiscovered. How much of myself lay dormant and undiscovered? When would I finally open the secret door and dare to climb the imaginary stairs to the new me? The rooms called to me, louder and louder each day. It was only a matter of time.

I've thought about my parents so much lately. The past year's events busted open a wound. Somehow, I know remembering is part of my healing, but I don't feel the healing yet. I only feel the ache. One memory haunts me. We had gone to camp in the mountains in Virginia. My parents had been there and knew of a cliff they wanted me to see. We walked along a path until the woods opened, exposing the waters below.

The sun beamed down on us. The three of us, suntanned and laughing, responded to the clear waters that beckoned to my parents more than me. A piece of me was terrified, and yet, another part felt exhilarated. My father jumped first, and I held my breath as he disappeared into the calm sea below. In my mind, I counted—*one, two, three*—until he burst through the water's surface. My mom reacted to his excited yell as if it were a mating call by leaping in after him. Her forty-something body resembled that of a teenager, yet it was her spirit that was contagious. My dad watched her reappear in the small waves. He swam to her immediately, meeting her with an embrace that I had become well-accustomed to through the years.

After a moment, they looked upward and called to me. My legs became rubbery. If I didn't jump with determination, I could tumble down the side of the rocky cliff. My pounding heart begged me to turn away, but I also wanted nothing more than to swim in their world. I craved the sensation of falling, of trusting the water to slow my speed enough so I could regain control and burst through the surface.

A smile lit my face as I gazed at the horizon, so calming, a place where two beautiful creations came together and sometimes melded into magic. I let my mind drift so I could coax my legs closer to the edge, and with one final breath, I jumped. I rose to the water's surface, laughing and feeling free and alive.

CHAPTER 30

Brent

*C*AN YOU MEET *me?* The words from Skylar waited for me on my phone as I stepped out of the shower.

Where and when? I responded with water still dripping from my fingers. I toweled off, never letting my gaze divert from the phone.

Now and at the diner across from my office. If we get there soon, I'll have time for coffee before work.

Be there in 15.

I raced around the bedroom and fumbled with my clothes while looking for a missing shoe I found tossed in the corner.

When I arrived, Skylar was already at the diner, coffee cup held in both hands while her focus settled on something outside the window beside her. I slid into the booth seat as she pulled herself back from her private thoughts and faced me.

"We have a lot to discuss," Skylar said.

The waitress poured my coffee as I mentally shooed her away. Instead of the waitress leaving, Skylar asked a few menu questions before she ordered oatmeal. Without looking at the options, I ordered a plate of pancakes and bacon. Once alone, Skylar took a moment to adjust her napkin. Was she stalling on purpose? What words were stuck in Skylar's mind?

"Skylar," I nudged. "You're killing me."

"Let's start with the easy stuff."

"Okay, and that is?"

"Chrissy reached out to me."

The news piqued my interest enough I momentarily forgot the proposition.

"Chrissy? Bruce's ex-wife? Don't you barely know her? Didn't you only meet her once at Bruce's funeral?"

"Officially, yes," Skylar said. "I'd seen her a few times before the funeral. Back when they were married, she would come in the office some. We were never introduced. She reached out to me because she said she had some interesting information. I'm not sure that it's really helpful to the case, but needless to say, interesting."

"Go on." I tore open my Splenda packet and started the coffee preparations.

"Sometimes I wondered why Bruce had such a hard time getting over a woman who had left him." Suddenly, my coffee lost its appeal. Did she really not understand? "It was because she didn't completely leave him. They met up secretly sometimes. I would say that she strung him along, but in all honesty, I think she loved him."

"She sure didn't look like she loved him when she came into the office all fired up."

"Chrissy explained that. She knew Bruce was doing illegal things to try to get money for a future with her. She warned him to stop and that it would never work. When he gave her the expensive necklace, it proved that he was still involved somehow. She wasn't mad that he'd bought it for her, just that he'd dealt with dangerous people."

"Still, what made her reach out to you? Isn't that a bit strange? She doesn't even know you."

"But we had a connection—Bruce. She couldn't tell her highfalutin friends that she was still sleeping with her ex-husband or that he was involved in drug smuggling. She asked me about what I knew of the case. I only said what was already public information, and I tried to leave myself out of it."

"How'd that go?"

"She knew a woman in the office was involved in Bruce's dealings. After our meet up at his funeral, she had a feeling it was me."

"What did Bruce tell her about you?"

"I'm not sure, but when I told her that Bruce once told me I was a diversion, she got a bit quiet. Then she denied knowing what he'd meant by that."

"What was your take? Do you think she was holding back?"

"Possibly, but I don't think she knows much. I believe Bruce would have protected her from knowing too much."

"Agreed."

"I think she just needed to talk to someone who'd known Bruce and the case. Pretty ironic that a woman who seems to have everything has to reach out to a practical stranger to speak about her deepest, darkest secrets."

"Yes, it is."

Skylar took in a breath. "It leads me to the next part of our conversation."

"And that is?" I asked, even though I was quite sure I knew what it was.

"I left rather abruptly last time we talked."

"Really? I didn't notice."

Skylar shook off my sarcasm with a slight eye roll. "Chrissy and I are as different as night and day, but we have some things in common.

"Such as?"

"We both had decisions to make, and we both went with the easy choice, the choice that didn't make ripples for ourselves or the majority of the others anyway. Chrissy is living with her regrets. I don't want that."

"What are you saying, Skylar?" I hoped my expression didn't show desperation.

"I'll keep my mind open about us. I owe myself that. And in truth, I owe Adam that. You were right. I either need to go into my marriage with my whole heart or not at all."

There was a hardness in her voice, but her words were exactly what I wanted to her. Part of her heart belonged to me, and I planned to do everything in my power to keep it that way.

"But, Brent, if I choose Adam, you and I will both respect my decision."

"Of course."

"You and I met in a unique situation. We could easily find that the best part about us is the fact that we could never be."

"I realize that." It crushed me to admit it, but it was a possibility.

"We owe ourselves some time to get to know each other."

"I couldn't agree with you more." I reached for her hands across the table. She gave them a slight squeeze before retracting.

"Nothing physical."

"Understood. So where does that put us?"

"It puts us at friends, which is a perfect place for beginnings."

For the rest of the morning, I tried to envision the possibilities, yet I had a difficult time ending my vision with anything other than touching Skylar. Anywhere would be fine—her cheek, her lips. The next month would be like going to Longhorn Steak House in handcuffs. Somehow, we would figure it out.

An idea struck me, due to the fact that every time I felt overwhelmed with some frustration or other, I ran. The idea of running was becoming an all-consuming need.

Meet me in the park at 6:30. Wear your running shoes.

Would those be my blue or black pumps?

You're kidding, right?

You'll find out at 6:30.

A smile edged its way across my face, but I pushed it aside. The more focused I was on the task at hand, the quicker I could get home for my run. I grabbed my wallet and keys, along with the necessary paperwork, and headed to my truck. Another of Henry's hotels awaited me. The story at this one was similar, but without the enticing secret room and drop-in from the additional special agents. The same went for the hotel after that. My job was pointless if we didn't find Nick and what he had stashed away in Room 432.

After lunch, I got word that Kemp and Hall were bringing Patrick in for more questioning, so I headed back to the field office. I slipped into the adjoining room and found Meghan already there.

She glanced my way. "This guy's a wreck." Apparently, she enjoyed watching criminals squirm.

"Maybe our colleagues should have sent him off with some Xanax after they last questioned him," I added.

"I almost pity him."

"Really?"

"No, not a bit," she said with a hint of humor in her voice. I leaned back against the table near the two-way glass and gave my attention to the show in front of me. "They're pressing the issue of him being so intimidated by Nick."

"There was definitely more to that part of the story," I said. "Agreed."

Patrick squirmed in his seat before clearing his throat. "They would have killed me. I didn't have a choice."

"Nick would have killed you?"

"No, not Nick. He kept me alive. Or, he did when I started working with him, at least." Patrick looked up and locked eyes with Gabe. "But now…." He ran his fingers through his hair as if he wanted to tear it out. "If they find out I talked, I'm dead."

"Patrick, the more you work with us, the more we will work with you."

There was a long uncomfortable silence. Patrick's shoulders slumped, an actual visual of his walls of reluctance collapsing before the truth started spilling over the top.

"I got in with the wrong people. It started small, in high school. One little step at a time. All of a sudden, I became a supplier to some big wig drug dealers." He glanced up, testing their reaction.

"Continue," Gabe urged.

"I was just a stupid kid, spoiled and angry because I didn't want to work at a fast food restaurant to earn spending money when I knew my father had it to give. I'd get a job, not show up, get fired, and expect my father to pick up the pieces by giving me whatever cash I needed. I thought he would cave before I did. I felt ridiculous wearing the apron and calling out orders, serving the kids from high school through a drive-through window as they tried to eat enough grease to stave off their hangovers."

"Weren't you working with other kids from your high school?"

"Yes, but as I told you, I was a spoiled punk. He was right to cut off all of the money. When I ran out of my meager savings and was going to have to take the bus to school, I got desperate. That's when a friend suggested I talk to someone who could help."

"Let me guess; you got to sell a few drugs for him."

"Bingo. It was easy. And I wasn't selling to little kids, so I felt better about it. I sold to friends at parties, people who were going to buy from someone anyway. Why not me, I figured? Why shouldn't I get in on the deal?"

Finally, Patrick's journey through his childhood was starting to connect to his current situation.

"Was the marijuana from Henry? No, but Henry got my name from connections I truly don't know, and the next thing I knew, I was selling Ecstasy as well. Funny thing, it wasn't a cop who busted me. One of my customers told my father. I was called into a room to make the sale and there she was. Tori sat on the bed with some friends. She will swear it was a set up, but I saw her face. Tori had no idea I would be the one selling the drugs. Her and her sister came from nothing. My dad made something of himself, while their father made bad choice after bad choice, leaving them to always try to find favor with my father. This was a perfect opportunity. My father had always taken pity on them. The girls, he often said, were the daughters he never had. In his opinion, they deserved better." Patrick's face contorted as he spoke, as if the memory stung.

"After going to my father, Tori felt obligated to also help him find the dealer. My dad wanted me out of their circle without consequence. My father went to meet with them, maybe to pay them off. They called him and told him to meet them at the park. After that, I don't know what happened to my father, except that I had put him in a situation that his heart couldn't handle. I literally drove my father to the grave, and for what? They still didn't leave me alone. It was little stuff through the years, and I never got caught; not once. My record was so clean, I was able to become a TSA officer.

"Tori started working at the club and met Nick there. I don't have all the specifics, but they approached me. Nick needed to expand his business, and I was just the shady connection he was looking for. I could get their supplies into the hands of dealers—not just me, but many others. They had this man park at the bar with a crap load of drugs in his car. I took the drugs, left him money in his glovebox, and never spoke to him. The guys above me came to enjoy my friendship with Nick."

"So, Nick threatened to cut off your drug supply?"

Patrick nodded. "The dealers would have killed me. I had to help get the money through security, or Nick wouldn't supply the drugs."

"You never spoke to the person driving the vehicle?"

"No."

"Would you recognize him?"

Patrick nodded. "I watched him walk into the bar before I went to his vehicle. He was a frumpy middle-aged guy." Gabe slid a picture across the table. Patrick nodded, confirming it was Bruce.

"Tell me a bit about how you helped smuggle the money through security."

"It was easy at first. Random people I watched for with minimal amounts. Nothing I would necessarily get fired over. After a few test runs, they sent Skylar through. Man, I've never seen so much cash in my life." He placed his head in his hands and gave his bangs a frustrated yank. "Damnit, I swear, I wouldn't have done it if it were a weapon. I swear. But it was only money. Money can't hurt anyone."

"Well, it does when it brings illegal drugs into our country. You had to know it was for something shady."

"The craziest part was, I didn't need any of their money anymore, but I was already in too deep. After my father's death, I wanted to live a clean life, to make him proud. And I was, sort of. But they wouldn't let me go."

"Are you ready to start naming names?" Hall asked.

"What the hell; I'm screwed anyway."

Kemp pulled out a pad, and Hall got comfortable in his seat.

"I think I've seen enough," I said to Meghan.

"Just another day of trying to solve one case and uncovering five others in the process," she added.

"I'll catch up with you later." I felt her watching me as I exited. I didn't look back.

Skylar showed up at the park wearing a brand-new pair of gray running shoes. A chill lingered in the evening air, and we stood together warming up not only our muscles, but our conversation as well. The words between us ran sluggishly at first. I wanted to move away from the case, away from the past, or at least our past.

I thought for a moment, as we jogged side by side, of what I wanted to know about Skylar, and I decided that I pretty much wanted to know everything.

The privacy of the park allowed our conversation to go places we had yet to discover together. For a moment, other experiences the privacy allowed for entered my mind, but another feeling crept in as well—the dreaded catch 22 of all catch 22s. If Skylar caved to temptation, how would I ever trust her if she became mine? At no other point in my life would I know this side of her. If I lost her to Adam, I'd concede his victory, step down from the podium and slip into the shadows. If she chose me, I would never again be the other man. I would be the one living blindly, hoping she was resisting all other temptations. Every misstep Skylar might take became a character flaw that might later come back to haunt me.

This was not a time for regretful decisions. As we jogged side by side, I brought my mind back to the purpose of our adventure. I wanted to know Skylar, and I wanted to know everything.

"So, tell me, if you weren't an accountant, what would you want to be?"

She laughed. "You would probably never guess." Although her words didn't come that easily. Breathing was already difficult.

"A teacher?"

"No. I could never deal with the disciplining part. Or maybe the teaching part either. Maybe just the planning." She grinned. "I could be a professional lesson planner."

"Does that job even exist?"

"It should. But seriously, I would have liked to have been a doctor, except that I really don't like dealing with people. I just like the idea of taking all the facts and figuring out what they mean. Kind of like on the show *House*."

"So, you want to be House?"

"I wanted to be." She smiled. "I'd like to think I would have had a kinder bedside manner."

"No doubt." I glanced her way. Her contented, faraway expression fueled my questions. "What happened? Why didn't you become a doctor?"

"Well, maybe I would never have made it through med school anyway, but it just wasn't going to happen."

"Why?"

"Let's save that conversation for another day."

"Will do."

"Your turn," Skylar announced.

"I was always drawn to police or investigative work. I've never regretted my decision, and depending on the day and the case, I still enjoy what I do." With a bit of hesitation, I decided to delve into a place I feared would change the magic of our evening. "Can I ask where Adam thinks you are?"

Skylar was silent for a moment. "Besides the whole Henry fiasco, I've never lied to Adam, or at least not big lies; not lies he would actually care about. To be truthful, I don't know how to do this, Brent. I don't want to be dishonest."

"So, what did you tell him?"

"Nothing. He started playing cards with a group of men from work. It's very unlike him, but after everything that happened, we both realized we should probably be more open to building some bonds outside of just us. I think it's good for us."

"I agree, but that's one time. What about the others—or at least, I hope there will be others?"

"I'll tell him I'm having coffee with a friend, I guess, which isn't completely a lie. We are only that—friends."

"Believe it or not, Skylar, I wouldn't want to be anything else, not until you have chosen me, and Adam is aware of that decision. I promise you; I will never ask more than friendship of you until that day."

"Thank you."

About a half of a mile had passed rather slowly beneath

our feet. "Do you think we can walk?" Skylar asked. It was quite apparent why Skylar didn't own a pair of running shoes.

Okay, so maybe asking her out for a run hadn't been the best idea. "Next time, maybe coffee?"

"I'm really not opposed to running. Actually, I can see why it might be nice to force yourself out here versus curling up in front of the TV, but I'm apparently completely out of shape."

"No worries. I'm trained in CPR." I saw her sideways glance. "It's not considered touching if I'm saving your life. In fact, I'm thinking you look a bit blue in the face." Skylar shot me another sideways glance, this one in warning. "Totally a joke; just trying to lighten the mood."

"I just found some more energy." With the slightest hint of a forgiving smile, Skylar trotted on ahead with me following wherever she chose to go, knowing that if I didn't, I was going in the wrong direction. The topics ran more freely, as did we, while we jogged along the water's edge. And sometimes, we let the silence pass as easily as our words. A peacefulness settled over me, despite the adrenaline bubbling at my core. The best part of being there was knowing it was the only place I would choose to be at that moment. When I glanced at Skylar, I was met with her soft smile, brightened by a hint of glow from the full moon's light, and I knew she thought the same.

We decided our next outing would be at a small movie theater, hoping the smaller crowds decreased the chances of being seen by anyone we knew. Nights later, I slipped into the San Marco Theater. I couldn't deny the excitement building inside of me, which in turn created a hint of guilt. I pushed the later feeling to the back of my mind. Time would be my judge.

The lights dimmed, and Skylar had yet to show. Maybe she'd

decided against it. Perhaps it had felt like more of a date than running in the park. She may have been right. The short time we had left was supposed to be about getting to know each other, the real us without the drama, but how could this be the real us, sneaking around? The guilt persisted despite my efforts. The credits began, a part of the movie others watched impatiently, yet I enjoyed the hints of what was to come, snippets of the future.

Just as the last trailer finished, the lights completed their final dimming and the movie began. How many times had I scanned the doors, hoping I would see Skylar enter? I would be watching the movie alone.

"Excuse me."

Skylar squeezed between the seatbacks and the people's knees seated in our row.

"I'm so sorry. I had a little trouble getting away." I looked into her eyes and saw through the darkness of the theater, a trailer of my future. It was worth waiting for, worth purchasing a ticket in advance.

"You're forgiven." I resisted the urge to lean in and kiss her hello. Even a friendly kiss on the cheek would have been incredible, but Skylar was right; no physical contact. It would be hard to get closer to the border without stepping over it. I had to respect her, and Adam.

It so happened the movie was a comedy/drama mix, so one minute we found ourselves laughing and the next I heard sniffling. I looked over and saw Skylar wiping away a tear—the second time I'd witnessed her crying. The first had been in the taxi cab when she wouldn't share what was going on in her life. I was happy to be beyond that but envied the moment long ago when I'd been allowed to wrap my arms around her and smooth her hair with the palm of my hand. The draw to touch her was a force almost tangible in itself.

Perhaps, for whatever reason, going to the movies together did resemble a date too much. Of course, it did. Who were we trying to kid? I reached into the popcorn only to touch her fingers. Electricity passed between us. I prayed that one day, I would be able to touch Skylar's hand often enough that my body would not become immune, but would grow used to the feeling of her skin against mine, that I would be able to think beyond the electricity. But today, the feeling was all consuming. Beyond any other woman in my life, I loved Skylar, and I might never get to realize a future with her. My initial exhilaration faded to sadness, and by the time we walked outside and bid each other farewell for the night, the feeling had grown to a giant black hole that could have sucked me into it. I spent my drive home mentally stepping away from a pit that I could very well have to face.

A few days after the movie, I finished work early and rolled into the parking lot of my apartment around six o'clock. As I stepped out of the truck, the air felt eerie. I glanced around the still parking lot but saw nothing out of the ordinary. Yet, some innate part of me knew I was being watched; an energy passed from an unknown source. The energy bounded up the stairs behind me and, refusing to be ignored, pummeled me in the back. As I approached my door, I saw it was slightly ajar. Never a good sign.

I pulled my gun. Letting the door slowly swing open, and without a sound, I entered the shadowed room. If anyone was inside, they had a better view of me than I had of them. Fumbling momentarily, I found the light switch and evened the playing field. With practiced precision, I checked each room, corner, and closet. Whoever had been here was long gone, or worse yet, they were watching my silhouette pass by the windows from a hiding place outside.

Gabe and Roger were soon at my door, along with a team to check for fingerprints and any tampering. They found nothing. I would say my apartment had been ransacked, but when you have little to no furniture, or belongings to speak of, it's pretty difficult to ransack a place. Only a few drawers had been pulled out, just enough to let me know someone had been creeping through my things.

"If you ask me," Roger said, "I think someone was sending you a message versus looking for anything. Maybe Nick saw you at the hotel the other day."

"Something tipped him off, causing him to empty the hotel room, so maybe. I'm sure I'm not his favorite person after helping to get his brother convicted."

I hadn't heard Meghan come in, but now she stood in my living room, sizing it up as if she was discovering a whole new layer of me. "You okay?"

"Yeah. I came home to find my door had been forced open. Maintenance will be around to fix it after everything's wrapped up."

"You think it's fine to stay here?" Meghan asked. Roger, acknowledging the possible invitation, glanced over her shoulder at me.

"Once the door's repaired it'll be okay," I answered, hoping to save her the time of continuing.

She glanced around the room. "Well, I'll give you credit, Brent. It's not that messy for a bachelor pad."

"There's not enough stuff in here to make it messy, I suppose."

After an uncomfortable silence, she said, "Well, since there's nothing for me to do here, I'll head home for the night. Let me know before it gets too late if they can't get that door fixed."

"Will do."

Again, Roger gave me his knowing look. As Meghan headed toward the door, something caught her attention. She walked over to my counter and turned around holding a movie ticket. When did you find time for the movies?"

"Excuse me?"

Meghan waved the movie ticket stub.

"Where did you get that?"

"It was sitting right on the counter," she said.

"I don't go to the cinema often, that's for sure." I took the stub from her and looked at the date. It was the ticket for the movie that Skylar and I had seen in San Marco a few nights ago, and I was reasonably sure I would not have left it sitting on my counter for days. Maybe I had missed it on my last swipe that I'd classified as cleaning.

"Sounds lonely, watching a movie by yourself."

I remembered sharing the popcorn with Skylar, our hands occasionally grazing, the comfortableness of just being together. "To be honest, it was quite pleasant."

"To each his own, I guess." She turned toward the door.

Once she was out of earshot, Hall said, "When are you going to toss that girl a bone?"

"When and if I'm ever ready to have her feed off me as well, and I'm nowhere near that time yet."

Hall shook his head. "It's just plain painful to watch."

"Well, we agree on that." I hoped the topic would fizzle out. "You about finished up in here?"

Kemp nodded. "I think we can wrap it up."

Maintenance showed up as my colleagues were heading out, so I decided to follow them to the parking lot. As soon as I had said my goodbyes, I headed straight to my truck and searched the door cup holder that doubled as my garbage can. Sure enough, there was my ticket. Skylar purchased her own pass so we didn't enter together, and I never had it in my possession. Today, someone had been letting me know he—or she— was watching me and reminding me of my vulnerability and Skylar's.

CHAPTER 31

Skylar

Journal Entry

ADAM SAT AT *a table surrounded by men I didn't recognize. They were all laughing. Empty mugs of beer filled the table, and a waitress held the next round on her tray. I hated him. Before entering the restaurant, two women divulged to me that they were both sleeping with my fiancé. They laughed when they told me, as if it was totally acceptable.*

Adam didn't look up until I stood beside him. The women stood behind me, entertained, I'm sure, by the show they inspired. In my hands, I held a bag of what appeared to be kitty litter, and I flung it in Adam's face. The kitty litter flew across the table. The group of men froze, and silence filled the room.

I deserved to be furious. I was, I suppose, which would explain why I threw the bag of kitty litter in his face. But after throat punching the women, I hopped into a red convertible Lamborghini and spun out of the parking lot, shifting gears and spinning tires until I hit the interstate. My anger remained on the table where I had thrown the kitty litter. All I felt was free and powerful. What was wrong with me?

I helped my parents plan the trip. Every detail, or so I thought at the time, but being older now, I'm sure there were decisions to which I was not privy. It was there anniversary—twenty years—and I wasn't invited on the adventure. There was so much excitement in the air. I even helped my mom pack their bags.

CHAPTER 32

Brent

CAN YOU MEET *for coffee?*

Our usual place? I replied.

What if you meet me at the pier? I'll bring the coffee.

The ease with which Skylar texted me gave me hope and also terrified me. I had set myself up for being crushed beyond any emotional beating I had yet suffered.

I wanted to tell her being alone with her was becoming too difficult, that standing side by side watching the sunrise might be unbearable for me, but instead, I replied, *See you at seven.*

Oak trees, dripping with Spanish moss, framed Rivertown Park and created a strange atmosphere of admiration and eeriness. From a distance, it would appear the moss was overtaking the trees, suffocating the oaks until the life had been strangled out of them, but it wasn't so. The trees still stood strong under the weight of the foreign growth. Together, it would appear, they formed a new species: a sturdy frame, dripping not with leaves, but a blanket; an unexpected, yet beautiful, creation.

Skylar waited at the end of the pier, a coffee cup in each hand, a smile from ear to ear. As I approached her, drawn to her with a force I had no chance of fighting, I wondered if she could possibly feel the way I felt at that moment—alive to the point of bursting, yet petrified at the same time.

"I thought it might be nice for us to come back to the place I first thought I might hate you."

"Hate me?" Letting my smile meet hers, I took my cup from her hand. "Those are strong words."

The wind gently blew her hair across her face, and I resisted the urge to tuck the strands behind her ear. How long could I last without touching her?

Adjusting the misbehaving strands, she explained, "You can't imagine my surprise when you led me up to the van with the special agents inside. Every moment I had shared with you flashed before my eyes; every word I had ever said. I felt so exposed."

"I didn't have a choice. You know that now, don't you?"

"I've forgiven you."

"I suspected maybe you had." We looked out over the river, both of us caught up in our own thoughts. In the waters around us, fish jumped, and we gestured to them as if we could catch them in our hands if we pointed to them fast enough. The wood on the pier, covered by graffiti, marked the moments shared by friends and lovers. Messages and faces were painted, somehow adding to the pier's beauty; a piece of each person's special moments engraved, leaving a lingering presence for the next visitors. Hearts encircled the names of young lovers, and I thought how the heart, an organ with the purpose of pumping blood throughout the body, incapable of thought, had somehow become the symbol of such a powerful emotion as love. But looking at Skylar, who had the excitement of a child, pointing out the next jumping fish, I understood. My chest filled with a fullness threatening to explode. I was in love with our past, present, and the future I imagined.

"What's wrong, Brent?"

A few more fish jumped in the distance. I watched them, knowing Skylar was waiting for a response.

"Maybe we should calm down on our outings."

Skylar's face went ashen. "What? Why? Did I offend you somehow?"

I shook my head. "No, not at all." I struggled to find the words. "It's too hard, being here with you." Skylar remained silent. "If you want to stick to the pact, then I think it's best if we just meet at the café."

Skylar nodded. "From now on, just a morning coffee, or maybe breakfast."

"I think that would be best." We walked back down the pier, our hands grazing each other's, yet not taking hold.

We met at the diner a few days later. Since finding the movie ticket on my counter, our moments felt tainted. Half my mind scanned the surrounding area the entire time we chatted. I didn't want Skylar to feel that same way, but eventually, I had to tell her about the finding. An expression mixed with fear and shock shadowed her face.

After letting the news sink in, I added, "We should let the other agents know you think you're being followed again. I can't mention the movie ticket. Ryan would insist our outings classify as a conflict of interest, and maybe he's right, but I want someone watching out for you. I might be able to explain an occasional cup of coffee."

"Then they'll know we're meeting."

"We'll make it seem like part of the plan. We can develop a routine. If Nick or one of his counterparts is watching us, then he'll figure out the routine and eventually Roger and

Gabe will find him lurking. We'll get our coffee, and it'll help catch Nick."

"I guess that's a good idea. It's just that…"

"I know. It's not the same. But Gabe and Hall won't be sitting in here with us, and they won't be listening to our conversations."

"Okay," Skylar said reluctantly.

"It's a good thing, Skylar."

She nodded, picked up her coffee, and stared out the window, as though wondering who might be out there at that moment.

The convenient part of the plan was that Skylar could let Adam know about our meet-ups. She explained we were trying to draw Nick in while she was in a safe environment. Special Agents Kemp and Hall would be outside of the diner and I would be inside. After a bit of convincing on Skylar's part, everything on the outside was almost as it was on the inside.

Unfortunately, or maybe fortunately, the case aspect gave us more almost guilt-free time to get to know each other, but it also brought the case into our time together.

Almost always we could shut it out, because almost always, Meghan's presence wasn't necessary. Occasionally though, it was decided she should join me, and I wondered if it was Ryan's way of keeping me honest. Those breakfasts with Meghan were less than comfortable. The conversations didn't flow, and the coffee tasted bitter on my palate. Meghan would rehash the case, and Skylar would politely answer any questions. But as suspected, Meghan would also let the discussion drift to more personal matters, such as Skylar's wedding, which turned things from uncomfortable to unbearable.

"Have you chosen your band yet?" Meghan's demeanor had

changed from special agent to friendly. Although, to be truthful, I believe she was just investigating other subjects of interest to her; testing whether Skylar was competition worthy of concern.

"No. We might have a DJ instead of a band. It's a small wedding."

"Brent, what was the name of that band? You know, the one that played at Beaches the night you took me there?"

Skylar's gaze fixed on me; not angry, because she couldn't be, but betrayed.

I cleared my throat to get rid of the sensation of it closing. "I'm, I think, maybe it…"

"Overboard, wasn't it?"

"Yes, I believe so."

"They were quite good. Once we walked over to the beach area and got away from the speakers, the band was very enjoyable. We should go back to Beaches sometime, Brent."

"Maybe." I kept my eyes on Skylar, hoping she'd heard my hesitation.

"Well, I'd better get back to the field office," Meghan said. "Are you heading over there shortly?"

"I'll be right behind you." Meghan opened her wallet. "I've got it." I told her. "No worries, Meghan."

"Thanks, Brent. I must say, I enjoy the hanging-out-eating-breakfast-at-a-diner, part of my job though."

"The job can have some perks, can't it?" I replied. Had Meghan noticed that Skylar and I had barely looked her way?

"I'll catch up with you later, Brent. Nice to see you, Skylar."

"You as well," Skylar said with little emotion.

Neither of us spoke until Meghan had passed through the doors. "Is she your plus one?"

"What do you mean?" I asked.

"On the wedding RSVP. Is she your plus one?"

"Good chance, but I haven't officially asked her."

More silence, long and intense, hung between us.

"I just…I guess…well, you never mentioned you were seeing anyone. You have every right. I just wasn't prepared."

"Skylar, I went out for a drink with Meghan once. I'm not seeing her."

"You can. I would have to understand, wouldn't I?"

"I suppose you would, but I have no desire to be with anyone but you. Sitting here, as your friend, is better than a night with someone else. Don't you understand that, Skylar? You will let me go when you walk down the aisle. Up until that moment, I'm not moving on."

Her eyes glistened, and the anguish cast shadows upon her face.

"I need to get to work." Before standing she gently rubbed my hand, but I couldn't decipher the source of warmth behind the action. I only hoped it wasn't pity.

Despite a few weeks of occasional breakfasts, Gabe and Roger had yet to witness any suspicious activity around the diner. Eventually, they stopped being our silent partners that we had somehow been able to forget existed, yet my mornings still began with her text.

Can we meet for coffee?

I can be there in an hour.

I slid into the booth seat across from her and allowed myself a moment to take her in before speaking. In the time I had known Skylar, I had never seen her accentuate the parts of her that were beautiful—the flawless skin, the perfect smile, the curves beneath her conservative clothes. Besides the few times she'd worn jeans to work, she may have been the most conservatively dressed woman I had ever met, never showing a fun side or trying to draw attention to her more than adequate shape. Did she know how attractive she was behind her armor? My guess was no.

"I wanted to show you something?"

"Okay."

Skylar reached into her purse and pulled out two pictures.

"Please forgive me if this seems cruel, but I have my reasons."

"Okay," I said again with a hesitation that had not been there before.

She turned the pictures to face me. One of them appeared to be a hole in the middle of the ocean; the other was of Savannah, Georgia. "I want you to tell me your thoughts when you look at these."

"Are you asking me to run away with you? I do have a little experience with scuba diving," I said with a chuckle. Then I prepared myself for a blow.

"They're my honeymoon choices. Adam and I are trying to decide where to go."

"And you don't mean for this to be cruel?" I sat back, my body's unintentional way of distancing myself from the source of the pain.

"Your choice is important to me."

"Why? If you make it to your honeymoon, then I shouldn't be anywhere in your mind. Why should I help you choose, Skylar?"

"I know it doesn't make sense, but the decision is metaphorical."

I didn't understand, but since I had already decided I would do whatever it took to change her mind, I went along with it. After sitting up, I moved the pictures closer to me and studied them. The first image drew me to it with a sense of curiosity and fear. The second picture was a horse drawn carriage being pulled down a street lined with giant oak trees covered with Spanish moss. A place where memories were created from the ghosts of the past.

"Skylar, they're both great, just different."

"Which one am I?"

I stared at her, searching her for the answer she wanted to hear, petrified I'd give the wrong one. But I answered honestly.

"I think you're Savannah." Somehow, I knew I had just told her to choose Adam.

She slid the pictures back over to her side. "You're wrong, Brent. I want to believe I'm Savannah because it's easy. It's who I chose to be a long time ago."

"Why are you second guessing yourself?" I sensed Skylar was somewhere far away, and if I spoke softly enough, she may allow me to go there with her. "It's not a bad thing to enjoy a calmer life, one without fear. You don't have to be adventurous for me. Not to mention, Savannah is crawling with ghosts. What's more petrifying than that?" I tried to calm her with a smile, but her expression was one I had never seen on her face. A deep sadness hovered over her.

"There are ghosts everywhere, Brent."

I reached for her hands, and for a moment she let me hold them before she picked up the pictures and placed them back in her purse.

"Skylar, if you want to know which one I like best, it's the one that makes you truly happy. Even if I don't get to tag along."

Skylar stood to go, and then surprisingly, she bent down

and kissed my cheek. "And that's why it makes it hard to picture either one of them without you."

CHAPTER 33

Skylar

Journal Entry

I STARED UP AT the hedge walls that extended up into the sky and created a labyrinth around me. A suffocating feeling overcame me. The sun beat down on me, yet I knew storm clouds rolled across the horizon beyond my sight. I walked aimlessly until, far in the distance, I saw the exit. It was nothing more than a pinpoint of light.

Tears streamed down my face as I broke out into a run. At first, my legs, as heavy as tree trunks, fought to move, and then some force released them. I raced past the hedges but got nowhere; the opening remained barely visible. I stopped trying to fight the need to flee and froze in my tracks. Instead, I circled in my spot and watched the clouds spin above me. I had built all the walls around me. Every time I'd said 'yes' to something that had made me feel ill at ease, another wall had risen up around me. Even in my dream, though, I knew that every labyrinth had a way out. I just had to find it.

CHAPTER 34

Brent

THE NEXT DAY, I found myself in Ryan's office explaining why breakfast with Skylar was still crucial to helping her feel safe and informed. With knowing eyes, Ryan warned me about the hazards of becoming personally involved. I left his office feeling as if I'd succeeded in instilling confidence in my professionalism, but knew I needed to tread lightly with Ryan's faith in me.

Cynthia entered my office just as my phone alerted me of a message.

Chrissy wants to meet again.

"Am I interrupting anything?"

I did one more double take at the message before giving my attention to Cynthia. "Nothing so pressing that I can't catch up for a moment."

"Sorry that you had to discover the owner of the SUV on your own. What luck, huh?"

"Well, I'm not sure it was luck. He was leading me back to the hive as he put it. Either way, no worries. I still have complete faith in your abilities." Cynthia took the seat near my desk. There was a different air to her that I could not quite discern. "Everything okay?"

"Oh yes. I just wanted to fill you in on Henry's stepmother."

"What did you find?"

"Well, I'm quite confident she's not Brenda Carter."

"What makes you so sure."

"She passed away five years ago. Breast cancer."

"That's a shame." Following Cynthia's lead that a slow casual conversation was what she needed, I sat back in my chair. "I didn't have a strong feeling about that hunch, but I wanted to rule it out."

"I've heard you've had coffee with Skylar quite a bit. Anything I should know about?"

"No. We're just friends watching the pieces after the explosion fall back into place."

"And seeing where you fit into the picture?"

"*If* I fit into the picture that's left is more like it."

Cynthia stood. "It will all work out, I'm sure."

"Are you sure you're okay?"

"Brent, I'm always okay." Cynthia's eyes sparkled when she spoke. "I'm just watching a few pieces fall into place myself, but it's all good."

"If you need to talk, I'm always here."

"I know. That's why I came to visit you." Cynthia showed the smile I had grown accustomed to through the years. "Let me know if there's anything you need me to investigate for you."

"You know I will." As the door shut, I turned back to my phone and responded to Skylar's text. *Did she say why?*

No, but I'm having a drink with her after work.

When and where? I want to be there. We can give you a device so Roger and I can listen in at the next table.

I cleared the arrangements with Ryan and gathered the necessary authority to record Skylar and Chrissy. At seven o'clock, Roger and I were ordering beers at our booth behind Skylar's. Each of us had an earbud in an ear. As planned, she'd shown up fifteen minutes before the scheduled time so that we could have her squared away.

"Chrissy's here," Roger said. "Man, I can see why Bruce didn't want to let her go."

I remembered Chrissy from the funeral and understood why Roger's attention had not strayed from the woman's God-given gifts lavished with the manmade embellishments.

"She's coming this way."

I sat across from Roger, impossible to be seen from her angle, in case she should recognize me.

"Thanks for meeting with me, Skylar."

"Of course. You sounded upset."

"Have you already ordered?"

"No."

"Let me do the honors." It took only a moment for a server to be at the table. "We'll have two Old Fashioneds."

"Umm, I don't really drink the hard stuff," Skylar said.

"You can handle this. Plus, I need someone to drink with me."

The ease with which Chrissy got Skylar to drink hard liquor served as evidence she generally got her way.

"I've been thinking about things; what to share and what not to share."

"There's more?"

"Not a lot, but I need to tell someone. I don't know who else it can be." The server set the drinks in front of them. "Cheers." Glasses clinked, followed by a small cough caused by, I assumed, the alcohol sliding like lava down Skylar's throat.

"Too much?" Chrissy asked.

"No. Just a bit shocking at first. I think I can get used to it."

"You mentioned Bruce once told you that you were a diversion."

"Yes. Do you know what he was talking about?"

There was a pause, in which I pictured Chrissy taking another sip of her drink. "Not exactly, but Bruce was trying to get out of working with Henry. I was angry about the necklace because he'd promised me that he was trying to cut ties. One night, after he'd called me, I went to his house. He was hammered. Bruce was drinking so much at the end, and I suspect doing other things as well. Henry scared him, he scared everyone really. In the beginning, Bruce signed off on a few forms and took a nice bit of money on the side. It was a risk, one he'd thought was worth it, I guess. The years passed, and everything went by unnoticed. I didn't get all the details at the time. I just suspected there was more to the connection than Bruce was sharing.

But that night, the night he called me hammered, he was so upset and nervous. He told me he was in over his head, that he had been doing things he'd never thought he would do. That's when he told me he was leaving drugs in the glovebox, going into the bar for a drink, and then going back out to find the drugs gone and the money in its place. Lots of money. He told me he had been stashing his money in case something happened to him. He wanted to get out, just run off and leave. He was hoping I would leave with him. If he stayed, his life would be in danger."

"Why would his life be in danger?"

"Well, I guess it wouldn't be if he continued to be Henry's puppet. The fact he wanted to clean up his act was going to kill him one way or another."

Again, I could only assume Chrissy appeared emotional when she'd spoken because of the pause.

"I'm sorry, Chrissy. I know this must be tough on you."

"When Bruce learned I would never leave with him, he went to Henry to try to find a solution. At that point, Henry knew he was on the FBI's radar and his house of cards was about to crumble. He offered Bruce a deal. When I pushed him to tell me more, he actually started crying and mumbling things like, 'It was me or her. I didn't have a choice.' I couldn't get much more out of him, nor did I really want to. Bruce passed out. He was so broken in the end, and the hardest part about it all is that I did that to him. I broke him. He was a good man, Skylar, before all this. He really was a good man."

"I believe you." Ice in the glasses clinked as she tried to wash down her sorrow, and then I heard the sound of Chrissy blowing her nose slightly.

"I'm sorry, Skylar, but Bruce had to find someone to start taking over his duties in order for Henry to let him out of the picture. That person was you. I'm to blame for your situation as well."

"I'm not quite sure what to say about that. I'd like to say no worries, but as you know, I can't. There have been a million worries over the past year."

"I know. I just hope that someday, you can forgive me. Maybe someday, I can make it right for you."

"Thank you, Chrissy. I guess that has to count for something."

"Would you like another Old Fashioned?"

"Yes. I would." Chrissy put in their order, followed by a pause, in which the waitress must have walked away. "So," Skylar continued, "what are you going to do with the stashed money?"

"I'm not sure. But I don't think it's just cash. Days before Bruce killed himself, he told me about the box again, and was rambling about stuff people might need to know."

"Chrissy, isn't there a part of you that wants to look at what Bruce was hiding?"

"I don't know. I've never wanted to see the contents. Whatever is there was part of why Bruce ended his life. I can't look at it, and I don't need any of his drug money."

"Where's it hidden?"

"Skylar, it would take a lot more than two Old Fashions for me to give that information up. In some ways, I feel it's my way of protecting Bruce's name. For all I care, the box and its secrets could have been buried in the grave with him. Maybe some mysteries weren't meant to be solved."

"To mysteries." I visualized Skylar raising her glass to Chrissy's before I heard the familiar clink as the two women bonded; both, I'm sure, in situations they'd never thought possible.

As I sat there, an invisible partner in their conversation, I realized that I had never heard Skylar have a genuine, honest conversation with another woman. As far as I could tell, she had closed herself off from her coworkers, and I'd never heard her discuss other friends, which didn't necessarily mean she didn't have any. Her and Chrissy's conversation drifted to more comfortable ground, and I bore witness to a new Skylar, forming what may have been the most unconventional friendship in the world. Still, I couldn't explain it in any other way.

Listening to her chat away, breaking off layers of protection that had built around her for reasons I could not completely understand, I struggled to comprehend my feelings for Skylar. To be in love with her, I had to love who she was today, and not only who I believed she might become. Maybe I didn't need to embrace every part of her personality, but I did need to accept every part. And I did. But it was the possibilities lying beneath the surface that begged me to not give up.

Adam was content—beyond content, actually—to watch her settle. Her breaking from the Skylar that was comfortable would create discomfort for both of them. Change was terrifying. But change was also living and experiencing. I needed to get to love the Skylar that Adam had spent so many years with, which was easy, but I hoped I would get to love the Skylar transforming into a fearless creature—fearless about adventures, but equally fearless about loving people, even the Liz's. Most importantly, fearless about loving herself, because the other issues would then fix easily.

After the two drinks, Chrissy picked up the tab, and they left the bar together. Roger and I waited until we got the all-clear from Skylar before exiting.

Five minutes later, my phone to rang.

"Did you get all that?"

"Yes, Skylar. You were great."

"I need to ask a favor."

"Anything."

"Drive me home. Two Old Fashioneds might get me arrested."

Adrenaline pumped into my veins, and I fought against the excitement the hormone created. I needed to be professional. "My pleasure."

Once in the truck, Skylar played with the radio station and rested on a beat one could dance to if so inclined. "Have you made a decision about your honeymoon?"

"We're at a standstill."

"Does Adam know you were going to be with me tonight?"

"Yes."

"And what'd he say to that?"

"He didn't say much. Lately, he just studies me, or at least, I feel like he does. Things have been a bit strained, with wedding planning and all. People are sending their RSVP's back, and we can't even agree on a honeymoon destination. It's too much pressure on a relationship."

I pulled into the driveway and left the truck running. "Should I walk you in and fill him in on the details?"

"No. I think it's best that I do it," she replied. "I'm sure he's eager to hear how it went."

"Very well." I considered leaving it there, but my mouth had other plans. "Do you think he trusts me?"

"He doesn't need to trust you. He needs to be able to trust me. Part of me believes I'm doing the right thing, taking some time to find out for sure before promising a lifetime with him, but another part knows that just being your friend is being unfaithful. That's a pretty hard thing to forgive myself for. This isn't easy, Brent."

"But we're holding to our promise. We are staying friends."

"Tell my mind that, Brent. I might not have many friends, but I don't think my mind would be struggling so much every time I found myself in the same room with them. I've always been a faithful person. I know what faithful feels like. This doesn't feel faithful."

Skylar hopped out of the truck. My heart pounded out a warning, and my mind scrambled to find the correct words. She balanced on the edge of her decision, and one wrong move could push her in Adam's direction.

"Thanks for the ride, Brent."

I saw the wetness in her eyes and couldn't let her leave that way. As always, I wanted—I needed—to fix what was wrong in her life. I got out of the truck door and took her arm. We stood in front of the headlights shining on us so brightly nothing could be hidden

"Wait, Skylar. Don't leave like this."

"You think you're saving me. You think you've done these great things for me. Well, let me tell you something that you're overlooking. I was happy. I was completely content, anyway. I would have gone to my grave not wishing for anything more than Adam and our bland little boring life. And then I met you, and you wrecked everything. You created a big frigging hole in the middle of my perfect little life. You think you can make me happier, but have you ever considered that you're the reason I'm unhappy? That maybe I hate you in some ways for making my life look pathetic? What if a boring and complacent existence is where I find my happiness? What if I chase something more with you, and in the end, I miss my boring and complacent life? I wish I had never met you. I wish you'd never had the chance to change my perception of my life. I hate you for that."

Skylar began sobbing. I took her in my arms, even though she had just been very clear about how I had been the reason her life was a mess.

"I'm sorry, Skylar. Maybe it's time I walk away. But I want you to know I never wanted to make you unhappy. And if it makes you feel better, you created a hole in me too."

I turned to go, and Skylar grabbed my hand. Tears streaked her face, and I felt them as if they were my own.

"It's too late to leave, Brent. When you find the person you love, it's not just about loving that person. It's about loving the person you envision yourself as being when you're with them, and to let that go is the hardest part of all."

Skylar spoke the words I didn't even know how to express, but the minute I heard them, they were mine as well. I caught one of the tears running down her cheek, and if it weren't for the opening of the door, I believe I would have experienced my first real kiss with Skylar. Instead, I stared into the face of the person I was destroying. Adam looked back and forth between the two of us. I was done. I couldn't hurt anyone else. We watched as he let the door close between us.

"What can I do?" I asked.

"Leave." Skylar looked toward the closed door. "I need to handle the rest on my own."

I just nodded, unable to find the appropriate response to the situation, and then left her alone to sort out the disaster I had created.

Two days later, Skylar called me in a panic. "Chrissy texted me the weirdest message this morning."

"What'd she say?"

"The text said, *I thought I could trust you. Now everything makes sense.* She won't respond to me. I've tried texting and calling."

Understandably, Skylar was confused, but I sensed something more; the pain of a friendship crashing to an end.

"What could she have meant?"

"I have no idea," I said.

"Did one of your men talk to her?"

"Not to my knowledge. I'll find out, Skylar. I promise."

"Please, Brent. I can't take any more not knowing. Something in my life needs to start making sense."

The phone went dead. I thought back to our conversation

from the night before. Again, I felt responsible for Skylar's life falling apart. I needed to fix it; I needed to talk to Ryan.

"Are you here about the recording?" Ryan asked as if expecting my visit.

"Maybe. Do you know why Chrissy would be telling Skylar that she thought she could trust her, and now everything makes sense? Did you send someone to talk with Chrissy?"

"Not yet, but we're going to look into that box she mentioned."

I was in the breakroom, drinking my second cup of coffee, when I got the call from Ryan. He sounded sterner than I had ever heard him; his tone had an unaccustomed urgency. After pouring the remaining coffee down the drain, I hurried down the hall. By the time I reached his office, a convention of people waited for me.

"I think you should sit down, Brent. We have something you may be interested in."

My legs gave way. I landed gracefully enough in the chair behind me that no one took notice.

"I've asked you several times if you thought you were too close to this case. Every time, you insisted you were not."

Without another word, Ryan hit a button, and Tori's voice rang out of the speaker. All eyes in the room were on me, and strangely enough, I forgot how to breathe. "Skylar and Chrissy are talking. I don't think we can trust Skylar anymore."

"Is Skylar still working that Brent guy?" Henry asked.

"Yes. He's still backing her side of the story. It's keeping her out of the spotlight a bit."

"She's good. I have to give Bruce that at least." Henry paused. "It's unfortunate Bruce's ex-wife knows where Skylar's stash is hidden. We should never have trusted him to hold onto it for her. He was obviously faltering in the end."

"Skylar just has to keep playing Brent until next week, when the next shipment will come in. We'll have her on the boat and out of here."

"Where's it coming in?" Henry asked.

"Same place as last time," Tori answered.

"Does Nick think it's secure?"

"Yes. There's no reason to suspect they know anything. We've had people watching the location. It seems clear."

"Tuesday, 8 pm, still?"

"Yes."

"Tell Nick I said good luck."

"We'll be toasting you in another week, Henry. Wish you could be there, too."

Henry's response wasn't verbal, so it was left to our imaginations.

My mind spiraled. How had it all started? I'd been selected to go on the trips to the Bahamas and Miami. Was it possible it was just by chance? Supposedly, I'd been selected because Bruce had suspected Skylar had feelings for me. That fact had been the beginning of it all.

"You're off the case, Brent." Sweat trickled down my neck. "Let us know if she reaches out to you in any way." My breath caught in my throat. "Your only job is to relay information back to us. Is that clear?" My world crashed around me.

"Yes." I managed to say. "Am I free to go?"

"For now." Yet, Ryan's stern gaze had not released me. "Be ready to answer some questions, Brent. My guess is there'll be plenty of them."

CHAPTER 35

Skylar

Journal Entry

I DREAMED I WAS *walking across the top of the water. Something floated in the distance—or rather, stuck up through the surface. As I approached, it became clear the object was not an object at all, but a living creature—a manatee. With childlike excitement, I quickened my pace toward the passive water cow munching innocently on some vegetation. I adored manatees. I had even swum with them once as a child, and in some ways, the memory had created an idolatry in my mind. If only I could once again let my hands graze the smooth, yet tough skin. If I did so, somehow, a supernatural moment of bliss would forever be embedded in my memory. Without owning up to my part in the idolization, the manatee became much more to me than a peaceful river creature, and instead became a direct link to the unknown.*

I approached the manatee and began to doubt it was a manatee at all. Instead, it appeared more like a large oil barrel, covered with a black sludge. The mystical feeling inside of me gave way to something darker. As I reached out to touch it, it sank into the water and quickly slid out of sight.

I awoke in a somber mood. That's the problem when we create idols. When we finally possess them, they never seem to measure up. We spend too much time chasing them, building memories up in our minds, creating scenarios we believe will become reality, giving qualities that are unearned to our treasured prizes. My melancholy mood hung over me throughout the day. What if I left the security of my shore to find my idol was nothing more than a soot-covered oil barrel? All day the question lingered on my mind. Finally, the answer became clear. The universe had sent me on a journey. She had tossed me off the shore where I found my security, and I had made a choice. I swam back to the shore, afraid the "manatee" would let me down. But what I needed to do, what I believe I was meant to do, was to learn to float on my own before deciding. Slowly, a part of me waded back in and let the waves lap at my ankles. I saw the creature in the distance and let my focus drift away. If I left, it couldn't be the manatee that called me away.

CHAPTER 36

Brent

I HEADED DOWN THE hall to my office as if walking through a dream. I'd never been with Skylar when she'd gone to the other "accounts." In all honesty, I hadn't been able to tell if when she'd gone into the banks, she'd been a willing participant. I remembered the night when Skylar had been uncharacteristically happy at dinner, angry only when my questions had dug too deep. My memory was very clear about her elated mood; I hadn't seen her that happy before then. On that trip, she'd opened her own account and had deposited a large sum of money into Brenda Carter's. Her mission had been a success. She'd wanted to be alone that night, to walk on the beach.

Although I was off the case, my colleagues couldn't make me avoid her. Well, at least that's what I told myself as I called her. I wouldn't question anything. My plan was to act as normal as possible and see where the conversation went. After a number of rings, the phone went to voicemail. Since the correct words to have recorded right after being told I was off the case escaped me, I hung up. After some thought, I decided to text instead.

When can we meet again?

For someone who couldn't answer the phone, she responded without hesitation.

I left Adam.

My heart pounded in my chest. Our journey could begin, well, as soon as I could prove that she wasn't a criminal about to run off with millions of dollars.

Why? I texted back. *I'm happy, but I didn't see this coming so quickly.*

For all the reasons I mentioned the other night. I wasn't being faithful to him if I was texting you and secretly meeting up with you. I couldn't keep doing that to him.

I can't say I'm not happy, but I'm sorry you're hurting, as I'm sure you are.

Brent, I have to stay away from you as well. I need to figure out some things on my own.

So where are you staying?

I'm going away for a bit. When I come back, I'll be able to be honest with everyone.

What do you mean? You'll be able to be honest with everyone?

I believe you know what that means.

Skylar. I paused. I had no idea what to say, or who I was really conversing with. Was it the Skylar I thought I knew, or the Skylar the FBI had painted a picture of? I was off the case, and because of that, I decided to momentarily ignore the fact that her criminal counterparts had just told an office full of FBI agents that she had played me and was in on the deal the whole time. *I'm here when and if you need me.* For just a moment more, I wanted to believe in her.

Thank you.

A telling silence fell over me. I wouldn't be hearing from her for some time.

CHAPTER 37

Skylar

Journal Entry

THE DAY MY world crashed, I was at Aunt Deb's, sitting on the bedroom floor, painting my nails a ridiculous green that I can still picture today. The phone rang. My aunt's voice resonated with the sound that no human ear can handle. It's the sound that, even before you know what caused it, makes you want to curl in a ball and close the world out. It's the sound where nightmares touch reality; the sound your soul makes when it cries. It's not a bumped knee or a lost gem whimper. It's the sound a person makes when they shatter. It's the sound you hear before curling up in a fetal position to protect the wounds that will never heal.

CHAPTER 38

Brent

FEAR RACED THROUGH me to know that the members of my squad, including Meghan, were on an all-out search for Skylar. Work was impossible, and I found myself spending more time pacing behind my closed door than doing anything else. Within the hour, Ryan entered, looking annoyed, and I dreaded hearing what he had to say.

"Do you know where your friend went? We stopped by Skylar's house to ask her some questions, and we were told by Adam that she'd moved out."

"I truly have no idea where she went." Knowing my job would be at risk if I didn't divulge everything, I added, "She just told me she'd left Adam and was taking a vacation to clear her head."

Ryan eyed me suspiciously.

"That's truly all I know."

"What would she have to be clearing her head about?"

Damn. I had just divulged too much. "She had cold feet about getting married."

"And you know this because?"

"I said I wasn't too close to the case to see things clearly. I believe that to be true."

"Then explain the conversation between Tori and Henry."

"I can't."

Ryan rubbed his hands together like a stern parent about to toss out a punishment.

"Is there anything else you want to share?"

I'd feel like a traitor no matter what I said, so I went with the truth. "One thing, I'm not sure if it's significant or not, but after the conversation in the bar, Chrissy reached out to Skylar and said stuff about not being able to trust her. Skylar couldn't figure out what she was talking about."

"Or so she says. It's a bit interesting that after Chrissy said that, Skylar skipped town."

The room began to spin around me. Maybe I had been played.

"I think it's time we find out what is in the mysterious box," Ryan said.

With a sickening acceptance, I agreed.

The computer stared blankly back at me. I didn't know where to begin. The new case I was on meant nothing to me. I found myself glancing more at my phone, placed beside my keyboard, than at the computer itself. Where was Skylar? What was she doing?

"Knock, knock." Cynthia stood in my doorway. "Rough day?"

"You might say that." I closed my computer screen and gave my full attention to the only person in the office from whom I stood a chance of getting any empathy.

"So, off the record, do you want to talk?" She closed the door behind her and took a seat across from me. Deciding if I could divulge everything, I crossed my arms and sat back in my chair.

"Come on. I'll share my secrets if you share yours," she said with a purposely youthful smile.

"I can't decide if I'm a fool or if Skylar is the one being played. One minute I'm positive I'm the victim, and the next minute I'm sure she is."

"You have strong feelings for her, don't you?"

"Is it that obvious?"

"Totally." Again, Cynthia smiled.

"I trusted her completely."

"Maybe you're right to trust her."

"Then why did she run off right when Chrissy acted like she'd found something out? Why did Tori and Henry have the conversation about her playing me?"

"Those are good questions."

"Do you know how much I wanted her to leave Adam? I should be ecstatic right now. She's having second thoughts. We stand a chance."

"That obviously makes you happy."

"Are you playing psychiatrist with me?"

"If it helps."

I rested my face in my hands. "I'm not sure if it does or doesn't help." I took a deep breath. "I don't know what I would do without you here."

Cynthia's expression became softer and kinder. "That brings me to my secret."

"Do I want to hear this?"

"I hope not. I'd like to think someone will miss me around here."

"You're leaving?"

"Not right away. That's why I'm trusting you with my secret. I still have several months."

"Why?"

"I need to get closer to my parents. I'm an only child, and it's time they have family nearby. They've lived in the same house since they were twenty, and until someone hauls them out of there kicking and screaming, they're not moving."

"Who's going to be my right-hand person here? You keep this place ticking."

"You're very sweet, and I can't pretend I won't miss it terribly, but there are criminals everywhere needing my attention."

Considering the situation, I felt it appropriate to give Cynthia a hug. "Well, your news certainly did not improve my day."

"Brent, there are times that you trust your gut, the one trained as an FBI special agent, and there are times that you trust your heart."

"Which one do I trust now, my gut or my heart?"

"I'm not sure, Brent." We released each other from our embrace. "Maybe if we can find out where she went, we can get some answers. Lucky for you, I'm good with that stuff."

"Yes, you are."

She patted my arm before turning toward the door. "We'll figure it out, I promise."

I watched as the most human part of my otherwise impersonal office headed for the door.

The hours dragged by as I sifted through the new accounts while trying to keep my mind from drifting to Skylar. Just when I thought I had won the battle, my phone vibrated. It was an unknown number, but not an unknown voice at the other end.

"Are you with her?" Adam asked.

"No, I'm not." Silence hung in the air. I sensed us both deciding how civil the conversation would be.

"Do you know where she went?"

"No. I promise you. Skylar didn't share her plans with me. She just told me she needed to clear her head."

"I guess whatever you were up to worked. Are you pleased with yourself?"

"Listen, Adam."

"No, Brent. You listen. You came into our home, pretending to be a friend or at least someone there to help us, and all that time you had ulterior motives. I knew it, or at least I always sensed it. First, you let her stay involved in a case that could have been dangerous to her, and then you made her question the one constant in her life that she has been able to count on through everything. You pretend you care about her. How's that caring about her? You could have gotten her killed."

"We didn't know she wasn't involved. She was part of the case."

"If you knew her, you would know how insane that idea is. Skylar would never choose to be involved in drug deals and money laundering."

I thought about all the times we had heard that through the years. There was truth in what he'd said. He had sixteen years on me. Sixteen years in which he'd gotten to know her deeply. Yet, how many times had we found that the ones closet to the situation were the ones most easily blinded?

"If you question her feelings for me then don't you want her to figure them out before you marry her?"

"I didn't say I questioned her feelings for you. I said I questioned your feelings for her. And no, I don't need her to work her feelings out. I need her to say we're together for life, and the rest will follow."

"It's not in my hands. It's in hers, but more importantly, we need to know where she went. There's still a case going on."

"Her part in the case is done. Leave her out of it. We haven't noticed anyone following her in some time. Just leave us both out of it."

"It's not that easy, Adam. I'm not at liberty to discuss everything, but this case has not been closed yet."

"What do you mean?"

"I'm not working the case anymore, so I'm going to leave it there. Adam, if you hear from Skylar, please let us know."

"Is she in danger?"

"Just…please, contact us if you hear from her. I need to go, Adam. I don't expect you to agree with me, but I'm not the type of person who goes around breaking up relationships. I care about her. And if she truly cares about me, too, then I guess it's a choice she needs to make."

Before he had a chance to respond, I hung up.

An hour or two later, I heard footsteps, with a persistence that caught my attention, coming down the hallway. My body tensed, despite not knowing why. At the same time, my phone lit up with a message from Cynthia.

They found the box.

I stared at the words. The message was too short; too abrupt. Why?

By the time Ryan appeared in the doorframe, I was already watching and waiting. Something told me I would not enjoy his visit. Without speaking, he approached my desk and slapped a passport down in front of me like a parent who had found a science test with a big red F on top stuffed under a child's mattress.

Skylar's face smiled back at me. What was he saying? Had they found her? I looked back up at him, questioning.

"Look a little closer, Brent."

I turned back to the passport, and the bottom fell out from beneath me. So many mysteries were solved, yet one question now begged for an answer. Why was Skylar's face on Brenda Carter's passport?

I needed air; I needed time to think. I pictured Skylar raising her glass at the bar with Chrissy and saying, "To mysteries," maybe encouraging her to never look in the box. I remembered the way Skylar had so abruptly asked where the box was hidden. Had her eagerness actually stemmed from fear of what was inside? Had she known the passport hid in the contents of the box? Had she wanted to find it before skipping town? As a special agent, how was I so easily blinded?

CHAPTER 39

Skylar

OF ALL IRONIES, on that fateful day, my parents didn't die scuba diving. They didn't miscalculate their air supply and become unconscious before ever seeing the surface of the water again. The sharks never swarmed; their parasail never crashed into the ocean.

No, none of that happened to my breathtaking, full-of-life parents. Instead, they died before reaching their scuba diving excursion, while siteseeing on their moped, a vehicle an elderly person might have cruised around on the day before. My life-changing moment happened as my parents drove around a chaotic traffic circle where lines blurred, and culture made chaos mundane.

Their faces, suntanned and glowing, are frozen in my mind. Not at the moment of impact, of course, but right before. Both of them were envisioning the day with all the magic and wonder it had to offer. My dad, I imagine, was looking at my mother in the side mirror like she was the fuel that kept his heart beating. It's the only image I want to remember.

CHAPTER 40

Brent

THE FBI HEADQUARTERS buzzed as each agent was briefed and assignments were handed out. My job was to review, with fresh eyes, every detail of every report I had submitted throughout my time at McClurry's. I needed to stop seeing Skylar as the victim and start seeing her as the woman with two identities. The image of the passport flashed through my mind—her smiling face next to the name of the third party, the one that owned all the shell companies. The one that held a large sum of the money in her accounts. The Skylar who'd gone missing at the most convenient of times.

After a couple of hours had passed, giving me enough time to revisit my past, I was called to Ryan's office. When I entered, he stood and, with arms folded, repositioned himself so that he leaned against his desk. Roger sat in an office chair next to him, torn, I'm sure, between being a comrade and a special agent.

"Let's start from the beginning, Brent." Ryan opened up a folder containing what I believed to be notes from the initial investigation. The room was silent except for the sound of the papers being flipped one by one, as he tried to find a place to begin his attack.

Who hasn't heard that when we die, we watch our lives flash before our eyes? All morning, I'd been forced to relive my life as if viewing it for the first time; an outsider to my story. I thought back to the very first meeting, when the temps had been introduced to the staff at McClurry's. Had Skylar had a description of me even then; the guy to watch for who would be working undercover?

The day she'd laughed—when we'd tried to decide who would go first through the door—I'd suspected something for the first time; a chemistry maybe, if not the budding of a crush. How easy was it to fake a small, girlish giggle? Shortly after, Skylar had locked her keys in her car, just to get a ride home on my motorcycle. Even then, I'd wondered how much of an accident it could have been, but it now screamed conniving rather than cute.

"Brent, the beginning? What made you feel Skylar was a person of interest in the case?"

"I'm not sure." And I really wasn't. For the life of me, I couldn't decide who'd been stalking who. "We were introduced; made small talk."

I heard her voice like a ghost, telling me how she'd been thinking of installing hardwood floors in her cubicle. Each time I'd looked at her, I'd seen something more shine through her conservativeness. Her humble beauty had become more intoxicating. At what point had I lost sight of the case and my purpose?

"Small talk about what?"

"The office staff. Coffee. Weekend plans."

"And then you were just told you were going away with her to Miami?"

"Yes. I thought it was weirdly convenient, but sometimes things like that happen."

Had Bruce truly been that in tune with each interaction that had taken place in the office? Bruce had often hidden himself behind his closed door. Those first days, I remembered studying each person, trying to find out who might be a part of Henry's dealings. My colleagues and I knew that someone in his office could be helping him, and I was to get to know everyone. What a fool I'd been, never sensing they'd been doing the same to me. Befriending me; keeping me just close enough.

Skylar had kept everyone distant, never attending a happy hour, never joining people for lunch. Only me. For God's sake, she'd never even gotten married.

"What can you remember about Miami?"

I thought back to our first trip together. Why had they selected me? We'd always believed it had been their way to start spinning the web to trap Skylar; sensing they could get something on her by sending her off with her office crush. Could it have been to get me away from the premises? Could it have been to make me Skylar's confidant, to keep tabs on me?

"Nothing big," I said. "Just a rundown hotel. I could tell why Bruce wanted someone else to cover the account. And I understood why Bruce wanted a man with Skylar. The hotel was in a rough part of town."

"How did they get the first picture of you with Skylar?"

"We took an innocent walk on the beach. We had some wine, shared a blanket. It looked worse than it was in reality."

"You're telling me this conservative woman, a woman who was angry about being sent off with you, so easily curled up on a beach with you, giving no thought to her long-term partner? Didn't that behavior seem out of character?"

I wanted to explain that she'd acted differently with me, that something between us had made her act out of character, but I couldn't. "I guess it does."

"Whose idea was it to walk on the beach where the photographers waited?"

"I can't remember."

"If there were photographers. She never was able to hand over the pictures."

"She said she destroyed them. Wouldn't you have?"

"Are you defending her? Still?"

"No, I just want to know the truth."

"As do I, Brent." Ryan shuffled a few more papers.

"She told me when we were in Miami that something troubled her about Henry's accounts."

"That could be because they actually troubled her, or she tried to gain you as a confidant. If Henry and Bruce knew you were FBI, it would make sense. They would know you were suspicious. This distanced her just enough."

"I guess."

"I have here that she called in sick during tax season, and her explanation seemed a bit vague. Isn't that a bit of a faux pas for an ultra-conservative accountant who never called in sick during the previous tax seasons? I would think an employee would have to be very sick to call in, yet it says here she showed no signs of any ailments the following day." Ryan eyed me over his readers. "And shortly after that she ran off to the Bahamas with Henry."

"It appears so."

As much as I tried to keep my cool, I knew my demeanor spoke otherwise. Ryan set the folder on the desk behind him.

"Brent, we've been through this all before. If something got missed, we all missed it. But now is the time we find it. I'm not interrogating you to find your fault."

But you are.

"Together, we need to see how they managed to hide all their money under a name they created, a name that just happens to be Skylar's alias, and then have them all just disappear without a trace."

"Understood. I'm an open book."

Ryan took a deep breath as he reached again for the folder. His attempt to calm the tension in the air hadn't succeeded.

"According to your notes, after the sick day, she seems to be distant from you. You fly to the Bahamas, and she barely speaks to you."

"Yes, but then she also broke down crying. Stressed about something she couldn't share with me."

"Once again, we can't prove if this was stress or acting. If she knew who you were the whole time, she needed you to be sympathetic to her. She needed you to move slowly enough that they had plenty of time to transfer all of their money."

I answered with silence, but inside, my thoughts were anything but silent. The movie reel was playing all the scenes back and making me look like an idiot.

Ryan flipped some more papers. "Then I see here you tracked her to the Starbucks where Bruce's ex-wife was getting coffee. Can you explain that?"

I shook my head.

"Because to me, spying on the ex sounds like a favor you would do for a friend. I see no other reasonable explanation, do you?"

Again, I shook my head. "No, I don't," I mumbled.

"How did she react when she learned our agents were in the office; when she found out they had stopped by her desk? She didn't know at the time that we were trying to make her open up to you. Which she didn't."

"She was a bit uncomfortable."

What I didn't say was the question I'd asked before she'd headed out the door to Henry's. *When are you going to give up being the mystery woman?*

I could still see her, smiling over her shoulder at me as she said, *Why should I? Don't men find mysterious women intriguing?*

She'd been enjoying it. She'd been enjoying the adventure and trying to lead me on in the process. I wondered then how much I actually knew of Skylar and Adam's relationship. She'd claimed this strong bond, yet they'd never married. How was I to know how many times she had flirted in the past? How many other temps had she used to break up the monotony of tax season?

"Then we have that she failed a drug test and didn't receive any repercussions."

"There was a repercussion. She needed to do whatever they asked." How did I go back to defending her so easily?

"Maybe." Ryan took a moment to read whatever was in front of him. "Up to this point, Skylar had shown interest in you, and you had reached out to her several times to let her know she could come to you. Still, this rule-following, innocent woman takes a suitcase full of money through security, risks being caught, before coming to you for help."

I pictured her, as if it were only yesterday, looking me straight in the eyes and asking, *Have you ever felt that somehow in your life you got in way over your head?* At the time, I'd felt for her as if she were strictly the victim, but now I heard the words differently. The wording now resonated more like the confession of a regretful criminal than a victim.

"And then she willingly walked into the bank, far away from the threatening people, and opened an offshore account in her own name with illegal money."

But there'd been reasons, hadn't there? Skylar had explained them so well. I recalled her defensive tone when I'd asked her about the carry-on bag she'd left Bruce's office with. I remembered her asking how I had seen her since I had already gone to my truck. Skylar had showed her deceitful side once again. Over and over, I'd asked about the carry-on bag's contents, and over and over, she'd lied—eventually, becoming frustrated and insisting that she walk on the beach by herself.

"But she did come to me. She did tell me we needed to talk."

"Let's revisit that, Brent. She came to you after finding out people had been at her desk, searching for something. Maybe she just knew the game was up, and it was time to try to save herself. Her confession carries little weight at the moment." Ryan paused, a triumphant warrior hovering over the fallen one before adding one more blow to end it all. "Meghan said that Skylar hadn't even picked out the band for a wedding that is supposed to take place in a matter of weeks. Brent, who hasn't chosen the band for her wedding with that little time left? Only a woman with no intention of ever going through with the marriage ceremony."

I slumped, defeated, hiding my face in my hands.

"Brent, have you ever considered that she never intended for us to rescue Adam from the Netherlands? Maybe she had wanted the money so she could disappear and start over without him."

Refusing to allow the vision to fade from my mind, I gripped the memory of Skylar's warm hand held in mine as we walked out on the pier. The details had not been strong enough to taint at least that, and then I remembered more of Skylar's words as we'd stood alone looking out at the horizon. *Have you ever wondered if you're really a good person or a bad person?* I released the grip of her memory, letting it fade away like the setting of the sun, making me wonder if it had ever possibly been as beautiful as I'd once believed.

Ryan left then, without another word and Roger followed. When I had the strength, I stood and headed back to my office where the new reality would have time to morph from the facts. As I let the story behind the sought-after intel transform into a truth, it burned. How had I not seen the holes? She'd sought me out, and I'd foolishly allowed myself to believe that I was a love interest. Maybe they'd known all along that I was FBI. Maybe they'd known the only way their plan could continue was to bring me in just enough that I'd felt I was in control, watching and gaining insight. Meanwhile, as I'd sat back, a pawn in their game, they'd been completing their mission. And it had worked, except for Henry's capture, but Nick and Skylar were long gone, no doubt in another country.

Maybe they were both on a yacht, crossing the Atlantic, sipping cocktails and laughing their asses off, specifically at me and how gullible I had allowed myself to become.

CHAPTER 41

Skylar

Journal Entry

LIFE IS MERELY a journey we endure in preparation for the big trip. As we scan our environment and decide what to bring with us, we toss the haggard garments to the side and neatly fold the ones deemed worthy. We tuck the secrets and private items into hidden pockets where we hope no one will discover them despite the knowledge of scanners. Nothing is truly hidden. Then we zip up our suitcase, content that it holds the very best of us, and with faith in that fact, we depart. It's almost time. There's only a few more things I need to say, but the words are difficult.

CHAPTER 42

Brent

TORI, ABIGAIL, CHRISSY, Patrick, Nick, Adam and Henry made up the list of people we could question. It would have been a very busy day, except for the fact Tori could not be located, and after Nick had cleaned out the hotel room, we had lost his whereabouts. Abigail was a lost cause; either the best actress in the state of Florida, or she legitimately knew nothing about her sister's location. Patrick was the only one willing to speak to save his ass, but he hadn't been able to offer much.

Adam came willingly to the field office. His interrogation dragged on for hours. I was only able to observe. The color drained from his face as my colleagues showed him the passport. That's how they began his questioning. They set the tone that made him willing to talk.

"She had been acting differently; secretive. She was changing—shopping for different things, wearing lipstick. I sensed she wasn't happy with our comfortable life any more. All of a sudden, she wanted more than I could give her. I had strong suspicions that her change had to do with Brent."

In the observation room, surrounded by coworkers, I tried to remain stone-faced and emotionless, but the air was thick, and breathing was difficult.

"Then her boss called, and he asked about all of her absences. I didn't get the chance to hear her excuses before Bruce told me to meet him at the hotel. He said he had proof—pictures. Bruce wasn't in the hotel, only this other guy, the one who was arrested with Henry during the drug bust. I never saw the pictures, and I wanted to believe Skylar. When the special agents brought me back from the Netherlands, and she begged me to believe her, I did. Plus, the story panned out. Brent was with the FBI. She was working on Henry's account. It was easier to believe that she'd been played than to believe that she was playing me."

"I know this may be difficult, but I want you to tell me anything else you remember. Can you give us more details on her strange behavior before she disappeared?"

"Yes. She was meeting that woman Chrissy for coffee and movies. Skylar had never needed girl time before."

"Chrissy said she only met with Skylar a couple of times before finding the passport."

Adam was silent a moment. "That doesn't make sense. Skylar told me she was with her many times, that they ate breakfast together before work. One time she bought sneakers so they could go running in the park. I thought that was very out of character."

My jaw tightened, and a bead of sweat formed on my forehead. I hadn't expected our secret rendezvous to become part of the investigation.

"Adam, this would not be the first time Skylar was dishonest with you."

"No, it wouldn't be."

I felt sick for Adam yet telling him the truth about her secret outings wouldn't help the situation at all. I'd thought Skylar had told Adam about our meetings in the end. Perhaps the number of times was just too much to pass off, and she'd decided throwing in a few coffees with Chrissy might prevent questioning. Eventually, my boss would find out the other outings were with me as well.

"Tell me what Skylar told you before she left. What led up to her leaving?"

"I saw her and Brent together. He brought her home from the meeting with Chrissy."

"What exactly did you see?"

"The way they looked at each other; it was obvious. They had feelings for each other."

Ryan would be finding out about the secret outings faster than I'd thought.

"Did you address it?"

"Yes. I hoped she would be apologetic. I expected her to beg for forgiveness. Instead, she told me she needed time to think."

"She didn't tell you where she was going?"

"No. I have no clue. She wasn't herself at all at the end. I didn't even know her anymore."

"Did you believe she was leaving you for Brent?"

"To be honest, no, I didn't. I felt like she just didn't know who she was anymore. She was quiet and distant most of the time."

"Are there relatives or friends that she may have gone to visit?"

"She has her aunt, but I already checked with her. I just want to know she is safe. I think she would have been honest with me."

"What about a place? Was there someplace she had talked about?"

"We were trying to decide on our honeymoon destination, but we couldn't agree."

"What were the choices?"

"I wanted to go to Savannah. She wanted some tropical place where we could scuba dive or at least snorkel."

"Did she mention where?"

"Nothing specific, really, but why would she run off to our honeymoon destination when she still hadn't officially called off our wedding, and I hadn't officially said no to the idea? I just let her know I wasn't happy with it." Adam thought for a moment. "It wouldn't make sense to run off to a place we were possibly going to go to when everything calmed down."

"I suppose not, but we need to check all the possibilities."

"Understood."

The interview wrapped up shortly after that, when the other agents concluded Adam didn't have the information they were seeking—or maybe they were eager to follow the one lead he did lay before them.

I went to my office and watched the clock hands as they refused, as always, to freeze for a moment, to give me one much-needed, unrecorded second to catch my breath. Another click of the clock hand moving forward reverberated through the air and warned me that it wouldn't take long. Sure enough, the tapping of footsteps could be heard drawing closer to my office. Ryan entered and closed the door.

"I was expecting you," I said, leaning back in my chair.

"Brent, I'm getting a bit exhausted by the denial game. It's time you come clean."

"I'm not sure what to say. Do you want me to say I had feelings for Skylar? I had feelings for her. I believe I kept those feelings in check. I believe I did my job even if it appears that she pulled one over on all of us. She was upset the night Adam saw us. She admitted she was confused."

"What made her confused?"

I took a deep breath. I hadn't broken a rule. I'd maybe bent a few, but not broken them. "She wasn't hanging out with Chrissy. She was with me. She wanted to make sure she was making the right choice marrying Adam. Our meetings were platonic. We just allowed ourselves to get to know each other better." Ryan paced a bit while rubbing his forehead. "I never specifically asked her each time who she'd told Adam she was hanging out with when she was with me."

"Stay away from this case, Brent. I'm not letting you in on any investigations pertaining to Henry or his counterparts. Skylar is not your friend. She's wanted for questioning. If you hear from her, you are to let us know. Understand?"

"Understood."

Ryan turned to leave and then added, "And Brent, the next reprimand you receive will be an official one. Don't taint your record. She isn't worth it."

Later that evening, when my eyes could no longer see straight, I hooked my phone on the charger and prepared for a restless night of sleep.

The phone rang, and Adam's sleepy voice replied to my hello.

"I didn't tell them everything."

"What are you talking about?"

"Quite some time ago, Skylar started keeping a journal. She wrote strange things, dreams I believe, and poems. I wasn't really hiding the journal from them. Well, not exactly. I just didn't want them to read it."

"Why are you telling me then?"

"Because I think you're the only one willing to go the extra mile to find Skylar, and maybe give her a chance to explain. You're the only other person who wants her to be innocent."

"Adam, you can trust—"

"Shut up before I change my mind. No, Brent, I can't trust you. I just need you to give her a chance."

"Okay." I didn't dare say anything else.

Adam took a deep breath. "Anyway, the journal doesn't make any sense to me, but it was important to her; private. I only know about it because I saw it sitting out on the bed when she was in the shower. I got home earlier than expected. I quickly glanced at the journal, but left the room when I heard the shower shut off and pretended I had never seen it. I forgot about it, since I couldn't see it as anything of interest at the time. But with all that is going on, I went searching for it. I tore the bedroom apart trying to find the damn thing and gave up. And then I saw it, clear as day, sitting on top of some books on her dresser. She had never kept it there before. It's almost as if she'd set it out for me to find, and it took me this long to notice it."

"So, did she write anything new in the journal? Anything that would help locate her?"

"Not that I can tell. In the end, she was writing poems, or copying other people's, at least, into her diary. It makes no sense to me."

"I'd like to see it."

"I expected you would. But if it doesn't look like it'll help, do me a favor and just give it back to me. I feel as if I'm betraying her by letting strangers read it."

"I understand. But please know, I will have to let the

other special agents review it if I feel anything could be used as evidence."

"Understood," Adam's tone changed. "Am I right? Do you still think she's innocent?"

"I hope so, Adam. I truly do, but for now, I need to distance myself from any personal feelings and look at the facts. If she is innocent, then we'll find that out as well."

"Let me know what you find."

Before I could reply, the phone went dead.

Before going to the office, I ran by Adam's house to get the journal which was an awkward and nearly silent exchange. Even Ted, sensing an energy, a storm that was about to rip his home apart, watched without barking. As soon as I found a private place to pull over, I studied the diary as if my world depended on what secrets it held. Skylar's penmanship, neat and practiced, felt more personal than I'd expected. I ran my hands over her words as if I could touch her through them. Suddenly, I remembered her mentioning the journal to me. I remembered wanting to know what dreams filled her mind.

The first entry was dated just about the time I had started working at McClurry & Associates. Flipping through, I saw that not all of them had a date, which might make it trickier to decipher. I began reading.

From the back seat of the car, I stared at the man driving. My heart pounded. Who was he? Friend or foe?

Snarling noises came from outside. The zombies were closing in on us.

I stopped reading and, feeling as if I was seeing too much, closed the journal, but then I remembered Adam saying it was as if Skylar had wanted it to be found. The journal although not too long, would be difficult to understand. The clock warned me of my tardiness and made me determined to continue. I finished the first passage.

Had Adam read this entry? Had he wondered, as I did, whose name she'd yelled, and did he suspect, as I did now, that it had been mine? I told myself it was just a silly journal, a nonsensical way to chart feelings that could never be admitted to the world. What I'd read were not the words of a criminal, just a woman suffering. The words so far had nothing to do with money laundering, or shell companies, or drug smuggling. And with that in mind, I tucked the journal into my bag where it would patiently wait for me and me alone to decipher its contents and get to know Skylar through her dreams.

CHAPTER 43

Skylar

Journal Entry

LIFE IS A concert filled with melodies that orchestrate a symphony of moods. My heart had stopped dancing in the middle of life's concert, stuck in the despairing lyrics of a song that ended long ago. My ears stopped listening to the change in the tempo, and I settled into a dark hole, watching as others made the room come alive.

Circumstances jolted me awake and pushed me back on the dance floor. Instead of dancing, I allowed myself to be bumped around by others' movements, never creating my rhythm. How did I let the melody of one song dictate my life? Did I love the song—the feeling of despair?

The song had ripped a hole open inside of me, and I'd settled into its depths. It was time for me to open my eyes and see the crater surrounding me—to understand it completely. It was time to seek the ones who had taught me adventures were a side dish to the entrée they enjoyed every day. I might not have understood all her lessons when I was younger, but I was starting to now. One more dance, Mom, one more adventure. That's all I need. One more dance with you, and I'll hear my song.

CHAPTER 44

Brent

I WAS AN OUTSIDER in my own place of work. Only Cynthia was brave enough to make eye contact with me, but our offices were far apart and our interactions sparse. On the positive side, my situation had become as close to paid administrative leave as I could get. I had a light workload and extensive spare time. I opened up my computer to begin going through my backlog of online mandatory training which also helped me look appropriately busy if I received a visitor. For a moment, I considered actually following through on the training idea, but I then sat back to read another journal entry.

I was in my backyard planting flowers when I noticed a small lake forming behind me. A childlike excitement intoxicated me as the cool water splashed across the backyard and slapped at my ankles.

I paused, allowing myself to feel Skylar's emotions, to be with her at that moment of self-reflection, and tried to understand. These were emotions experienced during the time Henry controlled her actions, or at least she claimed he had. She had felt in over her head, but what I couldn't be sure of from her dream was whether she'd felt over her head with committing crimes or being with me. Maybe both.

The waves softly lashed against the beach, as if tired from a day of hard play. I could see him waiting for me amongst the crowd, and I drifted toward him.

Due to the fact no name was mentioned, I let myself believe Skylar had envisioned me standing on the beach with her. It would make sense, since the beach had led to a significant change in both of our lives. If it was true, it was the moment Skylar had allowed herself to be blackmailed—the beginning of the spiral.

The office was quiet, or at least I was unaware of the rhythmic normal sounds…. My eyes were focused on the documents before me….

Something caught my eye, and I leaned in closer to better see it. At first, it looked like a smudge, and then it moved. I jolted upright as the blemish increased in size…. From the blurry image, a spider took form….

I had to ponder the interpretation. Spiders and danger and sexual feelings…. No wonder Adam had given up.

The room was hot and stale. Light filtered through the window, glistening off dust specks that floated in the air. Around me, my classmates' sleepy faces stared forward at the teacher who sat at his desk…. We sat in silence except for the teacher's thick finger, tapping out a hypnotic rhythm. A pendulum on his desk demanded my attention….

A gentle knock made me look up to find Meghan standing in the doorway. Sliding the journal from view, I said, "Wow, a visitor. It's nice to see I'm allowed one."

Her face showed no sign of amusement. "Can I come in?"

"Of course." An uneasiness rose in my chest.

"Do you know how they found the passports?"

"I wasn't told, actually."

"Gabe and Roger followed her."

"They followed Chrissy?"

"No, they followed Skylar. She led them to a marina, where she got out, looked around and then drove away. She never actually retrieved anything, but when Gabe and Roger investigated further, they found that Bruce had kept a run-down boat in a slip. The box was hidden in the live well."

"What? Why? I mean, how would she know where the box was?"

"That's a good question, isn't it?"

"There seem to be a few good questions lately," I replied.

"Do you still believe she's innocent?"

"I want to." I thumbed through some papers on my desk to avoid making eye contact.

"If you need to talk, I can listen." Meghan left without another word spoken from either of us. For a while after, I worked on the training, trying to push the investigation out of my mind, so far from me that I might just be able to see it clearly. After a couple of hours, I gave up and read another entry.

The phone rang with a faraway sound, as if muffled by a pillow…. The demanding device was nowhere to be found. I jumped from the bed and searched the room…. Digging through my shoes, I saw the lit-up screen, and answered the call before the ringing stopped.

"Hello. Hello," I yelled.

Through the static, I heard the familiar voice of a man, but I couldn't decipher a word he said. As if my life depended on the conversation….

"You have to listen to me," he said.

"I'm trying."

Before I could comprehend his words—and trust me, I wanted to understand him more than anything—the hotel phone woke me. On the other end of the line, Adam's voice reminded me that my reality was anything but blissful.

I had been the one calling Skylar that night. I remembered telling her what I believed the dream meant. The entry told me she would not use my name in the journal, and there was a good chance that when I suspected the dreams were about me, they probably were.

I was about to read the next entry when another gentle rap sounded on my door. Cynthia shut the door and sat. I could only be thankful for the few souls still wanting to speak to me.

"I can't stay. I know you're supposed to be left out of the investigation, but I trust that if I share something, it stops here." It was a statement and a question.

"Of course, Cynthia. I would never get you in trouble."

"We have a small lead."

Torn between the feelings of fear and excitement, I emotionally froze.

"Tell me."

"Skylar flew to Chicago with no connecting flight. She also took enough money from her bank account—about five thousand in cash over the last few weeks—to get her far away. Adam didn't notice until now. Do you know why she would fly to Chicago?"

"No clue whatsoever," I answered.

"I've got to go. I'll keep you posted.

Just as I was about to leave for the day, Cynthia popped in once again.

"Listen, I hate to be short and sweet, but I don't need anyone questioning my visits."

"Understood."

"We've found that Nick and Tori had aliases and fake passports as well."

"Doesn't surprise me."

"The good news is, we've tracked them."

"And the bad news?"

"They're traveling with Skylar, or I should say, they flew to Chicago the day after she did."

My heart stopped. Why was my mind insisting on trusting her? How much more evidence would it take for my loyalty to Skylar to cave. I welcomed the final blow. Let it end my misery. "Not really what I wanted to hear," I mumbled.

"I'm sorry, Brent."

"I know."

Cynthia began to leave. "Cynthia, wait." She shut the door and gave me her attention. "Do you believe dreams hold answers?"

"Excuse me?"

"Could the universe be hinting at things in our dreams?"

"Well, to me, the universe," she said with quotes, "is God, and yes, God whispers to us in many ways—dreams, songs, people. Most definitely." She gave me a concerned look. "Brent, are you okay?"

"Just confused. Very confused."

"Call me if you need to; off-hours is best."

"Thanks, Cynthia." Then she disappeared down the hallway, leaving me alone. I threw the journal into my bag, too sick to read more.

It was late by the time I reached my apartment. The hours until bed slipped away slowly, even if there were only a few left to go. After eating some leftover pasta, I cracked open an IPA and sat in silence, wishing for the time to pass so I could go to sleep, yet when the hours finally did, I was wide awake, unable to put my thoughts to rest. I flipped the television on and found a late-night show where the host did a sing-off with some musical talent I was unfamiliar with. Even though I knew I should be amused, I could not drown out the whispers, begging me to not give up, coming from my bag.

I reached in and placed Skylar's journal on my lap. Its leather cover had the year 2016 embedded in it. Apparently, journaling had not been a priority in Skylar's life until recently. In order to understand her side of the story, I had to read the diary in its entirety, even though I wasn't sure I cared to sympathize with her.

I was sitting at my kitchen table eating bacon, one of my all-time favorite foods. Ted sat next to me, whimpering for a taste, but I wouldn't share. I just looked into his sweet, desperate eyes and continued to shovel the calorie-free dream bacon into my mouth. As dreams go, I can't complain. Until I took another bite, and the rancid taste jolted me awake.

Again, I wondered if the forbidden situation had to do with me or Henry's money. Skylar had never seemed to care about money, but I didn't trust my mind anymore. If she hadn't meant money, then Skylar had just admitted to craving me deeply—and believing that had caused too much trouble already.

My only focus was on the hand I held. I knew the man, and in my waking hours I would have been aware of the fact I shouldn't be holding his hand. But I wasn't awake, and my mind allowed me a moment that reality could not. Only the image of our fingers locked together and the feeling of completeness the bond created within me stood out in the dream. I wanted to stay in the warmth of the moment forever, where everything felt good and right. The vision was the most intimate one I've experienced because the man touched places I've let very few people explore. Somewhere in my alternate world, his hand is still wrapped around mine.

That wasn't about Henry. My heart raced. Hoping. Wanting so much to believe in her; in us.

Something shifted in my mouth. I sprinted to the bathroom mirror and studied my reflection. One of my front teeth was missing. Suddenly, many of my teeth slid out of place and then fell from the sockets into the sink. I knew if a tooth is returned to its rightful place it might retake like an uprooted plant. One by one, I forced each tooth back into its hole. The mission was futile. For each tooth I replaced, another one fell into the sink. With each clink on the porcelain, panic filled me. The final clink jolted me from my sleep.

I walked along the paths of my college campus, going somewhere. I recognized the buildings, but suddenly, nothing made sense…. Frantically, I pulled out all of my books, realizing I didn't recognize any of them. The paper was nowhere….

I walked, hoping something would rekindle a memory but nothing came to me. Finally, I saw a blond, curly-haired friend I hadn't thought about in years. I ran toward he…. I stopped in my tracks, waiting for clarity, until reality brought me back.

A frozen river surrounded me. Up ahead, I saw a group of people and realized they were my childhood family. I raced toward them…. Right before I reached them, the ice cracked, and I dropped into the freezing waters. I swam with stiffened arms to the underside of the hole and climbed out….

Much of the ice around us disappeared before I could reach them, leaving only the shrinking island we stood upon. Below us, killer whales bumped into the underside of the island and bounced.... We stood in the center of our island, our hands clasped together, until a whale's head jarred into us, and I was jolted awake.

I stood in a field and out of the grass arose an impossibly large group of balloons. The sky hid behind the array of colors clumped together and held by a hand slowly emerging from the ground below it. Even though my very brain was creating the image, I had no clue what was coming next. Who would have expected to see an enormous Superman balloon being lifted by all the other little ones? For a dream, it was quite an impressive colorful sight, and I stood mesmerized by the image of the floating Superman until he drifted far enough into the distance that my brain became bored and brought me back to consciousness.

Skylar's sadness seeped into her dreams. Had she made up all these dream passages to fake fear and feelings? Damn, if I would play the fool again. *Distance myself*, I told myself over and over again, but something inside me screamed, *Keep listening*.

CHAPTER 45

Brent

I WALKED INTO RYAN'S office to complete my morning briefing. My accounts were so far on the back burner, it was embarrassing to report on them. My shoulders slumped like a benched baseball player delegated to ice duty and watching my teammates hit grand slams. What choice did I have?

"Good morning, Ryan."

"Have a seat, Brent." He would say those words anytime I entered his office, but today, they instilled in me a sense of doom. I slipped into the chair across from him. "Do you know of any connection Skylar might have with Guatemala?"

"Guatemala? No, she never mentioned Guatemala it. Can I ask why?"

"We have reason to believe that's where she was headed. Cynthia tracked her. She flew into Guatemala City and then into Flores, Guatemala."

"Do you have men there?"

"Not yet. Has she contacted you in any way?"

"I would tell you if she had. I've never forgotten whose side I'm on." No need to discuss the fact she was trying to speak to me through a journal full of dreams.

"I believe you, or at least, I believe it was never your intent to help her."

"What about the other people of interest? Any word?"

"They seem to be a step behind her at all times. They shouldn't be able to slip through any more cracks. We have alerts all over the place but unfortunately, they were able to get out of the country. Nick and Tori had fake passports."

I kept my expression blank, not letting on that Cynthia relayed the information to me already. "Do you think it's strange Nick, Tori, and Skylar aren't traveling together?"

"I wouldn't expect them to, to be honest. And since Tori is apparently Nick's love interest, he's keeping her close by."

"Why wouldn't they have a fake passport for Skylar? Besides the Brenda Carter one?"

"Maybe they ran out of time and couldn't get their hands on one. Hopefully, we'll have them in custody soon, and we get all of our questions answered. We've contacted our El Salvador legat. The agents there cover Guatemala. I don't think I need to mention the drug trafficking problems we have in Guatemala, and I don't think I have to point out that Skylar traveled there alone and willingly."

"It appears that way, anyway."

Ryan eyed me for a moment. "You understand any information I share with you is strictly to see if it triggers a memory that might be helpful to the case. You are not to be involved."

"I'm aware."

Ryan let out an exasperated breath. "One thing is for sure, we'll find them."

"Isn't cocaine usually the problem in Guatemala? Henry dealt mostly with Ecstasy."

"That's what they brought into the United States from the Netherlands. It doesn't mean that's the only place they were doing business. Nick's business of buying and selling yachts could have been active anywhere."

"Was the recorded conversation in the prison a hoax?"

"It appears they wanted to throw us off their tracks. First, they made it sound as if Skylar was the enemy. Second, they can't be meeting someone for a drug deal at the usual spot when they're now in Guatemala. They wanted to buy time for all of them."

"I guess it worked."

"For now. Listen, Brent, you're a good agent. Consider this case a rite of passage. Learn from it and move on."

"Thanks. I will." His words served as a small relief. Wanting to leave the subject on that note, I asked, "Did you want to hear about my other accounts?"

"Have at it."

Once back in my office, I pulled out Skylar's journal. Maybe I was a better agent than Ryan even knew. Just maybe I was onto the one true lead we needed to be concerned about, but before I said a word, I needed to be sure.

I opened to the next dream. All of them came back to the same idea. If I allowed myself my own interpretation, it would be that Skylar realized while she slept that she was much more than a woman trapped in a life of conservativeness and safety. She had a choice, and she had the power to make that choice. Apparently, her last dream solidified her feelings.

I was in Bruce's office. I'm not sure if it was the box that Chrissy had spoken of, but I needed to see what was inside. It was critical to me, as if my dream self knew of my conscious self's desires. Bruce's drawers had many keys, and I frantically tried each one while watching the door. I knew someone was coming, but in my dream, it wasn't clear who that someone might be. I tried about fifty keys, it seemed. Just as the time was about to be up, a small silver key slid into place and I heard the click of the lock. Maybe due to my excitement of finally knowing, I woke without ever solving the mystery that had been troubling my waking hours.

An urgency overtook me. I needed to find the box. Something crucial would be revealed within its contents. The problem was, I had no idea where it might be. I only hoped Chrissy's curiosity would also get the best of her. Which it did. Two days after my dream, I called her and told her that Henry was having me followed, and I feared that maybe his people were keeping an eye on her as well. If whatever was in that box could ruin Bruce's memory even more than his actions had, she should move it or at least make sure they hadn't already taken it. Then I waited.

The next day, I borrowed Adam's car so she wouldn't recognize mine, and I followed her to an old boat house. I parked in a secluded spot and watched her. She went into the boathouse. I couldn't be sure whether the box remained in its place or not, but she came out empty handed. Later that day, I went back to the boathouse to look for the box, but I couldn't find it anywhere. Maybe it was an irrational fear, but something about the contents terrified me.

I froze. Skylar had never known what was in the box. It was the first piece of evidence I should report, but I needed to finish reading her words before I let others see it. Due to the situation, the journal would probably be taken from me, the one person who stood the best chance of understanding Skylar's message. Although, much to my chagrin, it appeared the journal would end with poems. Not my specialty.

I put Skylar's diary to the side and typed Guatemala into the search bar.

"What are you up to, Skylar Shaw?" I whispered into the air.

At the top of the page were images of things to do in Guatemala. If Skylar sought a new life, one where she could live freely with her millions of illegally earned money, why would she choose Guatemala? I scrolled the page and studied the local attractions, while envisioning her at each one and allowing the anger to rise inside of me.

Tikal, an ancient Mayan citadel hidden away in the rainforest was at the top of the images on the screen. It stood one hundred and fifty-four feet tall against the blue backdrop of the sky. Structures of varying sizes surrounded it.

The natural limestone bridge at Semuc Champey and the Cahabón River was another hot spot. Would she stop to swim in one of the turquoise pools that were formed by the river? Or maybe she was choosing to check out Pacaya, a local active volcano. Was she tasting the bitterness of the fruit the town was named after?

Lake Atitlán was breathtaking and notable because it was formed in a volcanic crater. Was she hunkered down in some cozy hotel in the busy town of Panajachel or walking around the streets watching the vendors showcase their merchandise? Something made me pause as I looked out at the lake in the middle of that crater, but like a thought that disappeared before it could be expressed, my reasoning was gone.

I plugged in drug trafficking in the country. My experience as a forensic accountant had never circled me back to any Guatemalan cartel, although there was a serious problem with cocaine transshipment and Guatemala had recently reached out to the United States for help. Our president had frozen aid to countries that were not preventing drug trafficking, and even though Guatemala was putting in efforts, they needed more vehicles, boats, and helicopters to get the job done. When chasing down the drug trafficking boats, some Guatemalan officials would find themselves stranded hundreds of miles out at sea after running out of gas and would have to wait to be refueled or rescued.

Nick's speed boat had slipped in during the night to assist Henry in his last drug deal. Knowing Guatemala lacked the ability to catch a speeding boat that could disappear into a million-dollar yacht in the middle of the ocean, why wouldn't Henry and Nick consider using another country besides the Netherlands to increase their revenue? If they were willing to deal Ecstasy, wouldn't they also be willing to deal cocaine?

At a rap on my door, I looked up to see Cynthia slipping in again, probably sneakier than she needed to be.

"You know, I'm not in prison. You're probably allowed to still speak to me." I smiled at her, letting her know I meant my words lightheartedly.

"You're no fun. You think it's just the men in the field who enjoy being covert?" As usual, her smile outshined mine.

"Ryan filled me in a bit."

"You really are here to wreck all my fun, aren't you? What do you know?"

"I know they're all in Guatemala."

"Do you know their fake identities?"

I shook my head. "See? I still need you."

"The Tidwells. Arthur and Amy."

"How'd they get through security?" I asked.

"We're still investigating. Perhaps Nick and Tori have other connections with security. Another possibility is they slipped by security. Names are easy to catch, but facial recognition takes a bit more effort. They might have altered their identity. A few changes, like Tori's hair being dark brown and Nick's head being shaven, can throw a busy transportation security officer."

"Now what?"

"Our guys are searching, but as you know, it's a bit trickier to find people in foreign countries."

"If they get on some speedboat with their loot of cocaine, they could disappear anywhere."

"Yes." Cynthia put her hand on the doorknob and glanced back at me. "Have faith, Brent, even when it seems impossible."

CHAPTER 46

Brent

THE FBI HAD impressive resources—intel, computer access, men in Guatemala—and I was trapped in my office with but one hope, the journal. I picked it up once again and hid it behind the screen of my computer, so it appeared as if I was working diligently on another account.

I opened the journal to Skylar's poems. I'd never been good at poems. I had never written one, and the only time I'd read one was when I'd been forced to. The teenage boy inside of me remembered the dread of English homework. But I would give it my best effort. I had to.

I stared at the first poem, sketched in her hand, and took a deep breath to prepare myself.

You're killing me, Skylar.

My mom understood that the universe was always whispering secrets in our ears. It's all about deciphering the language. Sometimes the answers are hidden amidst the words. Sometimes the meaning's clearer than you think.

<u>The Hole Inside Me</u>
Some things are forever
Or at least they seem
Until they come crashing

Destroying all things
How petrifying
The moment had been
To see it demolished
Only a scar can remain
A hole so deep
No life could exist
The oxygen depleted
Death frozen in place
The process of dying
Stopped in its tracks
All knowledge says run
Stay safely away
But a hand makes me curious
to view the debris
Amazed and in awe
What do I see?
Not a hole
That is lifeless
But the beauty
In me
I creep closer
Timidly, and then
I am racing
Because inside the hole
Above the trapped past
Is where life is happening
It wasn't destroyed
It became something new
Something amazing
A place that is mine

A place to discover
To relish, to know
To swim in, to savor,
Make peace
With the death
That lies there below
There's a hole in the middle
Created through time
A chasm of hope
That contains my soul.
~anonymous

Letting the words rest in my mind like a fine wine on a connoisseur's palate, I leaned back in my chair. I didn't want to miss anything hidden in the words; clues that worked as ingredients only a true connoisseur could detect. Was the author, possibly Skylar, describing the hole her parents' death had created within her? After only a few moments, I sat back up and grabbed the journal again. How was someone who couldn't tell the difference between Two Buck Chuck and California's finest supposed to knowledgeably decipher the meaning of the wine legs sliding down the glass?

With a deep breath, I began again.

<u>*My Horizon*</u>
I touched the horizon
Just in my mind
A place only some
Have the privilege to find

I hoped in the moment

I wasn't alone
That in the past
The future was sewn
~anonymous

Maybe it was possible to touch a place that seemed out of reach. The first step was believing in the possibility, and knowing you were okay without it.

Frustrated, I ran my fingers through my hair. If this was a test, she may have overestimated me.

For some reason, I remembered a conversation I'd had with Skylar. We'd been talking about languages and trying to understand the universe. During the conversation, she'd mentioned poems and hidden meanings. A piece of the puzzle begged to be discovered, and I knew the one person who might be holding it. I found Adam's name in my contacts and hit call. He acted neither surprised nor expectant.

"I have a question for you."

"And that is?" Adam said, almost impatiently. He obviously had no intention of getting into a lengthy conversation.

"Did Skylar talk about her parents' death much?"

"Not in years. When we first got together, I asked about it, of course. Skylar was always a bit of a recluse, so to speak. She had a couple of close friends from high school. They speak every now and then, but mainly if they call her." Adam paused a moment. "Does this have to do with the journal?"

"Not necessarily," I somewhat lied. "Just trying to get inside Skylar's head."

"Good luck with that." He sounded angry, and I supposed he had a right to be. "Skylar said her parents died on some scuba diving adventure." Adam laughed, a frustrated, shake-your-head-in-confusion kind of laugh. "Did she tell you that for our honeymoon she wanted to go scuba diving in some hole?"

"Yeah, she did—or at least she showed me a picture of a hole." Something was clicking. The clarity flickered in my mind like a short-circuiting light bulb.

Adam was quiet for a moment. "Of course, she told you." After a momentary pause, he added, "She was happy with me before all this started."

"She told me that, too."

"She did?" Adam's voice softened just slightly.

"Yeah, she made me well aware of the fact."

"Then why are you still around?"

"The case is still ongoing." This time I paused for a moment. "So, she never mentioned where her parents died?"

"Maybe, a long time ago. I can't remember. Skylar didn't want to talk about it much. I knew it was a part of her life that had shaped her, and I loved her just the way she was. What reason did I have to dig into a past that had no meaning to me?"

"I guess none."

"So, is that it?" Adam asked.

"Yes, unless you have any new information."

"I've got nothing."

"Thanks for your time then." I said, although I was pretty sure Adam had already ended the call.

I picked up the journal again, just as I heard the familiar tap on my door. Sure that the visitor was Cynthia, I continued to scan the first line.

The gruff voice made me jolt.

I couldn't make out what Ryan was saying over the sound of my nervous heartbeat in my ears. Glancing around my desk,

I tried to find a way to hide the journal before he reached me, but there wasn't anywhere.

"I'm hoping you can wrap up the report by the end of the day. I have something else I need you to move on to," Ryan said, now hovering over my desk.

I cleared my throat that suddenly felt near closing. One more mess up and my job could be in jeopardy, not to mention the fact that I would never find Skylar.

Folding my hands over the journal, I looked directly at Ryan, as if, with the power of my mind, I could distract him from looking elsewhere. "Definitely, yes. I can definitely have it ready."

Ryan eyed me suspiciously. "You okay, Brent?"

"Of course. Any word on Skylar's case?"

With a sideways glance that let me know he was aware of my attempt at distraction, Ryan answered, "Nothing yet. How about you? Have you remembered anything that might be of importance?"

"I assure you; you would be the first to know. I want her found as much as you do."

"Maybe not for the same reasons." He studied me as he spoke, as if the pressure of his words would cause me to collapse beneath them.

"If Skylar is part of Henry's drug trafficking organization, then we are on the same page. She deserves her punishment if she played all of us that way."

Ryan nodded slowly and gave my desk a few gentle knocks before turning toward the door.

I prepared to settle into the piles of work that had built up around me, knowing the sun would set, the streets would quiet, and the rest of the world would be settling into their beds before

I typed the last words of my report. The rest of the journal would need to wait for another day.

On his way out, Ryan said over his shoulder, "I'm truly rooting for you not to be stupid here, Brent,"

"Me, too," I said to the empty room. "Me, too."

CHAPTER 47

Brent

SLUMBER BRINGS MANY changing tides, the calendar flips to a new day, the sunrise slightly shifts in time to meet the expectations of the solar year, and the thoughts of yesterday mingle in the crevices of one's mind to create the reality the next day was meant to begin with. I was never one to remember my dreams, or often anyway, but when I woke, I knew the genre they'd been written in by the mood that encompassed me. Apparently, Skylar had been wreaking havoc with my memories because there was a darkness in my mind when I thought of her. If there had been a court case playing in my mind, Skylar had gotten slaughtered by the defense. I felt angry and bitter toward her, as if her pleas for understanding had sat out souring on the countertop while I'd slept.

I tossed the journal I had pulled out the night before into my bag, and then headed to the office where Ryan would be handing over the information for the next case. *Give me something interesting,* I pleaded; *something to make my mind drift far away from the Guatemalan forests and its ever-present drug cartel.* If Skylar wanted to live some highfalutin life on the run, so be it. I recognized the sourness created from my dreams tainted my perceptions of her, but I couldn't shake my mood.

After tossing my bag on the passenger side of my truck, I settled in behind the steering wheel and flipped the radio on. For the life of me, I could not remember ever listening to the particular song that had played while I was with Skylar, but I heard her in the music. I changed the station, and there she was again, floating across the notes like a breeze with no end and no beginning. She wafted through my senses, an unwelcomed visitor. The image of her irritated me. I no longer wanted to think of her, to protect her, to care. What had changed in my sleep? I questioned why, if Skylar wasn't a part of Henry's plan, why would she not be reaching out to me? Why depend on a journal?

All the facts pointed to her guilt: How easily I'd gotten targeted to be the one to travel with her; how she'd signed the papers to become Brenda Carter; how she'd willingly traveled to the Bahamas with Henry. As for the failed drug test, there was no sign of it. Even if there had been one, who could prove she hadn't willingly taken the drug? She claimed to be straitlaced, but she also drank on any occasion alcohol was offered. When Chrissy had mentioned the box of money, Skylar had seemed very curious as to where it was. And then she'd followed Chrissy, for God's sake. What innocent person did that? Had she known the passports and ID were within it? But then the journal had made it sound otherwise. I couldn't let it fool me.

Anger welled up inside of me, yet she was there in the words I saw around me, in the words I heard in the lyrics of songs—words that should have had no meaning otherwise, that should have passed my ears without impact. Have patience. Wait. Trust. I didn't want them to, but they softened my mood like a deep breath. Neutral ground—that's what I would allow myself, for today. I was neither a friend nor a foe. I needed to rest my mind from trying desperately to understand a riddle that had not finished giving its clues.

I reached the office with just enough time to drop my bag off, and in almost a laughable fashion, as I gently tossed it to the side of my chair, the journal fell out, mocking me. She would not be forgotten that easily. Firmly, I stuffed the diary back inside. Today was my day off from her.

Ryan was at his desk when I went in and took the seat in front of him.

"Did you get my report this morning?" I asked, while trying to get comfortable in a chair that offered none. "Sorry it was a bit late before I finished."

"It was perfect. I wouldn't have had a chance to review it until this morning anyway." He closed the folder that sat on the desk in front of him and set his readers on top of it before leaning back in his seat. "Not a trace of them. It's as if they've disappeared."

My heart sank. Not all of me was resigned to hating Skylar or adjusting to the idea that I would never see her again.

"Not the news any of us want to hear, that's for sure," I added.

Ryan folded his hands across his middle-aged belly. "No, Brent, it is not. We've reached out to Abigail. She's a frantic mess. Either she is a wonderful actress, or she is legitimately concerned about her sister's welfare. I don't think this is the first time Tori has made her lose sleep." He eyed me quietly for a moment. "Any ideas?"

"Not yet."

Ryan lifted an eyebrow. "Not yet? That sounds a little open-ended."

"Hopeful, only."

"Well, hope is about all we have to go on right now. Our agents have been to the hotels, motels, shacks—nothing. I'm afraid Nick, Tori, and Skylar have already left Guatemala. We have agents on alert in the Netherlands, but our suspects could have gone anywhere. In fact, they would be a bit foolish to go to the Netherlands at the moment. We're tracking other yachts they may have purchased, but with their history of fake identities and bitcoin purchases, it's difficult for sure."

"So, what next?" I asked.

"From us, patience, I suppose."

There it was again, the word that for unexplainable reasons resonated Skylar's presence. The only reason it comforted me was that somehow, if I felt her strongly in the midst of clues I could not verbalize, there was a reason, and if there was a reason, then there was a plan, and if there was a plan, then there would be answers. Someday, there would be answers.

While I walked down the hallway to my office, a new folder of shady accounts in hand, I felt my footsteps quickened and my heart raced as if I was on a ride rounding the top of a precipice and ready to view the world from new heights, for good or for bad. The feeling manifested from the journal. I was rounding the top and needed to open my eyes and be ready to see what the ride tried to reveal.

Damnit. Today would not be a day off.

Tossing the folder on my desk, I grabbed the journal and began to read. This time, there would be no pausing, no trying to understand. I would let the words rush past me and hear the messages they were screaming.

The next poems weren't anonymous. They were all by the same author, Rahima Espat.

<u>The Wishing Star</u>
<u>Rahima Espat.</u>

Cold dark night,
I look up with fright.

I see you flash,
Tearing the sky with a gash.

Faster than lighting,
Your transformation was striking.

Something I had never done,
Wishing for you to come.

I made nothing out of it,
A lost wish on a universal pit.

The moment I had you before me,
And it was then I knew you had to be.

You are everything I asked for,
I would say even a bit more.

When you wish upon a star,
The universe knows who you are.

I carefully read the next one, "Beauty in Death." The poem spoke of death and finding the meaning in life. There could be something to the words in this poem, but something told me otherwise. Only the author's name was underlined again.

I moved onto the next one, titled "Ode to H^{2}O." Again, no underlining in the whole poem except for the author's name— the same woman, Rahima Espat.

I read on. The next poem, Desde El Silencio," was the biggest mystery because it was all in Spanish. Once again, Skylar only underlined Rahima Espat.

That was it, the last of the poems, the last of the journal, and in the last part of the diary, I couldn't even understand the language. I plugged the title into a Spanish to English translator site, my younger self wondering why all these conveniences hadn't been there for my generation. The title in English was "From the Silence." Starting with the first verse:

Cuando de reojo veo tú silueta;
Paran mis latidos,
Mi cuerpo se estremece,
Y se alborotan mis sentidos.

I began the translation.

When out of the corner of my eye I see your silhouette;
Stop my beats,
My body shivers,
And my senses are upset.

The silence of this cold loneliness;
I scream what I feel,
I reveal my wishes,
But there is nobody who can listen.

I look back just to see you pass;

Losing myself in you to walk.
My eyes taking care of you,
While I'm wondering, who will you think of?

I continue my path in silence;
Everything goes back to normal.
In writing I keep these feelings,
For them never to speak again.

I read the words over and over, trying to make sense of them, knowing that meaning is often lost in translation. The message did not sound like Skylar, no matter how hard I tried to decipher it. I supposed I could have tried harder, but again something told me I wasn't supposed to. Skylar had left everything untouched except the author again. It was the fourth poem by the same author. Why?

The clock on my wall ticked, warning me I did not have forever to figure out the clues hidden in the poetry and that's when it hit me. Skylar had chosen one in a foreign language because the answer wasn't in the words of the poem. I had to focus on what she had pointed out to me by underlining certain words.

Quickly, I typed Rahima Espat into the search bar. Obviously, she was a poet. I would not be winning any investigative awards for that discovery. I scrolled for a bit to learn Rahima was a Belizean poet, and even though I may not have majored in geography, I knew Belize bordered Guatemala. Skylar didn't care about Guatemala. She was just making her way to her destination. But why Belize?

"Didn't you hear me knock?"

"Cynthia, no. Sorry, I didn't." I closed my computer. "Any news yet?"

"Nothing that I'm aware of. As of now, they've kind of disappeared in Guatemala."

"I heard. Let me ask you, if you were traveling from Guatemala to Belize, how would you do it?"

"What are you onto, Brent?"

"Maybe nothing," I said with a small smile I hadn't quite intended. Cynthia's gaze turned questioning. "But I think it's something. I think Skylar was heading to Belize. Guatemala was just a pit stop."

"Why not just fly to Belize?"

"Because that would be too easy to trace. She's taking her time. Skylar flew to Chicago, waited a few days, and then flew to Guatemala, right?"

"Now you think she doesn't want to be traced?"

"No, she doesn't want to be traced right away. This might sound crazy, but I think she wants me to be patient; to give her time but not to give up."

Cynthia's smile lit the room. "Well, this could be fun. Looks like I've got my work cut out for me this afternoon."

I would have said more, but like an excited child on a scavenger hunt, Cynthia had hurried out the door. After opening my computer back up, I typed 'things to do in Belize' into the search bar of my computer, and what I saw hit me like a speeding train—the answer. Skylar's journey was not about becoming lost; it was about finding herself and seeing who cared enough to discover who would emerge from the adventure. Adam just didn't realize he had handed over the treasure map to the finish line and the woman that would be waiting there.

CHAPTER 48

Brent

I WENT BACK TO the poem I suspected Skylar had written. It wasn't about the hole in her—well, maybe it was that, too—but after seeing the picture, the picture Skylar had shown me of where she wanted to go, the picture of a hole staring back at me from the middle of the ocean, I knew the poem was truly about the place her parents had gone to for their last adventure.

From the word 'hole' in the title, everything described The Great Blue Hole off the coast of Belize. Things that go crashing—it's a sinkhole four hundred feet deep that formed after years of dripping water created a wonderland of stalactites and stalagmites. I'd read the scar as a scar inside of Skylar, but the hole was also a scar on the earth's surface. The article talked about an H^2S layer that I had no desire to read about in depth, except for the fact that the layer separated the good ocean water from the anoxic water. No oxygen exists. *A hole so deep, no life could exist, the oxygen depleted, death frozen in place, the process of dying, stopped in its tracks.* In the anoxic waters, researchers had found the remains of scuba divers that would not decay because there was no oxygen in the water for bacteria to live on in order to do their job.

But she'd said that above all that, life was happening, and

a hand made her curious. I reread the line. *But a hand made me curious to view the debris.* Me; I made her curious. She wanted to be a part of the life that was happening outside of the past and the death of her parents.

I reread the next anonymous poem, "My Horizon," and envisioned Skylar and me at the pier; the sun setting in the distance. The words I believed to be hers said *I hoped in the moment, I wasn't alone. That in the past, the future was sewn.* Skylar wanted whoever she'd intended the journal for to be there with her, and even though she'd never mentioned my name in the entire book, something, maybe just hope, made me adamant it was me.

But why hadn't she just said it? Maybe she needed time to figure things out on her own? Maybe she wanted to know which one of us truly cared about knowing who she was and which one of us was willing to let her be that person?

While racing to Ryan's office, I nearly took out three unaware agents. Excitement and adrenaline caused me to barge in without knocking, and I was met with Ryan's hand up, an irritated hold-on-a-minute expression on his face as he spoke into the phone receiver. As he watched me, the irritation slowly faded into curiosity, and he wrapped up his call.

"You got something?"

"Skylar's in Belize." My excitement had also made me forget the fact I had never mentioned the journal. The realization hit me almost simultaneously with Ryan's words.

"You just left my office knowing nothing, and suddenly you're sure of her whereabouts?"

"I remembered something that had seemed like nothing."

"And that was?"

I knew that mentioning the journal needed to be handled like stepping on hot coals with my bare feet. If my words were carefully spoken, they might not leave blisters.

"A picture she showed me, before leaving. She was trying to decide which place to go to for her honeymoon. The choices were Savannah or…well, she didn't say the other place, but she showed me a picture. It was of a giant blue hole in the middle of the ocean."

"What makes you think she went there? We've already discussed this, and as per our discussion, she would have no reason to go to her honeymoon destination without being on her honeymoon."

With a final step, I placed my foot on the glowing ember. "Skylar kept a journal of meaningless dreams and random poems. Adam gave it to me thinking it might mean something to me, but it didn't. I thought nothing of the journal's contents at first—just a woman's unexplainable thoughts. Then I decided to give the diary another look. When we knew Skylar was in Guatemala, the journal took on a new meaning."

"You didn't think to share it?"

"It was gibberish. A zombie bit her, and then a killer whale tried to push her off an iceberg, and a tidal wave attacked her in her backyard. It didn't seem to be solving any case. What resonated were the poems. Most of them were written by a woman who lives in Belize. When I searched things to do in Belize, the picture Skylar had shown me was one of the first things to show up. When I read about it, it brought me back to one of the poems; I believe Skylar wrote it. It's called "The Hole Inside Me," and it talks about a place where no life exists."

"Slow down, Brent. You're losing me."

I took a deep breath and started again. "The Great Blue Hole actually has a layer at the bottom where all of the oxygen has been used up by bacteria eating decaying matter. Now if something falls beneath that layer, it doesn't decay." I went on to explain a few more facts, to make sure Ryan would understand the metaphor.

"Skylar never told me where her parents died, only that before they could reach their destination, their moped got sideswiped by a bus. Adam told me they were on a scuba diving adventure, and that Skylar had wanted to go scuba diving in some hole for their honeymoon. She showed me the picture. I know it's what the poem is about. Skylar said she needed to clear her head before getting married. Her parents' death changed her life more than anything else.

"I'm telling you; Skylar is not hiding from us. She's not part of Henry's plan. She probably doesn't even know that Nick and Tori followed her there."

"If you're correct, Brent, if she isn't part of the getaway, then you know what that means, right?"

I nodded; my excitement suddenly vanished. If Nick and Tori weren't escaping with her, then they had one thing in mind by following her to Guatemala. They were cashing in on Nick being her beneficiary. Skylar was being hunted.

"You have to let me go to Belize." Ryan had to have heard the desperation in my voice.

"Why is this so important to you, Brent?"

"Because, since I don't believe Skylar is a drug smuggler, I'm quite sure I'm going to be spending the rest of my life with her."

Ryan nodded, a hint of a smile on his lips. "I'm not all in, but I'm willing to give your story some credit."

"That's all I ask."

Within an hour, a group of us sat around a table being briefed.

Skylar's flight had taken her to Flores, Guatemala, where she'd seemed to disappear. The searches of hotels and motels had turned up with nothing, but if Skylar had paid in cash, which she would have, and if the employee who'd checked her in hadn't been working at the time the agents had searched that particular place, Skylar could have very well gone unnoticed.

Agents also checked the airlines that flew to Belize, and since she'd have used her passport, we could safely assume she hadn't flown to her destination because there was no evidence of her showing her passport to board a plane. Another option was she could have taken a boat across the Gulf of Honduras from Porto Barrios or Livingston, Guatemala to Punta Gorda.

Skylar could have also rented a car. Most rental agencies didn't allow their vehicles to be taken across the border, so she would have had to walk across the border and then rent another car once in Belize. Did Skylar have any idea of the dangerous situations she could find herself in, a woman alone and trying to cross the border? Panic filled every inch of my body, and I begged the universe to protect her from the groups of men that impersonated border control and at best would only steal her money. There was no evidence thus far that she had rented a car in Guatemala. Relief washed over me as I assumed that she'd gone with another form of transportation.

The final option was for her to have taken a bus from Flores to Belize City. This mode of transportation was still risky, but at least she wouldn't have been alone, and the process was a bit more official. Ryan already had agents on their way to the Línea Dorado bus line to seek answers. The border into Belize sat between the two countries at Melchor di Mencos in Peten, Guatemala. The border ran forty-four miles along the Guatemalan border that connected the roads heading southwest to Flores, which lay eighteen miles away. She would have needed a valid passport whether she crossed the border by car, foot, or bus so she should be able to be traced.

Once the possible routes had been laid out, there was nothing we could do but wait. People drifted in and out while others, waiting for word, paced the room. At the first hint of proof, I would be on a plane to Belize. Eventually even I had to go back to my office to work on my other case.

At nearly five o'clock, my phone buzzed.

"Come back to the conference room," Ryan stated, his tone too flat for me to decipher.

Nervous could not begin to describe the feeling inside of me. My life rested on the what I would discover in the days to come— or at least the life I dreamed of sharing with Skylar.

Everyone was seated around the table when I entered, and I hurried to join them.

Ryan nodded at me. "Skylar did in fact take a bus to the border of Guatemala. From there she crossed into Belize on foot. This was two days ago. As for the rest of her journey, they are still working on that."

I released a huge sigh of relief. We had found her, and as of two days ago, she was alive and well.

"The concerning fact, if Brent is correct," Ryan continued, "is that Skylar could be in danger. The agents in Guatemala have found that an Arthur and Amy Tidwell rented a car and also took it to the border, and from there, they crossed the border on foot one day ago. They are definitely following her."

Everyone's attention became focused on me. They knew that this was not just another case to me, and I no longer cared.

"Brent, you and I will be flying out tonight. We'll be in Belize City by tomorrow evening."

"Thank you," I said with a slight nod.

"Go get packed. We have a long night ahead of us."

I'd almost reached my truck when I heard Meghan call to me. Reluctantly, I turned to face her.

"I just wanted to wish you good luck." She avoided making eye contact. "It's very noble of you to go after Skylar."

"Thanks, Meghan," I stammered, uncomfortable and unsure of what else to say.

"You love her, don't you?"

"To be truthful, I've loved her, or at least, I've loved something about her, since the first day I met her. I can't explain how or why, just that I did." Meghan looked off into the distance. "I'm sorry, Meghan. I—"

She raised her hand, as though demanding that I stop talking. "If we could control our feelings I wouldn't be standing here, would I? You're no more to blame for not caring about me than I am for my lame attempts to pursue you. I'm a big girl, Brent. I'll survive this." Meghan turned to go, and I slowly opened the truck door, not wanting to show how desperately I needed to get away from the guilt that snaked its way around me. "And Brent, I truly meant it when I said good luck."

CHAPTER 49

Brent

THE FLIGHT TO Belize was exhausting and exhilarating at the same time. I tried my best to rest, because once we landed, I would need all of my energy and focus. One of many thoughts that had bounced around my mind was that Skylar, the most conservative person in the world, was going scuba diving. How? When would she have been able to get her certification? While packing my bag, I'd texted Adam and asked if he knew of Skylar recently completing the requirements.

He'd texted back that she had earned the certificate back in high school. At one point, her parents had considered taking her on the very trip that had killed them, so they'd all gotten their certification at the same time. I wondered to myself, had they taken Skylar, would everything have been different? All three of them surely wouldn't have been on a moped; maybe Skylar would have ridden behind her father on one, with her mother following on a separate one. But then everything would have changed. Not just in Skylar's life, but mine as well.

I did a little research and found that even if it wasn't particularly smart of Skylar to scuba dive after decades had passed since she'd received her certification, it was possible. Scuba diving certification was good for life.

Sleep had overcome me by the time we touched down at

Phillip S.W. Goldsen International Airport. Opening my eyes, I met the bright Belizean sunshine promising a new day. Surely, the local FBI agents would have made progress on locating Skylar. Hope washed over me, even if in the back of my mind something else wanted to creep from the shadows. We stepped off the plane, and as soon as the airplane mode on our cell phones was off, Ryan announced there was news.

"Skylar took the Muy' Ono Explorer tour. It has three possible drop off spots: Dangrigia; which is three and a half hours away; Hopkins, which is four hours away; and Palencia, which is four and a half hours away."

All of the destinations seemed impossible after a long night and day of travel. "Three and a half hours to the closest destination? Nick and Tori could be planning their attack as we speak."

"It's three and a half hours to Dangrigia by car but only fifteen minutes by air," Ryan said. "There's a plane waiting for us." In the distance, a small puddle jumper with what I assumed to be other agents waited for us to head out. We walked across the hot tarmac and Special Agent Kaufman introduced himself and his partner, Special Agent Daniels. "We're heading straight to Dangrigia. If we don't track them down there, we'll go the rest of the way by car."

"Has there been any word?" I asked, hopeful.

"No. They didn't rent a car or fly. That leads us to believe they have someone in Belize ready to help them with whatever plan they have. By the way, what makes you so sure Skylar isn't involved now? I heard something about a journal and dreams."

Ryan looked over at me as if saying, *You explain it*. I knew he was still doubtful.

"Skylar was about to get married. She had second thoughts

and left a journal. It appears to be only a journal of dreams, but it's more like about how her mind transformed her experiences throughout the investigation and being pulled into Henry's scheme. I believe it was coincidence that the other agents found the passport showing she was Brenda Carter at the same time that she decided to run off to figure things out."

Kaufman stole a glance at Daniels. "I'm missing something."

"The dreams only led up to the present time. In order for her to tell the future, or at least where she was heading in the future, she turned to poems. Some of them, I believe she wrote herself, and many others were by a Belizean poet named Rahima Espat. The poems for the most part have nothing to do with her situation, but one describes the Great Blue Hole. I believe it's where her parents were heading when they died. I believe she needed to come here before knowing if she was doing the right thing by getting married."

Kaufman and Daniels looked at each other and after a moment, Kaufman shrugged. "Women. They sure know how to complicate things."

We all climbed into the small puddle jumper, and within minutes, it raced down the runway. The small plane was loud, and I watched Belize pass by below. The blue-green water spread out before us, and before long, I felt a tap on my leg. Kaufman pointed, and in the distance, I saw The Great Blue Hole, and I understood not only Skylar's draw, but the draw upon her parents' spirits before her. An overwhelming feeling—as if I looked at the past, present, and the future all at once—spread through me.

An excitement arose inside me, but not for me, for Skylar, as if she were a marathon runner about to cross a finish line that had seemed impossible. I thought about the journey she had taken, all on her own—the secretive planning; the plane trips; the bus rides; and walking across a border in a foreign country she had never stepped foot in before. She was absolutely crazy, and exhilarating, and brave. And then I thought of Nick and whoever was helping him sneak around Belize undetected, and my heart sank. Skylar had come so far to discover herself. The universe could not possibly mean for her to come this close, only to be taken out by, ironically, the people who had caused the whole journey to begin with. They couldn't win. Could they?

With a thud, the plane landed, returning me to the world, no longer able to dream and admire from afar; no longer in a place where beauty and serenity shadowed the chaos that could be seen under the microscope.

As we stepped off the plane, a tropical heat surrounded us. A couple of black sedans, along with local law enforcement, awaited us, and the tedious tasks of going from hotel to hotel began. Armed with pictures, Ryan and I set out in one of the sedans with our target hotels in hand. Each time, we were met with the same shake of the head. No one had seen Skylar, Nick, or Tori. At the last hotel on our list, discouragement had set in, and the idea of getting in the car to start the whole process over again seemed impossible.

"I think we're out of luck here, Brent."

"Now where?"

Before Ryan could answer, the hotel manager, a short man with a thinning head of hair, spoke up. "Did you try the island?"

Hope rose inside me. "Excuse me?"

"Thatch Caye. It's a very popular destination for tourists. It has those over-the-water bungalows people are fond of nowadays."

"Could you get to The Great Blue Hole from there?"

"Oh, yes. They do excursions right from the resort. I highly recommend—"

"How do we get there?"

"Just go to the dock at Pelican. The boat will pick up the people there going to the resort. It's just about a twenty-five-minute boat ride."

Ryan was on the phone, letting the other agents know to meet us at the dock. Once there, we pulled out the pictures, hoping that before we bothered trying to explain why we would be needing a ride to the resort as non-guests, the photos would confirm the need. Finally, I saw a look of recognition.

"Yes, she took the boat out to the island two days ago, I believe."

"What about these people?" Ryan showed him a picture of Nick and Tori.

"I can't say for sure. They look familiar, but…Sorry, I can't be sure."

"Thanks, you've been very helpful. We'll need to get out to the island."

"The boat is for resort guests."

Ryan pulled out his badge, and the rest of us followed suit. The man looked across the ocean as if wondering what the consequences would be on the other side of the water.

"I assure you; your boss doesn't want the people we're looking for hanging around his resort."

The man nodded. "Come aboard."

The touristy pace of the boat was enough to drive me officially crazy. Skylar was almost within reach, but anything could happen, anything could be happening as I puttered across the blue waters. Just when I had reached the point that I thought I would jump off the side and swim the rest of the way, I saw the island in the distance. As soon as we reached the dock, we were directed to the check-in area. The urgency inside me rose, like an animal sensing danger in the air. The four of us walking across the lobby drew attention. Conversations stopped, and the desk attendant stood, as though knowing we would not be checking in, that something larger was happening.

Our badges were out before Ryan said, "We need to find this woman. We believe she may be in danger." Creating urgency was one way to ease the defensive nature that is naturally aroused when addressed by authority and to get them willingly and quickly on your side.

"Yes, she is here. She is staying in the bungalow suite, but I'm afraid she is not there right now. She's on an excursion."

"The Great Blue Hole," I said, trying my best to hide the franticness inside of me.

Ryan pulled out the next pictures. "What about these two?" The clerk searched the pictures. "I can't be certain, but I believe the man is on the excursion with her. I didn't see the woman, although he is here with one. It may be her, but I believe she's a brunette."

"The man went on the excursion alone then?" Ryan asked.

"No, not alone. There was another man. I believe he had a Dutch accent. I remember him. It's not an accent I hear often."

"We need a boat," Kemp said, "and scuba diving gear."

The attendant opened his mouth, as if to tell us why it couldn't happen. And then he picked up the phone. "A boat and your gear will be waiting for you at the dock, but I should warn you, it's a three hour drive out to Lighthouse Reef. The people on the excursion should be arriving there shortly."

As we raced to the boat launch, a million thoughts crossed my mind. One of the most prominent of them was Skylar hadn't taken a scuba diving class since high school. It would be too easy to make her death look accidental.

CHAPTER 50

Brent

A SPEED BOAT SAT at the end of the pier. Maybe it was the look on our faces, the blue vests with the bold FBI logo, the local law enforcement officers pulling up behind us or, most likely, the guns being tossed beside us in the boat, but we'd barely had a chance to settle in our seats before the driver had the boat going at full speed. There was no way to easily communicate with the ocean air whipping by us at seemingly hurricane speeds.

I covered my wind-blown face, and after hours, even breathing became tedious, but finally, in the distance, I saw a few boats settled around the hole. For the most part, the vessels were empty—the inhabitants were near, yet in another world deep beneath the ocean's surface. Once we were almost to a stop, a few black heads of scuba divers came to the surface. The idea that one of those heads could be Skylar's gave me hope. There was still a calmness in the air. No one suspected the danger that swam beside them.

Our driver pulled up next to one of the boats that also was from the excursion that had left Thatch Caye. A man, large in stature, eyed us curiously, waiting for an explanation. The myriad of thoughts running through his mind as he scanned the men in their FBI vests would remain a mystery, but I envisioned him seeing his life flash before his eyes as he analyzed what detail could warrant such a visit.

"We need the swimmers to return to their boats," Kaufman said to the curious driver. I scanned the water, even though the depth made it impossible to view all of the divers below the surface.

"That's not an easy request. Even if I can get through to the guides, the divers have to come up slowly. It's very dangerous for them to rise to the surface too quickly."

"Then have ascend slowly," Kaufman said with an air of irritation.

"Listen man, I want to help, but like I just said, it's not easy."

"Try."

The man picked up his device. "Lucas, can you hear me?" He held the COMM device away from his mouth while he waited for a response. "Can I ask what's going on?" he asked Kaufman.

"One of the divers may be in danger."

"I haven't heard anything from Lucas if that makes you feel better." The moments ticked by, and my anxiety level increased. "They're pretty far into their dive. These COMM devices are only so good."

"Try him again," Kaufman insisted.

"Lucas, can you hear me?" Silence. Minutes passed, and nothing. The driver shrugged, and in a fashion of *I'll keep doing this, but nothing is going to happen*, he spoke again, and then we heard a muffled, "Russell, we've got…"

"What did he say?" I almost yelled.

"I'm not sure," Russell said nervously, but I was quite certain he knew exactly what Lucas had said.

"Lucas, come to the surface."

"Diver…missing…going to the bottom."

"What?" I shouted louder. Russell looked panicked. "What's going on?" I yelled again.

"I'm not sure." He turned to the COMM system again. "Lucas, what's going on? Can you hear me?"

Silence. I grabbed one of the extra suits and slid my legs into the tight rubber. Finally, about twenty feet from our boat, a head emerged from the water. Whoever it was swam to the boat, and we pulled in the diver—a woman, maybe in her thirties, breathless. "One of the divers…something went wrong."

Kaufman placed his hand on my arm, politely telling me to be quiet. "What are you talking about?"

I zipped the suit and grabbed the oxygen tank.

"She sank," the woman panted. "A problem with her gear or something. She just started sinking. Two men are helping the guide search for her…she went so far down." The woman was crying. She had no right. She didn't even know Skylar.

Russell helped with my final adjustments. The dive would be challenging, and I had little experience. The suit fit appropriately, or so I told myself, knowing that if it did not, stabilizing myself would be difficult. Within priceless minutes, I flipped off the side of the boat, while listening to the woman, who had managed to catch her breath, direct me to where they'd last been seen. Other divers were returning to the surface. All of them seemed to be swimming easily on their own, making me certain that Skylar was not one of them.

As I searched the waters, scuba diving facts from my past dives swirled in my mind. Descend no more than sixty-six feet per minute. Stop at one hundred thirty feet and wait twelve minutes. How far down could they be? Recreational divers shouldn't be going down farther than that anyway. The words of the panicked diver came back to me. *She went down so far.*

The clear blue waters made visibility easy, yet I still could not find them. I forced myself to abide by the sixty-six feet per minute rule. I would be of no use if I got myself into trouble as well. In the second minute, I descended more than one hundred feet below the surface. The Great Blue Hole was clear but also a labyrinth of stalactites and stalagmites. I couldn't find them anywhere. In my panic, each shape jumped out at me; instead of fearing the larger objects could be sharks, only disappointment flooded me when I realized they were not other scuba divers. Finally, a large object approached me—too large to be a person.

Adrenaline raced through my veins making me feel certain that if it were a twelve-foot bull shark, I could just shove him to the side and continue on with my mission. Luckily, I did not need to test my strength against a species much more equipped to win a war fought in the depths of the ocean. The large form began to take shape, and I found that it wasn't one being, but three or four. Nick and his accomplice had to be pretending to be allies in the rescue mission. As I drew closer, I saw one figure holding onto another as the other two swam closely by but not touching. The body I feared was Skylar's appeared more like a rag doll than a human. She was unconscious at best.

The two figures swimming together had to be the guide and Skylar while the other two figures, I feared were Nick and an accomplice. As I approached, chaos ensued. One of the figures reached toward the tank of the man helping Skylar. Pretty quickly, he must have realized the intentions were not a friendly pat on the back for a job well done. With one hand still on Skylar, the guide pushed at the diver who was reaching for his tank while the other man came from his opposite side.

I raced toward them. If their purpose was to make sure Skylar never reached the surface, then if I could get to her, the men's attention would be diverted from the guide.

In moments, I was on them, pushing the two to the side and grabbing Skylar from the guide's grasp. As expected, their attention was quickly diverted to Skylar and me, giving the guide time to adjust to any instability he may have suffered. In the midst of the chaos, it appeared that the guide had succeeded in protecting his gear from their grasps.

The man I assumed was either Nick or his accomplice was on me quickly, and my eyes locked onto his. Could he even recognize me? As he closed in, I became more and more certain it was Nick and that he was well aware of who I was as well. Between our masks and the water, I could not sufficiently read his expression. Was it one of fear or victory? Did he know his job was complete—that Skylar had already died? Even so, he must know that if I had tracked him to the middle of the ocean, trouble awaited him at the surface. Would this stop him from tampering with more gear, knowing he would eventually have to face the consequences? Murdering a special agent would not settle well in court.

Whether due to recognizing me or the fact their attempt had failed, Nick and the other man began to swim away. Their escape plan was a mystery, since they needed to get to a boat at some point, but what mattered most was that we were able to stop momentarily to allow our CO_2 levels to adjust before going further. The guide made sure Skylar was receiving oxygen. Out of my element, I had to trust his call. I did not know what was more important—getting Skylar to the surface or avoiding the bends. And then he adjusted Skylar's suit so that she was one-hundred percent buoyant and, motioning to me to follow, let her drift to the surface. He had decided to go for a happy medium, giving her some time, but for his own safety after being so deep in the hole trying to save her, intending to take some more time to allow his own body to adjust.

The waters became bluer and bluer, and finally Skylar and I burst through the surface. The agents had their guns poised, while the other guide stood at the side of the boat ready to pull Skylar aboard. She was limp. A sickness took over me at the thought Skylar might gone. Before I knew it, I was on the boat beside her. Russell checked Skylar's vitals.

"Where are they?" Kaufman demanded.

"They swam that way." I pointed in the direction they had traveled. "Lucas is below us." As I finished saying the words, Lucas appeared and was brought onto the boat.

"I see them," Kaufman said. One of the agents took over the helm and we flew toward the escaping scuba divers. All the while, Skylar remained unconscious. The boat came to a stop, and I heard the sounds of their weapons coming to attention.

Behind me, agents shouted orders, and then Nick and his sidekick were being dragged on board. Sounds that were meaningless static. Then Lucas said something about having gotten the oxygen back on quickly but not quickly enough to prevent her from losing consciousness. Skylar had been getting oxygen for most of the time. There was hope.

"She has a pulse," Russell announced.

I held her hand in mine, whispering words like "Please," but not consciously choosing my words at all.

And then her eyes opened.

CHAPTER 52

Skylar

SOMEWHERE IN THE back of my mind, I remembered where I was and why, but the details were distant and unwilling to unveil themselves from behind the cloud, an obstinate child unwilling to face her consequences. But what had I done? What punishment awaited me? The sky shone blue above me, an amazing yet blinding brightness, a brightness so promising that fear faded to the background and something else took its place. Hope. Hope in the new day before me, where aliens were nothing more than childish nightmares, and spiders spun glistening webs to be admired not feared, and surfboards could glide above waves—even tsunamis.

For a moment, I was alone in my new world, and I was at peace with my aloneness, and then forms took shape out of the shadows. A face, a familiar one, smiled down at me, and I could almost feel my lips smile back at Brent, although I'm not certain they did.

"We need to get her back to shore," a voice said.

People propped objects around me, and they put something soft under my head. And then, at a fierce pace, we were off. My body bumped across the waves; jolting and exhilarating at the same time. Brent stayed beside me, watching closely. After some time, I looked around. There were several FBI agents wearing blue vests with bold letters across the front. I could make out other law enforcement men and the other divers, sitting in their seats, with concerned, pained expressions on their faces. The guide, Lucas, stood at the helm next to another man, both of them peering out at the ocean in front of us. We weren't on the boat we'd gone out on, and some of the divers were no longer with us. On the floor, near the agents, sat two men with their hands behind their backs as if they were handcuffed. I recognized them as two of the divers. We had even talked briefly—the weather, how many dives we had been on. I'd lied, knowing that my refresher course I had snuck in before the trip did not count as an actual dive.

How had I gotten here? Flickers of memories sparked in my mind. The journal—the idea started to form when I wrote about my parents. Every entry created a need for more memories—more closeness to them. By the time I'd wrote the poems and researched the poet from Belize, the plan had been devised. I'd needed time and distance to see my life clearly. Was I wrong to go to my honeymoon destination without Adam? No. I'd decided that if I were to choose Adam, I would go to Savanah and never experience the depths of The Great Blue Hole. This was my chance.

I'd felt the presence of my parents the entire time, at first holding my hand, and then walking beside me, and finally trying to keep up as if I'd grown to an adult within the short time. The fear that threatened to overtake me at times was replaced by excitement. The plan was in motion, and I wanted to enjoy the ride. Chicago was easy. Crossing the border on foot, not as much, but, in the end, the world opened up to me, and the possible hazards stepped from my path and let me pass without harm.

By the time I'd reached The Great Blue Hole, I'd felt unstoppable. Not once had I suspected danger lurked around the corner. The guide had taken us down the wall of the hole where marine life had drifted in the waters as if they were Chinese lanterns lighting the skies. As we'd descended farther into the depths, the waters had remained clear. Stalagmites and stalactites created a different world for us to explore.

When we'd reached our maximum depth, the instructor, staying close, had given us time to tour around. Something had changed, something I hadn't been able to put my finger on. Instead of the energy of a child on Christmas morning, I'd felt the ominous weight of a storm forming in the distance, yet nothing looked different. I'd thought about the information the guide had shared with us before leaving the resort.

Far below the maximum dive rate we will be descending to lies a H^2S or hydrogen sulfate layer. The entire hole is covered by it at about 290 feet below. At this level, it's very dark and nothing can survive below it. Hydrogen sulfate is a flammable, colorless, corrosive, toxic gas. The gas is dissolved in the water making it less toxic but still sea life will not pass through it. In fact, ocean explorers have found tracks of marine life that accidentally found themselves slipping below it and had tried to crawl out.

The interesting fact about the waters below that level is that whatever falls below it will never decompose because there is no oxygen left down there for bacteria to live on. In fact, two divers are still down there today. It was decided to leave them there in their final peaceful resting place.

Of course, I'd known all those facts. I'd used them to write the poem, hoping someone would read it and know what I'd been trying to say. And maybe even use the poem to find me.

But at that moment, when the eeriness had settled over me, all I'd been able to think about was the two bodies beneath me. They weren't decomposing, but I couldn't stop envisioning the pruny skin clinging to soggy muscles. What would their eyes look like after so many years under water? Inside my wet suit, I'd felt shivers, and I'd decided to swim closer to my guide. That's when I'd seen the two divers approaching me. For a moment, relief had settled over me, until all I could envision were the eyes of the dead scuba divers, watching me, warning me—and those two dead divers had become my parents screaming something to me I hadn't been able to understand.

One of the men swam uncomfortably close to me and set his hand on my tank. Suddenly, I couldn't breathe. Searching for my guide was futile, but I did it anyway, until my panic calmed into nothingness. Whatever else had happened between that moment and when I'd opened my eyes on the boat were lost. But why? Why would someone mess with my tank? I glanced around again at the agents, Brent, and then the handcuffed men. One of them had to be Henry's brother. I saw the resemblance now. How could I have missed it before? How much could Henry hate me to have me followed all the way to Belize to have me murdered? The more I tried to tie everything together, the more exhausted I felt. A welcomed sleep overtook me.

CHAPTER 53

Skylar

WHEN I AWOKE, I was in a hospital bed. Brent, staring out the window, had his back to me. I felt his concern in the way his shoulders slumped, as if the world had beaten him down.

"Brent." My voice sounded raspy. There were a million words I wanted to say, but I couldn't, not yet anyway. He was beside my bed immediately.

"Skylar, thank God. You took a really long nap." His teary gaze was as warm as his smile.

"Could I get some ice?"

"Absolutely." Brent disappeared for a moment, and when he returned, several agents were with him.

"Skylar, I'm Special Agent Kaufman. This is Special Agent Daniels. I think you know Special Agent Nelson."

"Yes, we've met." I couldn't imagine what I had done wrong, but my heart raced, guilty by association, I supposed.

"You're a very lucky lady."

"I suppose I am, but right now, I'm too confused to feel anything."

"This might clear things up." Special Agent Kaufman handed over what appeared to be a passport. "Open it."

Timidly, I studied the front as if preparing myself for what

I was about to see, and then I slowly opened it. The first thing I noticed was a picture of myself. Still confused, I looked at Special Agent Kaufman.

"Skylar, it appears you have two identities."

I looked again, this time studying the name on the passport. "Oh, my God! How could this be?"

"Do you remember getting this picture taken?" Special Agent Daniels asked.

I looked back at the picture and was slammed with the memory of being at Henry's after being drugged on the ship. "Henry had some man come to his house and take the photo. He said it was for my personnel file. When I told Henry that I wasn't part of his personnel, he laughed." I couldn't help but relive the memories I had tried to put behind me. "I can't believe this. I was Brenda Carter the whole time."

Brent sat on the chair beside the bed. "Skylar, remember when they told you that you were a diversion?"

"This was it. They were loading me with their money knowing no one could find a person who didn't exist."

"And then they added Nick as beneficiary," Brent continued. "All they had to do was wait for the waters to calm and then…" Judging by his expression, he couldn't get the words out.

"Then they just had to kill me to collect the money."

Brent nodded.

"Well, they must have loved the fact that I ran off to a remote island where they could get the job done without interference." Tears welled up. Trying to contain them caused a burning sensation so I let them flow. "I was so dumb."

Brent took my hand. "You had no way of knowing they would follow you all the way here, or that you were Brenda Carter. Going on this trip was brave of you, really, Skylar."

His hand— warm and strong— brought back memories of my dream where my world seemed complete when his hand wrapped around mine.

Special Agent Nelson cleared his throat. "Brave may not be the exact word I would use, but it all ended well. At his point, we believe we have everyone in custody."

"What about the woman?"

"Tori was waiting for Nick in their hotel room. She was much easier to track down than the other two," Special Agent Daniels added with a smile.

"So, you really think this is all over?"

"We really believe this is all over, but don't get too excited. You don't get to keep the cash."

"Too bad. It could come in handy, since I may have lost my job doing my little adventure."

"Well, Skylar, it's been a pleasure," Special Agent Kaufman said, "but I think Brent has it from here."

Special Agents Kaufman and Nelson both shook my hand gently as they bid me goodbye.

"Brent, I expect you back within a couple of days unless I hear otherwise," Ryan said as he put his hand on the doorknob.

"See you in a couple days," Brent said, but his eyes stayed focused on me. For a moment, we stayed like that, silent, enjoying the transition taking place between us—from 'what could never be' to 'what looks like a strong possibility.'

"I think I might have a wedding to cancel."

Brent's face brightened. "I think that might be best."

Just when I thought he might lean in and kiss me, the nurse walked in the room. "Well, Miss Skylar, things are looking good, but the doctor wants you to be observed overnight. If all goes well, you'll be out of here tomorrow."

"Sounds great."

"But I am afraid visiting hours are ending, so you will have to say goodbye to your guest until tomorrow."

"But…"

"It's okay, Skylar." Brent leaned in and kissed my forehead. "I know of a nice bungalow calling my name. I'll be back first thing." His smile was the last image I saw before being left alone for the first time, and I knew what I had to do before I could start anew. I picked up the phone and dialed Adam.

CHAPTER 54

Skylar

I AWOKE TO THE smell of hospital scrambled eggs and coffee. Brent asked if they had any French vanilla creamer, which apparently, they did not. A giddiness arose inside of me, and I regretted nothing—not the waiting, not the trying to see where things went with Adam, not the reckless adventure that could have killed me, and not the telling Adam it was over—nothing, because it had all brought me to this moment. But the giddiness wasn't all about Brent; in fact, maybe it was mostly about something else. I needed him to understand that fact most of all.

The discharge process seemed tedious, but I also relished the everydayness of our time together, already such a natural feeling that was both exciting and familiar. Brent walked beside the wheelchair and then opened the car door of the taxi he had called. I chose the back, and I listened in on the predictable chatter between the two men who were no more than strangers. Peace washed over me as I watched the Belize countryside speed by me. I thought of another time, so long ago it seemed, when Brent had crawled over the taxicab seat to comfort me. When the chatter paused, I looked up. Brent smiled back at me. Maybe he was reminiscing as well.

The short amount of travel was welcomed. It served as a

time of reflection, of letting go, of savoring what was before me. For the first time in what seemed like forever, I wasn't afraid. Not of Henry, not of Nick, and not of living.

The sun was becoming lower in the sky when I finished showering and getting ready. Brent had run out to grab take out. Neither one of us felt like being anywhere but alone inside our bungalow, but the sunset called to me, and I walked out onto our balcony and down our short private pier. I felt him rather than heard him and turned to see him watching me in a way that could finally feel welcomed.

"You're so beautiful," was all he said. It was all he needed to say, because I knew he was looking at all of me, and I knew he loved what he saw. He took a step closer, and my heart raced, but first I needed to explain my journey.

"Brent, wait. I need to tell you something. I need you to know that I didn't need you to find me. And I didn't need Adam to find me. I needed to find myself. My adult life has been dictated by fear, not faith. This journey was about me remembering that when the universe nudges me, it's for a good reason. I had to rebuild my faith in the fact that even when things appear to end very badly, the story is still being told. My journey's not over."

"Skylar, I know you needed this. I've known it about you before you hopped on the first plane, but if you didn't care if anyone found you, then why the journal, why the dreams leading me here, the poems?"

"Because, as much as I know I'm okay doing this life thing on my own if I need to, I was kind of hoping someone would want to go on the rest of the journey with me."

"You were kind of hoping someone would want to. So that someone could be…?"

"Let's just say, I had more faith in one of you having investigative skills than the other."

A gentle wind picked up, and the thatch roof rustled. Brent took another step closer to me, slowly but not cautiously because he knew what the outcome of his steps would be. I wanted to savor every breath, to be wholly in the moment. When he reached me, he touched the side of my cheek with his palm, and I wrapped my hand around his. Brent waited a few breaths before leaning in and letting our lips touch for the first time—or at least, the first kiss that would mark our official beginning.

"If you'll allow me, I would like nothing more than to walk beside you for the rest of your journey."

I wrapped my arms around Brent and rested my head on his chest so we could both watch as the sun touched the faraway waters. Maybe the horizon did exist in an untouchable place, but at that moment, in Brent's arms, I was quite sure we had accomplished the impossible.

EPILOGUE

Skylar

Jacksonville FBI Headquarters
One Year Later

SOME WOULD SAY it's a bad idea to work with your spouse, but then some people aren't solving FBI cases. Cynthia stayed until I could complete my training, and she showed me a few more of the ropes. I wasn't House solving the medical mysteries the way I'd once dreamed, but every day when I walked into my office and booted up my computer, my heart raced with excitement. My job was new, and scary, and exciting.

My life had a completeness that I had never felt before, and the strange part about it all was that it came about by making sure nothing was set in stone. Living in a self-created bubble only creates fear of tomorrow, instead of excitement of the unknown.

I had lacked faith in the whispers of the universe, and the paths its nudges were sending me on. Now, I was ready for the next adventure, to be carried to places I had long forgotten to dream of exploring. And for that, I gave thanks to the universe for reminding me to let go of the steering wheel and enjoy the ride I'd been created to take. Because, if the universe has something in store for me, who am I really to question it?

THE END

ACKNOWLEDGEMENTS

Without the help of others, I would be lost. Thank you to Edward Mickolus for all of your advice with anything pertaining to the FBI. I take full responsibility for any detail that is not exactly as it would be done outside the world of fiction. Other professionals that were resources in the areas of government organizations, banking, and accounting include; Andy Macey, Tim Proper, Jordan Jenks, and Lisa Cascanette. I take full blame for any errors or stretches of the imagination.

Many thanks to my friends Christine Schmitt and Meg Balke who graciously read my manuscript and offered advice. As always, my family members: Steve Tripp, Judy Deon, Karrigan Deon, Kim Stone, Gail Sheehan and Lisa Cascanette cheered me on, read my drafts, and suggested new and better ways. I am forever grateful for the time each one of them took to help me once again.

I am also grateful to Rahima Espat who gave me permission to use her poetry in my novel and to Catherine Kean for helping me with the final edits.

The following sites were used for dream meanings and interpretations:

http://www.dreambible.com,

https://dreamingandsleeping.com,

http://www.dreammoods.com.